E.A.C

A STONE OF FIRE

THE LOST GODS,
BOOK ONE

Because writing a book is easier than trying to find a husband.

Copyright © 2024 by E.A.CAMPION

Illustrations by Emma Hartley

All rights reserved.

No portion of this book may be reproduced in any form without written permission from the publisher or author, except as permitted by U.K. copyright law.

GAIA

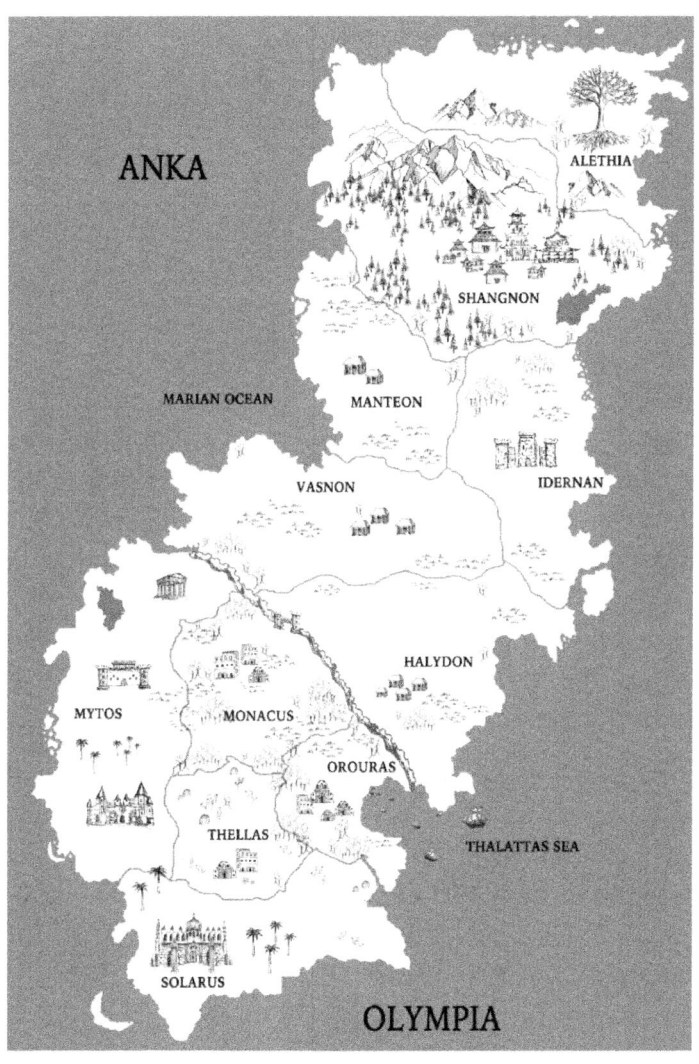

PROLOGUE

Rosalyn could sense something was wrong before she even opened her eyes.

Bolting upright in bed, her right hand instinctively reached for a dagger strapped to her waist, an automatic reflex from a past life. Yet, all her fingers brushed against was the soft, warm fabric of her nightdress. Letting out a shaky breath, she scanned the darkness of her small room, trying to shake off the lingering sleep clouding her mind. It was the middle of the night, and the only light came from the flickering flame of the small torch mounted in the wall sconce by her bedroom door. It cast elongated shadows that danced across the walls.

Moments ticked by, and an unsettling feeling crept over her—the hair on her arms stood on end, and the back of her neck prickled. It was a sensation she recognised, one that often accompanied the feeling of being watched. Squinting, she tried to focus on the shadowed corners of her room, searching for the source of her unease, but everything seemed in place. Then, a small movement caught her eye. She swung her head to the left, towards the window. The delicate voile curtains fluttered gently in the summer breeze, the soft rustling filling the otherwise silent room like a whisper. Strange. She couldn't remember leaving the window open.

A faint knock on her bedroom door shattered her thoughts, the unexpected sound startling her slightly. She pulled back her bedsheet and moved almost soundlessly as she slid out of her bed, her feet finding the cool wooden floor with unsurprising steadiness. She had been trained to remain composed under pressure—her years of combat experience having practically stripped her of fear. The rickety floorboards creaked beneath her weight as she made her way to the end of the bed, picking up the light dressing gown carelessly draped over the foot of it. Closing the distance to her bedroom door, she smoothed down her long brown hair with her palms and took a deep breath to centre herself. Flicking her eyes to the dresser, she quickly calculated the time it would take to open the top drawer and retrieve the knife she had concealed beneath her folded undergarments. Ten seconds at most.

With a swift motion, she swung open the door, bracing herself for an assailant on the other side. She paused, a frown knitting her brow as she surveyed the empty corridor before her. It took her a heartbeat to look down and take in the small figure standing in front of her.

Not a threat at all.

Jesper. One of the children she had been caring for over the last couple of years, when she first joined the orphanage. He was now around the age of four or five, but had been left here when he was just a few months old. His parents had perished in a house fire in Monacus, and his grandmother had reluctantly brought him here shortly after, unable to care for him, overwhelmed by her grief and age. He had a small scar from the fire, a burn just above his right temple.

He was a quiet child, but Rosalyn often found herself moved by his small acts of kindness toward the other children and his gentle nature. Though unsure of what magic he possessed, if any, she suspected it was one of the lesser gifts—perhaps water manipulation or wind bending.

Jesper stood in his pyjamas, a size too small, clutching his favourite grey teddy bear tightly in his left hand. His bronze curls were slightly dishevelled, one side flatter than the other—a clear sign he had been asleep—but his wide, brown eyes were alert as they looked up at Rosalyn.

"What is it, my love? Did you have a nightmare?" Rosalyn asked softly, her voice a soothing balm meant to comfort the boy, but also to ensure she didn't wake the other children in the neighbouring bedrooms.

"I… I got woken up. I heard a baby crying," Jesper replied in a small voice, equally as quiet. Rosalyn frowned.

"We don't have any babies here at the moment, Jes. The youngest is Agatha, and she's in your room."

Jesper shook his head, pursing his lips.

"Aggie is still asleep. I made sure I was super quiet when I came to find you; I didn't wanna wake her up."

Rosalyn offered him a gentle smile as she bent down to his level, extending her hand and running it gently up and down his tiny arm in a comforting gesture. Such a sweet, considerate boy, she thought.

"Are you sure it wasn't one of your dreams, sweetheart?" she asked cautiously.

Jesper often had nightmares, recounting them as if he were trapped behind bars, unable to breathe, surrounded by darkness as screams echoed all around him. Rosalyn often wondered if it was his subconscious replaying the trauma of losing his parents in these terrors, even though Jesper insisted he couldn't remember anything from that night, having been so young.

He shook his head emphatically at her question, his messy curls bobbing with the movement.

"No, Rosie, I could still hear it when I was coming to find you." He reached out a small hand, adjusting his grip on his teddy in the other hand to clutch it even tighter. He began tugging on her fingers with surprising strength for such a small child, pulling her towards the end of the landing. Rosalyn swiftly reached back to grab the flaming torch from the sconce by her door. Lighting their path, she followed Jesper down the dim hallway toward the stairs.

• • •

Placing her torch in the empty sconce beside the heavy front door, Rosalyn pulled it open with a soft grunt, the effort causing the hinges to creak loudly in the stillness of the night. She peered out into the dark street, noting the full moon hanging high in the sky, casting an ethereal glow that created a beautiful yet haunting ambience. Jesper remained close, clutching her hand tightly, positioned slightly behind her.

"See, I told you!" he exclaimed, his voice echoing off the surrounding buildings. Rosalyn looked down, and sure enough, a bundle was on the doorstep.

"Go and get Nanny Liria," Rosalyn instructed, turning slightly to guide Jesper back inside. He complied, his soft footsteps fading as he hurried up the stairs to the second level, where the Directress of the Orphanage resided.

Turning back, Rosalyn crouched down onto her haunches and carefully picked up the small bundle from the stoop. A soft woollen blanket enveloped a tiny body, and Rosalyn frowned as she ran her fingers over the fabric. The wool was incredibly soft and plush, clearly imported from the colder climates of Anka, suggesting it was an expensive purchase. She hadn't seen such quality since working at the orphanage, as poverty was one of the main reasons they had to take in so many children.

"Hi, little one, what are you doing out here all alone?" Rosalyn cooed, cradling the bundle closely to her chest. With gentle hands, she pushed back the soft blanket to reveal a small face crowned with blonde hair and striking blue eyes. Rosalyn sucked in a breath at the colour of the baby's hair, already putting the pieces together as to who this might be.

A pink bow adorned the infant's hair, indicating she was a girl. Rosalyn noted the full, rosy cheeks and the size and weight of the child; she couldn't have been older than nine or ten months. The baby grunted and gurgled slightly at the disruption, but as soon as their eyes locked, the baby settled, a calm seeming to wash over her. A small zing of energy sparked through Rosalyn as their gazes met, and she shuddered involuntarily. The babe wriggled and managed to free a chubby arm from the safety of the blanket, reaching toward Rosalyn's brown hair that had fallen forward over her face as she peered down at the infant. Rosalyn smiled at her before noticing a small note clutched in the baby's hand. Rocking the baby in one arm, she carefully plucked the note free from the child's grip and unfolded the scrap of parchment with her free hand.

Rosalyn's bottom lip trembled as she read the few hurried sentences scrawled onto the paper.

She knew that handwriting.

She would recognise it anywhere.

Several words were smudged, likely stained by her friend's tears as they were written. Rosalyn looked back at the innocent eyes still focused on her, a single tear tracking down her cheek as she did so.

"I vow to love you as if you were my own; it's what your mother would wish for, my sweet Aela."

PART ONE

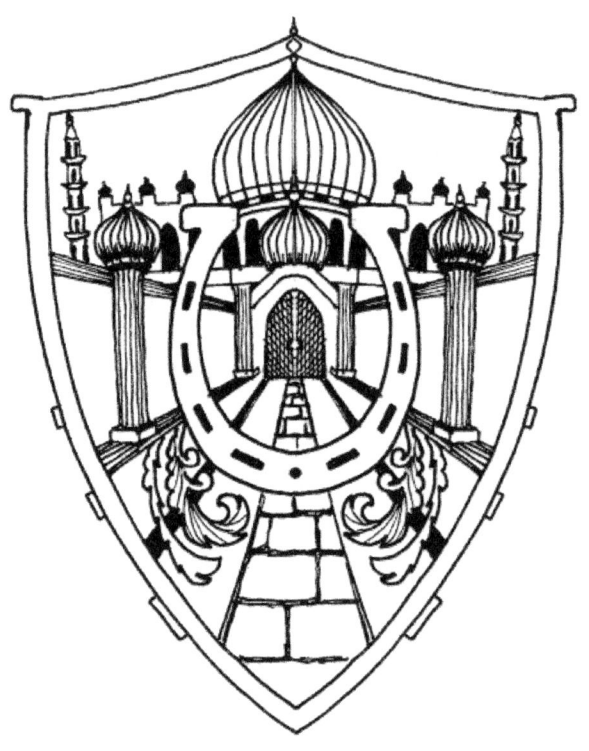

Protect her,
Daughter of my soul,
Daughter of your blood.
For she is the key to both halves,
The end to suffering,
The bringer of war,
The eye of the storm.

CHAPTER ONE

Seventeen years later.

The heat of the morning sun enveloped me like a thick, suffocating blanket as I stepped out of the cart, struggling under the weight of my two heavy bags. Sweat trickled down my forehead, and I wiped it away with the back of my hand, my heart racing with anticipation. Before me loomed a massive temple-like structure that shimmered in the sunlight, its colour a similar shade to that of the golden sand adorning the coasts of Olympia.

I took a deep breath, inhaling the scent of sun-baked stone and distant sea salt, hoping it would help ground me in this moment. I still couldn't believe I was finally here, after so many years of dreaming and practically wishing my life away, I was *actually* here.

The War College of Solarus.

The fortress's shining marble had clearly seen its fair share of fire damage over the years, as faint scorch patterns marred several of the walls. On top, two immense spires, each towering at least two hundred feet tall, reached for the sky, their surfaces catching the sun like polished gems. Between them, several domes punctuated the skyline, the largest positioned directly above the central grand archway that beckoned students inside.

I knew from my previous visits that the structure was at least a hundred thousand square feet. If you were to look at it from a bird's eye view, the fortress was an oblong shape, meaning it was deceptively much deeper than how it appeared when you were standing directly in front of it. On average, around three to four hundred students were living, learning and training here at any given time. I frequently imagined the countless students who had walked these paths before me, honing their abilities and learning the weight of their magic.

Apart from the spires and domes at the front of the building, the roof was entirely flat, with a roof terrace covering its entirety. It was a verdant expanse of grass and pebbled walkways, feeling like an oasis amidst the surrounding desert, and I often wondered about the resources needed to keep such greenery alive in this arid landscape.

A glimmer caught my eye, and I tilted my head back, craning my neck to look up to the top of the spire on the left. It was crowned with a torch of flame that flickered bravely in the breeze. On the opposite side, the right spire bore a torch of shadows, dark and swirling like ink in water. The two towers symbolised the two most revered magical abilities of the Continent.

I was a Fire Wielder, or a 'Flame' as we preferred to call ourselves, and a pretty terrible one at that, as I only had a few embers in my arsenal. Still, I tried to make up for it with my strategic thinking and the wealth of knowledge I carried about the history of Olympia and Anka, thanks to Nanny Rosie's teachings.

Every Fire Wielder and Shadow Summoner (also known as 'Shades') that resided in Olympia were obligated by the Crown to attend the infamous War College when they turned eighteen, as it was too dangerous for the Realm to leave such strong magic untrained.

Both Flames and Shades with relatively strong abilities could master their magic into tangible weapons, such as an extra pair of hands, a sword, arrows and so on. A useful skill, especially when it came to battle.

Once graduated, it was an unspoken obligation that Flames were to become a member of the Olympian Army, due to the destructive and devastating nature of their magic. On the rare occasion that a graduated Flame decided that they didn't want the life of a soldier to be their destiny, they would find themselves with an invitation to meet and discuss the reasonings behind their choice from General Zaneer, the head of the Olympian Army. She would arrive at their homes shortly after the invitation had been received, and by the time she left, she would have recruited another member to her ranks. She was either extremely convincing, or extremely terrifying.

Due to the centuries' long rivalry between both fractions, Shades very rarely entered the Olympian army's ranks. The General seemingly didn't contest this, as it was most likely easier for her to manage her soldiers when they weren't fighting amongst each other. Instead, the majority of Shades gravitated towards the shadowy underbelly of society that consisted of spies, thieves, and the infamous fighting pits that thrived in the darkness. I regarded those who fought in the pits as the cockroaches of our world, scurrying to survive, hidden yet everywhere. Although the pits were illegal in both Olympia and Anka, for each one that was stopped, three more seemed to spring up in its place. After so many failed attempts at shutting them down, the Crown's and their armies finally chose to turn a blind eye to them, pretending that they just didn't exist, ultimately leaving the pits to spiral out of control and remain unchecked.

Although Shades didn't cause as much physical destruction as those of us who had flames at our fingertips, Shadow Summoners were known to be just as dangerous for a number of reasons. For one, their magic allowed them to hide in plain sight. You could be talking to them one minute, blink, and they would seemingly disappear the next. In reality, they had just wrapped their shadows around themselves, but your eyes still convinced your mind that they were no longer there.

The deadliest of Shades were known as '*Shadow Whisperers*'. Shadow Whisperers were so rare that many people considered them a myth. They were rumoured to possess the power to manipulate minds and emotions, their shadows' voices filling your head and ultimately turning people into puppets of chaos. Some people swore that they had seen loved ones burst into a seemingly random fit of rage, a lust-filled frenzy, or sometimes into such a state of panic that they would go permanently mad.

Beyond Flames and Shades, others with diluted elemental gifts walked the Realms. These gifts consisted of abilities such as wind bending, water manipulation and even those that could control the soil and grow plants; 'earth-workers'. Unlike those of us who had inherited fire or shadow magic, elemental abilities had become diluted over the generations.

Therefore, they were often consigned to gentler pursuits, a reflection of the fading power from their ancestors; earth-workers often went on to have jobs in agriculture, and so forth.

My own aspirations were to join Olympia's war council. I knew that my limited magic would make me a liability in battle, so I believed my knowledge of strategy and history could serve the Realm better from behind the front lines. The most I could probably do to terrify our enemies was to light a candle and dance around with it, and something told me General Zaneer wouldn't be too impressed by that. In contrast, Nathaniel, my best friend, was an undeniable force among Flames. There was no doubt that he was fated for the Olympian Army and might even lead it one day.

As I approached the front steps at the end of the wide cobbled path where my cart had dropped me off, a plethora of friendship groups were clustered in front of the fortress, most of whom were wearing black tunics and breeches or dark fighting leathers. It was hard to tell which abilities each person held just from looking at them.

"Aela?!" a male voice shouted over the commotion of the morning rush. I swivelled my head from side to side, trying to locate the source of the sound.

"Nathaniel?!" I squealed back, my eyes searching for him through the sea of faces. The drumming of my pulse filled my ears as I scanned the crowd, excitement and nerves pumping through my veins. Then, as if he parted the crowd himself, Nathaniel now stood just a few steps before me. The sun reflected off his golden chestnut hair, highlighting the enormous grin that split his face. He looked like a God amongst mortals.

I leapt forward, closing the small distance between us.

"Oh, Aela, it's so good to see you. I've missed you so much," Nathaniel said, wrapping his arms around me and lifting me off the ground in a bear hug, squeezing me so tightly that air had no choice but to leave my lungs involuntarily. "Have you signed in yet? Do you know where your dorm is?" he asked, his cheek pressed against mine, a small zing of electricity dancing over my skin where we touched, the familiar comfort of our friendship settling around us.

"No, not yet. I just got here. I wanted to find you first," I managed to rasp out when he finally set me back down. I smiled up at him, so happy to see him but also relieved I could finally breathe again. The skin crinkled at the edges of his moss-coloured eyes as he took in my tired and slightly dishevelled appearance—his tell-tale sign that he was happy to see me. My arms were still wrapped around him, not wanting to let go just yet, and I subconsciously noted how much larger he felt since our last embrace; clearly, the combat training was paying off.

Releasing him, I stepped back, and a low whistle escaped my lips as I looked him up and down.

"You've filled out, Everflame," I exclaimed, offering him a small wink and biting my lower lip in a teasing gesture.

On my last visit, about three months ago, it was obvious from Nathaniel's aura how much his power had grown. It was a considerable difference, which only spurred my eagerness to join him here and train what little magic I had. At the time, though, I hadn't noticed the change in his physique. But now, as I ran my eyes up and down his body, I observed how tight his sleeves were around his biceps and how much broader his shoulders had become compared to his hips. I would have to be blind not to notice it now.

Nathaniel lowered into a mock bow at my words.

"How kind of you to notice, m'lady. Why don't you do this strong, handsome man the honour of carrying your bags and assisting you to your dorm?"

I rolled my eyes at his words and shrugged my bags off my weary shoulders. He straightened, his eyes still twinkling with amusement as he reached to take my belongings.

Nathaniel and I had grown up together, and I had yet to meet anyone with stronger fire abilities than him. He was a year older, so already a second-year student, and I had only seen him a few times since he had enrolled.

The three-day cart ride from our village in Thellas to the War College in Solarus cost six drachmae alone—more than half the monthly wage I earned at the orphanage. I could barely scrape together enough coin to feed and clothe myself, let alone put money aside for visits. The dusty, bumpy roads of the parched lands—the standard for our Realm—didn't make for a particularly relaxing journey either.

Even though they were neighbouring sectors, Solarus was almost triple the size of my home sector, and the War College was the furthest point south of Olympia. I had never seen the ocean before my first visit earlier this year, having grown up so far inland. When I arrived this morning, the first thing I did was look out at the glittering waves where the Marian Ocean met the Thalattas Sea, no more than a mere mile away.

The last twelve months had been tough for me. Nathaniel and I had been inseparable for the last fourteen years, having met at the orphanage when I was four, and he was five. When Nathaniel had first arrived at the orphanage, it was like we were instantly drawn together. Most people said it was because we were both '*children of the flame,*' but I often thought Fate's hands were more involved.

I had been a quiet and withdrawn child those first three years at the orphanage, but Rosie said I became an entirely different person when Nathaniel came into my life; "*he was the spark that re-lit the fire inside of you,"* she would often say. I truly had him to thank for all my fondest memories growing up, and I was eternally grateful for him.

I had been barely ten months old when I was abandoned on the doorstep of the orphanage. It was Nanny Rosie who found me, bundled up in nothing more than a soft woollen blanket, with a note clutched in my tiny hand, stating that my name was 'Aela'.

I had no memories of my life before that, but Rosie often told me she believed I had been very loved before she found me that warm summer night. This sentiment used to bring me comfort when I was younger. It was nice to believe, even if just for a while, that I had a family who cared for me—that I had a father who doted on me and a mother who wanted me to grow up to be just like her. Maybe I even had a brother or sister.

Yet now that I was older, I knew that Rosie only said this to soothe a lonely child who felt unloved and unwanted—feelings I still carried with me to this day, like an ache deep within my bones.

I used to hound Rosie with questions about where I came from, but as the years went on, she would either change the subject or spin outlandish tales from a storybook whenever I asked. Eventually, I gave up trying to find out who my parents were. It was clear that no one was searching for me, that no one was missing me. These days, I reminded myself that Rosie and Nathaniel were my family now—they were all I truly needed. They were enough.

As Nathaniel and I made our way up the steps to the large central archway under the main dome, we stopped in front of a wooden desk covered in scattered parchments, names written beside numbers. Clearly, this was where I was meant to sign in.

Sitting behind the workbench was an ebony-skinned woman with long braids that reached down to her waist. When she looked up at me with a welcoming smile, I noticed her eyes were the colour of honey, and her long, thick lashes reached her eyebrows. My jaw dropped slightly as I stared at her. She was possibly the most beautiful woman I had ever seen.

Several seconds passed before Nathaniel had to nudge me gently, his quiet chuckle pulling me from my daze.

"You might want to shut your mouth before you start drooling," he teased, and I felt my cheeks flush.

The beautiful woman looked over my shoulder at Nathaniel as I stepped forward, and her eyes twinkled slightly as she dipped her head in greeting.

"Name?" she asked, looking back at me, thankfully not commenting on my obvious admiration. She must be used to it.

"Aela Everflame," I replied meekly, still embarrassed. Her eyes softened upon hearing my last name.

"Are you Nath's sister?"

"No!" Nathaniel and I responded in unison. I felt a pang of sadness as I noted her familiarity with his nickname—one I never used—knowing she had spent more time with him in the past twelve months than I had.

"Oh, sorry, we don't get a lot of Everflame's here, so I just assumed. My mistake," she said, floundering slightly as she looked back down at her papers, aimlessly touching them to occupy her fingers, clearly an anxious movement.

'Everflame' was the surname given to all orphans throughout Olympia. Queen Elena Everflame, or 'The Fire Queen' as she was often called, had no children of her own. Instead, she opened orphanages all over the Realm after her husband passed. We were affectionately known as 'the Queen's children' throughout Olympia. It was a bittersweet title—a reminder of our shared upbringing and collective sorrow.

"This is my friend Aela, the girl I grew up with," Nathaniel told her. "Aela, this is Leena. She's a Flame in the dorm opposite me and one of my sparring partners in Combat Studies."

Nathaniel gave my shoulder a light squeeze, encouraging me to speak for myself as he always did when I was in a social situation. Leena's smile returned, and I managed to muster up the courage to introduce myself properly.

"Lovely to meet you, Leena, and please don't worry, people always assume we're related," I replied, still unable to meet her eyes.

I was always like this with new people. After spending the last four years working at the orphanage where I grew up, I found myself much more comfortable interacting with children than adults. It was their innocent nature and how they always spoke their minds that endeared me to them. I found that most of the adults I encountered in Thellas withheld information or were just outright dishonest.

Nathaniel had always been the confident one out of the two of us and was the main reason I had made any friends growing up. Unfortunately, in the past year, I had definitely reverted back to my shy and awkward ways without him.

"You're in room 266," Leena said, her tone cheery, as she looked back up from her list of names. She held out a large bronze key in front of her, attached to a worn leather keychain, with the room number faintly carved into the metal.

"266?!" Nathaniel said. "That's... in the Shade side of the building."

I turned to him, my heart picking up pace slightly with the implication, to see that he wore a bemused and slightly horrified expression. Yes, there was rivalry, but Shades and Flames didn't hate each other; it was just rare that we became the best of friends. Why did he seem so worried?

"We've had an unusually high influx of Flames this year," Leena said, shrugging slightly, unperturbed. "We either put her with the Shades, or she can write to the General to request a year's deferment, which Zaneer almost never grants. At least Aela's in the dorm next to Jaxon. He'll keep an eye on her."

"I'll be fine!" I exclaimed, taking the key with slightly shaky fingers. "I'm sure my roommate will be nice enough. It can't be that bad. I'll be fine. I'll be *fine*," I repeated, trying to convince myself more than anyone else.

No, the living arrangements weren't ideal. I had hoped to be near Nathaniel in the Flame side of the building after so much time apart, but if I had to suck it up and be with the Shades this year, I would. There was no way I was going back to Thellas and working with Nanny Rosie for another year at the orphanage just to wait for a different room. I had come this far; there was no turning back now.

I forced a weak smile to mask my rising trepidation, but I caught Leena and Nathaniel exchanging a look, confirming my suspicions that it might, in fact, be *that* bad.

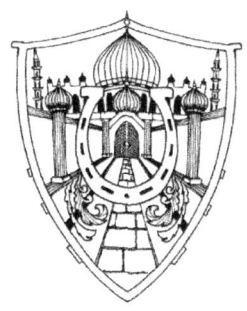

CHAPTER TWO

Nathaniel and I trudged our way up to the second floor of the Shade side of the building, to the right of the main archway, beneath the Shadow Spire. Although I could no longer see it, it somehow still felt like an ever-looming presence above us, beckoning me to my doom. I didn't have many belongings with me, only the bags that Nathaniel still dutifully carried for me, so it didn't take us long to reach my new living quarters. It was quite a depressing realisation, to know that my entire life could be packed away into two small bags.

We approached room 266 in a stilted silence, my nerves almost getting the better of me. Taking a deep breath, I slid the key into the lock. It clicked open, and the door creaked as I pushed it inwards, my eye twitching at the ominous sound.

A woman with hair the darkest shade of brown, currently tied up into a knot on top of her head, was sprawled across a bed on the left-hand side of the dimly lit room, with nothing more than her undergarments on. Not quite the sight I was expecting.

From her partial nudity, it was obvious she was a Shade. Having originated from the colder climates of Anka, they suffered from the heat of Olympia more than Flames; most at least had the decency to wear clothing, though.

"Um… hello?" I said, standing awkwardly in the doorway as my eyes darted around the small space that was devoid of colour. The room was sparse, with not much more than the two single cots pushed against opposite walls, save for an armoire, two trunks and a sink with a vanity below it. As my eyes settled back on the sharp-featured woman to my left, I noticed that she was flipping a dagger in her two fingers, already glaring at me. She was attractive, in a *'cut your hand on her cheekbones'* sort of way.

"Who the fuck are you?" She responded in a cold, monotonous voice.

I blinked back at her, slightly taken aback by her cursing. It wasn't in my nature to use such profanities, especially spending so much time around children.

"I'm your new roommate. My name's Aela," I replied cautiously, forcing a smile to my lips as I walked through the doorway, slowly closing the distance to her side of the room. I extended my hand to shake hers once I reached the foot of her bed.

She looked at my outstretched arm as if it was covered in manure and then back at my face, a sneer already starting to appear on hers. I quickly dropped my hand back to my side. I knew I should have just gone with an awkward wave. Damnit.

"Do you always speak like someone's got their hands wrapped around your throat?" She looked me up and down, her sneer developing into a full-on look of disgust. "You're not even a foot away and I barely heard what you said. The mice in the walls make more noise than you."

Horrified, I looked back over my shoulder to Nathaniel, who had edged his way into the room. I tried to convey a look of {*save me*} in his direction. Nathaniel noticed my expression and dramatically sighed as he lowered my bags to the floor with a thump – already knowing that his duties of being my social crutch were back in full swing after what I could only imagine was a much-needed break for him the last year.

"Don't be difficult, Alexis. Aela doesn't want to be in here, *almost* as much as you don't want her here, but you're just going to have to get over it. You're stuck with each other, I'm afraid." He flashed a smile at her as their gazes met, but the smile didn't reach his eyes. Instead, there was a hard glint to them, and I could tell it was his version of issuing her a warning. His look said {*behave, or you will have me to deal with*}.

"You know I hate it when people call me Alexis, orphan." She growled back.

Ah, I'm guessing it's a firm no to them being pals then.

Nathaniel released another exacerbated breath and turned his focus back to me.

"Aela, this is Lex. Even though she might be a Shade, ironically, she tends to spit fire. Once you get to know her, though, you'll realise she is all bark and no bite." He said, winking in her direction.

Before I could even process what he was saying, something zipped past my face as I was looking at Nathaniel, close enough that I could feel a stirring of air at the tip of my nose. A loud thud sounded from just behind me. *Way* too close for comfort. I whipped around to the source of the thud.

Lex's dagger was embedded into the wall behind me, still rocking from the force of the throw. It had missed me by only a few inches. Twisting back to her, my eyes were wide, my breathing much shallower than I cared to admit. My chest tightened with the start of panic. Thankfully, Lex didn't notice as her eyes were locked back on Nathaniel.

"Go careful what you spread, Everflame. People will start mistaking you for a Shade if you carry on with those lies, and we wouldn't want the little mouse to get hurt now, would we?"

• • •

A couple of hours later, the sun was approaching its full height as early afternoon loomed. After saying goodbye to Nathaniel so he could get to Combat Studies, I had managed to unpack my scarce belongings and put on the new bedsheets that had been very neatly folded at the foot of my bed in anticipation of my arrival. I'm guessing it wasn't Lex who had done something so considerate.

I was now laid back on the mattress, staring at the ceiling, waiting for the afternoon bell to chime to indicate my first official lesson. My stomach grumbled. I had missed lunch as I didn't yet know where the food hall was, but I wasn't sure whether the churning in my stomach was from hunger or nerves.

Lex had left the room not long after our charming first interaction (still partially nude) without uttering another word to me, so I didn't get the chance to ask her for directions by the time my stomach initially started to protest about an hour ago. She would have probably pointed me to the dungeon anyway, knowing my luck.

By the sound of it though, she hadn't gone far. For the first hour after her departure, all I could hear were her over-exaggerated moans and a bedpost knocking against the adjacent wall to mine. A part of me had wondered whether she had done it to unsettle me and make me even more uncomfortable, and the other part of me wondered whether she was just working off the fury she felt at having to share a room with a Flame; a fairly pathetic one at that. I wasn't exactly the formidable roommate she had probably been hoping for.

The guy that she had been entertaining herself with had stamina, though; I'll give him that.

Finally, just as boredom, hunger and irritation started to work me into a nervous frenzy, a distant bell chimed. Springing to my feet, I grabbed the small leather bag that Nathaniel had gifted me for my last birthday, now stuffed with parchments and pencils in readiness for the day, and lurched for the door in an excited hurry.

As I reached the end of my dormitory's hallway and made my way down the stone staircase to the ground floor, I realised I had absolutely no clue where I was going. Lex still hadn't returned to our room after her morning encounter with the misfortunate male next door, and although I was grateful for the peace, it did leave me wondering if she had forgone clothing for the rest of the day just to avoid me.

To my relief, when I reached the bottom of the stairs and passed through the small archway at the bottom of them, I managed to reorientate myself. I was back in the main hall, and the wide cobbled pathway outside was visible through the large entrance archway, which stood around two hundred feet high and was open to the elements.

The main hall was a vast, cavernous area, its grandeur amplified by the smooth, cool terrazzo floor beneath my feet and the tall, white stone walls that soared upward, disappearing into the dome above. The ceiling was painted with intricate, ornate images in a vibrant array of colours, though time had dulled their brilliance, giving them a faded elegance. As I gazed upward, I could just make out the distressed scenes. They depicted a fierce battle, warriors clashing with swords and shields, their faces filled with determination and valour. At the very centre of the dome, commanding attention, was a striking depiction of a beautiful blonde woman in a gilded chariot, her hair flowing like rays of sunlight. She was undoubtedly Helin, the Goddess of Sun and Fire, her expression fierce yet serene, embodying both the warmth of the sun and the power of flame. Surrounding her, swirling clouds and bursts of colour seemed to dance, lending an ethereal quality to the scene and making it hard to look away.

After several moments, I finally managed to pry my eyes away from the beauty above to scan the space around me once more. Many small archways were intricately carved out of the main hall's stone walls, each leading to shadowy passageways, much like the one I had just emerged from. People darted in and out of these openings, reminding me of gophers popping their heads in and out of their holes, their movements quick and unpredictable. As I scanned each archway, a knot of confusion tightened in my stomach regarding which direction I was meant to go. You'd think they would have provided a map or a friendly tour guide in a place this big.

Out of the corner of my eye, I noticed Leena still standing behind her table, her brow furrowed in concentration as she gathered up the papers that had previously been strewn across it like fallen leaves. I took a deep breath, the air thick with the scent of old books, summer air and sweat. Small talk had never been my forte, and I usually avoided conversations with strangers whenever possible. However, after racking my brain through all the potential outcomes of remaining silent, I concluded that I would only appear more awkward if I didn't ask for help, stumbling around like an aimless fool.

With a resolve I didn't entirely feel, I straightened my spine and donned the veil of fake confidence I had mastered years ago when Nathaniel and I ordered ale in Thellas' dimly lit taverns—very clearly under the legal drinking age. As I strode over to her, Leena's attention shifted in my direction. Her honey-coloured eyes, warm and inviting, ensnared me as they appraised me from head to toe, and a small, genuine smile graced her lovely face, making the surrounding chaos momentarily fade away.

"Aela, so nice to see you again!" She beamed, her voice bright and melodic. "Have you managed to get settled in? How is Lex treating you?"

I blushed, flattered that she remembered my name after all the people she had clearly been introduced to that day. The tension in my shoulders eased slightly at her apparent genuine warmth; she was like a sunbeam breaking through a cloudy sky.

"Hi, Leena, all sorted, thanks, but I have a class now and have absolutely no idea where I'm meant to be heading. Is there any way you could point me in the right direction for Realm History?"

There, I did it, and to my relief, my voice didn't come out as squeaky as I had anticipated. I also decided to ignore the question about Lex; it was best to avoid sharing that she had thrown a weapon at my face within the first sixty seconds of meeting each other.

"I'll do you one better; I'll walk with you!" she said, continuing to beam at me, her enthusiasm infectious.

Well, shit. I hadn't expected her to join me. Did this mean I had to engage her in conversation while we walked? Did I just stand still while I waited for her, or did I help her pack up her papers? Should I ask how her morning had gone?

Instead of doing any of these normal, logical things, I ended up bobbing awkwardly on the spot, nervously playing with the strap of my bag, looking anywhere but directly at her. My gaze landed on a particularly interesting brick at the centre of the grand archway, just above Leena, and I stared at it much longer than any sane person should, trying to will my racing thoughts to settle.

Once she had gathered her belongings, stuffing them into a satchel of her own, she passed by me, and I followed her like a baby duckling for a couple of steps. When she noticed I wasn't beside her, she paused and looked back, quirking a perfectly sculpted eyebrow in my direction.

"I won't bite, you know; you don't have to walk behind me like a creepy little ghost."

I closed the gap between us, a flush creeping up my cheeks, not entirely thrilled with that new nickname.

"Sorry," I responded, my voice barely above a whisper. "I'm not very good with new people and small talk; normally, Nathaniel is the one that wins people over."

"Silence works for me, too," she said sweetly, shrugging one of her shoulders as if to brush off the awkwardness. We walked a couple more paces until I realised she was heading toward an expansive staircase situated directly in the centre of the main hall, leading to a grand mezzanine level. Gods, how in the Realm had I missed that? It was almost precisely beneath the centre of the domed ceiling, but I must have been too busy looking up to notice it before. I wrinkled my nose. Great, not only did Leena think I was a weird, creepy lurker, but she probably now thought I was an idiot, too.

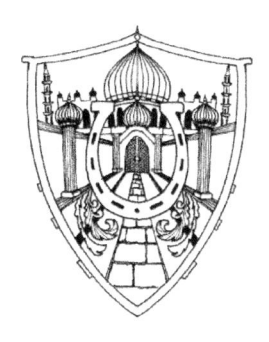

CHAPTER THREE

As Leena and I ascended the large marble staircase, the steps widened beneath us, each one polished to a high sheen that gleamed in the warm afternoon light pouring in from the archway behind us. The air around us buzzed with the sounds of laughter and conversation, punctuated by the rhythmic thud of boots on marble.

I took in those who moved around me, a vibrant tapestry of students, each a unique blend of sizes, shapes, and colours. Some Cadets smiled broadly, their voices rising in cheerful banter, while others moved with purpose, their heads buried deep in the pages of thick tomes, lost in worlds far removed from the bustling reality of the college.

As we climbed higher, I spotted a group of third-year Cadets descending the staircase. They were clad in worn fighting leathers, the fabric scuffed and stained from rigorous training. Sweat glistened on their foreheads, and mud clung to their boots, evidence of the gruelling exercises they had most likely just endured. A few of them bore the unmistakable marks of recent combat — flecks of blood splattered across their faces, a stark reminder of the realities of combat training.

Steel weapons adorned their sides. It was well-known that students, or 'Cadets' as they were known, were not permitted to wield real weapons until they had completed several years of rigorous training; this rule was in place not only to prevent injury but also to symbolise their rank and readiness.

On one of my visits to the War College, Nathaniel had explained to me the intricate process behind the steel weapons carried by the third-year Cadets and Olympian warriors. Each blade and spear was not merely forged; it was actually individually crafted by the Crown's personal Mage, a master of the ancient art of imbuing metal with magic. This skill allowed the Mage to weave threads of enchantment into the very core of the steel, so that when the weapon fell into the hands of its rightful owner, it would amplify their innate abilities.

For some, this bond was almost instantaneous, a moment of connection that ignited a surge of power. For others, however, it could take years of training and persistence before they truly felt the weapon respond to them. The process was deeply personal, and it was said that if anyone else were to wield your weapon once it had bonded to you, it would be nothing more than a basic piece of metal in their hands.

Whispers floated throughout the Realm that some weapons were so fiercely bonded to their owners that they possessed the ability to drain the magic of anyone else who dared to pick them up, leaving the intruder utterly defenceless. If the rumours were true, it would be an unfortunate reality that could spell disaster on the battlefield if you were to pick up the wrong blade from the ground amongst the chaos.

Stories also circulated that King Aadhar, the ruler of Anka—the Realm shrouded in shadows on the other side of the Continent—had a Mage who had mastered the ability to create magically enchanted steel collars and bracelets. This 'jewellery' could apparently drain you of your magic, strength, and sometimes even your consciousness, rendering you powerless and vulnerable in an instant. The thought sent a chill down my spine, a reminder of the dark and treacherous nature of power in a world where steel and magic intertwined.

As we finally reached the top of the staircase, Leena pointed to the left.

"That way leads to the huge roof terrace where Combat Studies takes place; you'll get there through the Fire Spire. Opposite that, there's another archway that takes you to the cafeteria. All our meals are served there, and it is also where we gather every Saturday morning for the Realm Announcements. Sunday is the only day we don't have any lessons, but most Cadets use the day for combat practice sessions to make sure what we have learnt that week has sunk in, with third years overseeing us."

It's no secret that I was absolutely terrified of my first Combat Studies lesson, as I was no better than a newly-born fawn when it came to balance and coordination. Fortunately, that wasn't until tomorrow, and today's lesson was supposedly held in more of a classroom environment. We turned to the right at the top of the flight of stairs as Leena continued her tour guide audition. "This way leads to the library, the War Room, and Professor Sephere's classroom at the end of the corridor."

My ears perked up. Safe to say, this was more my side of the building.

"War Room?" I asked excitedly.

"Yes," she smiled. "Every week, a different group of students is selected to take part in a mock war council; this can range from debating the previous week's Realm Announcement to how you would react if there was a skirmish in one of the Realms' Sectors. If you are lucky, you might even take part in a discussion of how you would navigate a war between Olympia and Anka if it were ever to happen again."

Her eyes sparkled when they met mine, and I had no doubt that mine were doing the exact same thing.

The Continent was divided into two Realms, Olympia and Anka; both were then split into what we called 'sectors.' Although Anka was larger than Olympia, much of its northern landscape was dominated by towering mountains, their peaks often cloaked in a thick blanket of ice and snow that glistened under the pale sun. The jagged cliffs and treacherous slopes made traversing that portion of the Realm perilous, with narrow paths winding through rocky outcrops. The harsh northern terrain left only a few areas in the southern sectors of Anka habitable, and even these flat plains were subjected to the relentless chill of a seemingly endless winter. The biting winds swept across the land, making it nearly impossible for crops to thrive; fields that should have flourished were often left barren, with frost clinging to the ground long after the last harvest.

This unyielding cold drove many Shades —the main inhabitants of Anka — to seek refuge in the warmer, more hospitable climates of Olympia. Most of the Southern Realm was enveloped in lush greenery that stretched between the bustling towns and villages. Rolling hills and fields undulated like waves across the landscapes of Monacus, Orouras, Thellas and northern parts of Mytos, some adorned with a vibrant array of wildflowers, patches of delicate daisies, and tall, thick trees that provided shelter for a variety of animals, creating a harmonious blend of nature and life.

At the southernmost tip of Olympia lay the hottest sector, Solarus. Here, the landscape transformed dramatically. Dry, dusty soil that cracked under the relentless sun created an almost otherworldly terrain. As one ventured closer to the coast, the earth turned to sand, stretching out into golden dunes that shimmered in the heat. Despite its beauty, Solarus also bore the scars of its harsh climate, with vegetation so sparse that what survived practically clung to life throughout the year. The stark contrasts between the tips of both Realms felt like two different worlds entirely, much like the sun and the moon.

As Leena and I stepped through the final archway of the corridor into the room designated for my first lesson, I was immediately struck by the change in architecture. The air felt heavier here, infused with a sense of history that clung to the dark stone walls, each surface looking rough and cool to the touch, unlike the polished marble of the mezzanine and main hall we had just passed through.

The room was circular, its proportions strangely small yet dizzyingly tall. I squinted, straining to take in the distant details of the ceiling, which seemed to stretch far above like some ancient, unreachable sky. A single small window faintly illuminated the space, casting dim light that made the dust particles in the air shimmer like ghosts. Long shadows sprawled up the walls, twisting in unsettling patterns, as if the room itself were alive. We had clearly entered the Shadow Spire.

Refocusing my attention ahead of me, I noticed there was a small central area where an older gentleman stood. He was surrounded by stone seats that were arranged in concentric circles, gradually rising with each layer. The seats, carved from the same dark stone as the spire, bore the marks of countless students who had come before, their surfaces polished from years of use. Students were trickling in around us, their conversations echoing off the stone as they settled into the multiple tiers leading up to the back walls.

The space reminded me of the amphitheatres in the north of the Queen's sector, Mytos—or at least, how Nanny Rosie used to describe them. According to her stories, they had once been grand spectacles, hosting plays, music, and tournaments. Now, though, they were little more than crumbled ruins, lost to time.

"I think we should sit on the bottom seats so we can hear Professor Sephere; his voice doesn't carry that well to the back," Leena said.

I turned to her, a frown on my face.

"Wait, you're in this class? I thought you were a second-year?"

Leena let out a frustrated huff.

"Yes, I am, but they're making me retake Sephere's class. My father is a dock worker at Orouras, and my mother is one of the Passage Guardians at the Wall, so no one ever really had the time to teach me our history growing up. Whenever my mother returned home, which is only a couple of times a year, she would spend that time teaching me how to fight. I am almost always top of the class in Combat Studies, but Commander Bellum constantly shrieks at us that '*an uneducated warrior is a dead warrior*', so here I am, luckily for you!" she said, offering me a small wink.

Slightly taken aback by how transparent she was about her upbringing, I couldn't help but feel a little awed by the fact that her mother was the warrior of their household. None of the men, let alone the women, in Thellas knew how to fight, which often made me fearful of how defenceless we would be if there was ever an attack, especially given how inland our Sector was.

We moved to take a seat on the stone bench in front of Professor Sephere. He was a small, stout gentleman who clearly had a passion for woollen cardigans. As I bent down to pull a pencil and parchment from my bag, a set of large boots appeared directly in front of my face.

"Well, who's this pretty lady you have here, Leena?" came a male voice from above me. As I looked up, my eyes landed on an extremely broad man with auburn-coloured hair, cut shorter on the sides and left longer on top. Bright blue eyes stared down at me; a few shades lighter than my own. He had pale skin with freckles, and a boyish grin appeared across his face as he took me in.

"Leave her alone, Jaxon. I'm trying to make a good impression here, and the last thing she needs is for you to be wittering in her ear all afternoon," Leena responded, applying pressure to her eyes with the heels of her palms, seemingly already annoyed.

"Ah, c'mon, Leena. You know I'm like a moth to a flame when it comes to an attractive lady." He darted his eyes between Leena and me, waggling his eyebrows, clearly proud of himself for making a pun about me being a Flame.

"More like a fly to shit," she retorted, and I let out a surprised laugh at her dry, quick wit as I sat back in my seat—pencil, parchment, and writing board now resting on my lap. She swivelled her head to me, and a stunning smile appeared on her face.

I couldn't help but meet her smile with my own. I'd only spent a few minutes in her company, but Leena simply radiated warmth, even if her potty mouth could rival Lex's.

I felt body heat on my right side as Jaxon sidled up close to me, pulling out his own writing equipment. He was an oaf of a man who completely invaded my personal space; I couldn't help but feel slightly claustrophobic, squashed between the two of them.

"Aela, this is Jaxon. He's also a second-year, having to retake the class after proving he's even more hopeless than me when it comes to academia," Leena sighed.

"What can I say?" Jaxon shrugged, the movement knocking my shoulder slightly as he invaded my personal space even further. "There's only so many times you can get hit over the head with a wooden sword in a year before the signs start to show." He winked at me. "So, Aela, you're a Flame, I take it, given the colour of your hair?"

Although there were many colours of hair and skin among Flames and Shades, my blonde hair was a beacon to the fact that I was undoubtedly a Fire Wielder, as there had never been a fair-haired Shadow Summoner throughout history. It was commonly believed that blonde hair only appeared in those with the strongest fire abilities, many believing it was a sign that you were a direct descendant of The Goddess Helin herself. However, my lacklustre performance when it came to summoning my magic clearly proved otherwise.

"Flame," I nodded in response, still smiling from Leena's previous remark.

"That's a shame; it would have been nice to have you on my side of the building with me and the rest of the Shades." He genuinely looked slightly disappointed, like someone had dangled a shiny toy in front of him but he wasn't able to have it.

"She's actually sharing a room with Lex!" Leena cut in. I glared at her, not wanting everyone to know where I would be sleeping at night, although I imagined no one would dare barge into a room with Lex and her daggers on the other side of the door.

"Lex?!" Jaxon snorted. A moment passed before he tipped back his head and roared with laughter. As he tried to catch his breath, he continued, "Damn girl, has she tried to attack you yet? Or better yet, tried to sleep with you? I never know which way it's going to go with her."

"Errr," I stammered, "Well, she did throw a dagger at my head when I tried to say hello," I replied, my voice slightly quieter than before, my cheeks turning a light shade of pink.

"What!?" Leena shrieked, and Jaxon's laughter resumed.

"That's foreplay for her!" he said, wiping away a stray tear as he attempted to compose himself.

What I found even more surprising than Jaxon's crude comments was the fact that he had absolutely no problem laughing and joking with two Flames. I looked between Leena and Jaxon while they continued to make barbs at each other and realised there was genuinely no hostility between the two of them.

"Wait," I interrupted them, "Are you two actually friends?!" My voice came out slightly louder and squeakier than I intended. Gods, I was going to be crowned this year's social pariah if I couldn't get my act together.

"Of course," Jaxon said without hesitation, his face suddenly becoming more serious. "Leena's mum is one of the Guardians who helped my parents cross the passageway when my older brother, Ollie, was just a baby," he went on, "They couldn't afford a third license for him at the time, but Leena's mum helped them out anyway, as she knew that's what Queen Elena would have wanted. Leena's mum told my parents her husband would help them if they could make it to the docks of Orouras, which, thankfully for my family, they did. Leena's dad spoke with one of the noblemen there and managed to barter for lodgings for my family so long as my father took a position with the rest of the dock workers."

He was on a roll now, the words spilling from his mouth. "We grew up across the street from Leena, and she hasn't been able to get rid of me ever since." He smiled across at her, and there was no longer a hint of a cheeky smirk on his face—just a look of adoration for his childhood friend. "My family raised me not to care what kind of magic you have; if you are good people, you are our people."

His statement surprised me, and as I waited for the class to start, I found myself thinking it might not be so bad here after all.

CHAPTER FOUR

"Settle down, Cadets, settle down!" Professor Sephere's nasally voice bounced around the room and up the spire, the space acting like an echo chamber. I looked around and noticed that the room had substantially filled up since my new friends and I had been talking; there must have been almost two hundred people squeezed into the space.

"Today, we are going over what you know about the current rulers of Olympia and Anka. Hopefully, this is an easy topic for your first lesson, and second-years, Gods help me if you still don't know the answers to these questions." He took a deep, wheezing breath, and I sensed that he had never partaken in a single day of action on the front lines.

"So, an easy one to start: who can tell me how long Queen Elena has held the throne for?!"

"Fifty years!" a voice in the back of the room shouted in response.

"Correct!" Sephere returned to the distant voice, shaking a pudgy finger in the Cadet's direction in confirmation.

Apparently, in her first few decades of ruling, Queen Elena had been celebrated far and wide for her radiant kindness and striking beauty. Tales of her golden hair cascading like sunlight and her warm, genuine smile that could light up even the darkest corners of her court often circulated throughout the Realm. Noblemen would practically trip over themselves to secure an audience with her, eager to bask in her presence rather than endure the gruelling hours of meetings with her husband, King Gerrard, whose assertive demeanour often overshadowed the gentler aspects of his wife's presence.

Their marriage, forged not long after her coronation, was often viewed as a storybook romance. Although they married at a young age, not much older than I was now, their bond was said to be unshakeable, rooted in mutual respect and deep affection. For decades, they had been the envy of the Realm, exemplifying a partnership that blended strength and compassion seamlessly.

However, the shadows cast by King Gerrard's untimely death, just shy of twenty years ago, had transformed her entirely. It was as if the vibrant colours of her spirit had dulled to muted shades of grey.

The soft, endearing qualities that once defined her reign hardened, and soon became stories of the past. The Realm, which had once thrived on her warmth, fell silent, replaced by an atmosphere thick with tension and uncertainty. Although Elena still ruled with a sense of duty and responsibility, her decisions increasingly lacked the compassion that had once been her hallmark. The once-lively halls of the palace were rumoured to feel cold and distant, reflecting a ruler who had become a mere shadow of her former self. It was as though part of her essence had withered and died alongside her beloved husband, leaving behind a queen who bore the weight of the crown but not the heart that had once made her so adored.

Elena remained vigilant about maintaining a strong army, even though Olympia and Anka hadn't warred in nearly seventy years. Almost all of Olympia's taxes still went toward feeding and housing the troops, with the remaining drachmae going toward the orphanages. I often pondered why she had such a vested interest in looking after those of us with no parents. In response to my questions, Nanny Rosie always said to me, "*Well, my little ember, it is believed that when King Gerrard died, Queen Elena vowed she would never love another and therefore, would never bear an heir of blood. This is her way of having children without breaking those vows. It is said that anyone who bears her last name, Everflame, if they have enough power and prove themselves worthy to rule, with the Gods' permission, they might one day take her place."*

This always sounded too good to be true to me, and I often thought that it was just the Queen's way of ensuring that everyone across the Continent was reminded that we grew up without families or wealth; a subtle way of weeding out the weak and holding us back. Nathaniel didn't share this belief; in fact, I could tell it filled him with hope. We often talked late into the night in our shared room as children.

"You know, one day Aela, an Everflame orphan will lead the Olympians into battle and will go on to rule over not only Olympia, but Anka too."

I had no doubt that he was envisioning himself on the throne. I used to laugh and think it was a stupid boyish dream, but given the amount of power he now wielded, and his dedication to ensuring he would be a key part of the Olympian army once he graduated, a part of me wondered whether he might one day achieve it.

"Now for the Ankans in the room, how long has King Aadhar ruled the Shadow Lands?!" Sephere's question jolted me back to the present.

"Three hundred years!" Jaxon shouted back.

"Correct!"

Jaxon fist-bumped the air in triumph, and I rolled my eyes at him. If he was going to celebrate getting something that easy right, it looked like he was going to spend a third year in this classroom.

King Aadhar, the current ruler of Anka, or the 'Shadow Lands' as some called it, had been in power for nearly three centuries. The crown's power led to a much longer lifespan, making the rulers and their chosen inner circle seemingly immortal. When a ruler died (often by assassination due to their lack of aging), the crown's magic then selected the next worthy heir within the bloodline. In some cases, second or third cousins were chosen, as there only needed to be a drop of royal blood in their veins. I often thought it must have been a startling way of finding out your family member had been killed when the crown suddenly magically appeared above your head.

Over the millennia, only a few rulers had been given the gift of physically passing the crown onto their chosen heir while they still lived, the process allowing them to grow old with grace. It was believed to be a blessing from the Gods, a sign that you had ruled honourably and that the Gods trusted your choice of succession.

"And what about Queen Alinoura, Elena's mother? Can anyone give me any information about her?!" Sephere questioned.

There was silence throughout the space. I knew a fair bit about Queen Alinoura, but there was no way I was going to spin a tale in front of two hundred people on my first day.

The Professor puffed out his chest at the lack of response and took another deep inhale. "Queen Alinoura was, and remains to be, Olympia's longest reigning monarch, having overseen many battles in her six hundred years on the throne. She was an enviable fighter and was often on the frontlines, something that not many rulers did. Countless believed she was the daughter of Helin herself."

A few gasps were heard throughout the auditorium at the insinuation that Alinoura was the Lost God, but they were silenced by a raised hand from Sephere. He continued his tirade.

"It wasn't until after the Treaty of Peace was signed just over fifty years ago that she decided to hand over the kingdom to her seventeen-year-old daughter, Elena; a choice that the Gods granted. Although Queen Alinoura was known to be a mighty warrior with the strongest Flame Wielding abilities in history, she is now known as 'The Peace Bringer' throughout our lands."

Of course, I already knew all of this from Nanny Rosie's bedtime stories; however, Sephere's musings continued once more. The man liked the sound of his own voice, that was for sure.

"Queen Alinoura lived another thirty-three years after she passed on the crown, which allowed her to watch her daughter marry and then mourn King Gerrard alongside her. It was rumoured, however, that Alinoura could no longer watch her daughter grieve and that it was that very sorrow that led to her death. A death of a broken heart."

I had been just three years old when I learned of Queen Alinoura's passing; the news swept through our village like a tornado, a storm of grief that left devastation in its wake. The sky seemed to darken as whispers of the tragedy spread, and the very air itself felt heavy with sorrow. Many of the nannies at the orphanage dropped to their knees, their faces twisted in despair, as tears streamed down their cheeks. Some clutched their hands to their hearts as if the weight of the news had struck them physically. I remember that the sound of their weeping had filled the air, a mournful chorus that echoed in the hearts of all who heard it.

In those moments, I couldn't fully grasp the significance of Alinoura's death, but the palpable anguish that surrounded me at the time had seeped into my small bones. I could see the way the older children looked at each other, their eyes wide with a mix of confusion and fear, reflecting the loss of a figure who had seemed larger than life. It became clearer to me, as I grew older, why Queen Elena had hardened into the cold and distant ruler she was now. The unbearable weight of losing both her beloved husband and her mother in such a short span of time must have been a crushing blow, one that shattered the light within her.

To add to her grief, the immense pressure of living up to her mother's extraordinary legacy surely loomed over her like a dark cloud. Alinoura had been a revered warrior and a beacon of hope for the Realm, her name synonymous with strength and compassion. The burden of expectations, coupled with the rawness of her losses, had undoubtedly etched lines of sorrow into Elena's heart, transforming her into a figure of regal indifference. I could only imagine the internal struggle she faced, caught between the memories of her former joy and the relentless duty that now defined her existence.

However, Queen Elena was still like a ray of sunshine in comparison to King Aadhar. Aadhar's reputation as a cold-blooded ruler preceded him; he was known to play the long game, using diplomacy as a tool to buy himself precious time. He exuded an almost oppressive shadow that seemed to drain the light from his Realm. Whispers of his cunning and cruelty circulated among Olympians, painting him as a master tactician more interested in power than in peace, despite the fact that he initiated the 'Treaty of Peace' with Queen Alinoura.

The last Realm war, seventy years ago (twenty years prior to the Treaty being signed), ravaged Anka's resources and depleted its ranks. Many Olympians, including myself, believed that the Treaty was merely a strategic manoeuvre, a façade to cloak his true intentions. I truly believed that for Aadhar, the Treaty was an opportunity — a chance to regroup and fortify his forces, to rebuild the Ankan Army into the formidable force that it once was, while maintaining an air of legitimacy. The people of Olympia remained blissfully unaware of the brewing storm on their borders. It was only a matter of time until havoc rained down on us once more.

"What can anyone tell me about the Treaty of Peace?" Sephere asked, his eyes searching around the room. I frowned; it was almost as if my thoughts had summoned his question.

"It allowed for the Passageway to be built!" Leena shouted back, pride in her eyes.

"Well done, Miss Du Preez!" Sephere nodded in our direction. "It looks like you did learn something last year after all."

Leena rolled her eyes.

"My mother's a Passage Guardian, arsehole." She muttered under her breath, and I couldn't help but let out a giggle.

"Is something funny, Cadet?!" Sephere barked, his focus snapping to me. All eyes turned in my direction, and I could feel myself living out my worst nightmare in real time. I instantly felt my face turn red and a rash appear on my chest around the necklace Nathaniel had made for me when we were children.

"Um, no Sir, I mean, Professor." I managed to force out. Gods, my voice sounded like I had just eaten a mouthful of potato and hadn't quite managed to swallow it all.

"What's your name, child?"

Oh good, he was patronising me now too.

"Aela," I responded, spluttering over my name slightly as I attempted to clear my throat.

"Well, Aela, how about you tell the rest of the class what you know about the Treaty of Peace and the Passageway, if you find my teachings to be such a joke?"

Fantastic. Absolutely *fantastic*. It looked like my coronation as this year's 'social pariah' was going to take place any day now. I took a deep, shaky breath and pictured myself as that confident fourteen-year-old trying to buy ale from my local tavern in Thellas. Clearing my throat for a final time, I began.

"Well… throughout our history, there has always been a divide between our two Realms, with the Crown of Flame ruling over Olympia, and the Crown of Shadow ruling over Anka. It used to be strictly forbidden for a Flame to enter Ankan territory, and vice versa. The border was, and still is, separated by a huge wall running from coast to coast."

I took another deep breath; my potato-throat seemed to have subsided, but I still needed to breathe; otherwise, I would pass out before I finished; black spots were already starting to swim in my vision as panic and embarrassment threatened to overwhelm me.

{Here goes nothing} I thought to myself.

"The wall used to be magically warded, so either ruler could feel if someone with unwelcomed magic entered their Realm. It was known that once found, the intruder would be executed on sight."

I gulped at the thought of this, trying to suppress a shudder as I imagined the countless Shades; desperately cold and starving, trying to find solace in the warmth of Olympia, only to be murdered for doing so.

"This separation led to many wars over the centuries, and Anka's population started to dwindle due to their harsh winters and their food becoming sparse with the King trying to keep his army fed. King Aadhar appealed to Queen Alinoura for a peace treaty between the Realms, which after careful consideration, Queen Alinoura accepted, having also grown tired. This led to a Passageway being created in the wall that is now fully monitored by guards on both sides, who are known as the Guardians." I cast a quick glance toward Leena as I finished and offered her a small smile at the mention of her mother's role.

"You go, girl," Jaxon whispered, bumping my shoulder in a supportive gesture.

"Very good, Cadet," Sephere said after several seconds, although it was evident in his tone that he had been hoping I would flounder. I sagged in my seat, relief washing over me.

Sephere finally turned his attention away from me to address the room, my moment of glory quickly over.

"As you all know, for safe passage between the Realms, you need a Permit of Passage that is to be authorised by the leading noble of your Sector; however, if you are looking to relocate entirely, you have to obtain a License of Residence from the Crown or a member of their inner circle, known as the *Elite*." He said matter-of-factly.

A License of Residence could often be bought for around five thousand drachmae; it would take me over forty years to earn that working at the orphanage, and that was without me buying any food or clothing. That being said, if you had a particular skill or magic that was useful to a Realm, the license would also be considered. This was how most of the lesser elementals, mainly those with earth-working abilities, ended up living in Anka, so they could assist with growing crops in the frost-ridden soil. It's also why the wealthier now saturated the Sectors of Olympia, as they were able to buy their way to a warmer and easier life.

Unsurprisingly, there were no orphanages throughout Anka under King Aadhar's rule, which led to a lot of infants being smuggled across the Passageway. It was an unspoken law among the Olympian Guardians of the wall to allow the children entry and to bring them to the closest orphanage, even if they didn't have a permit or license. This must have been why Leena's mother helped Jaxon's family smuggle his brother into Olympia.

It was said that if Aadhar caught wind of a child crossing without the appropriate documentation before they could reach the safety of an Olympian Guardian, well… let's just say that neither the child nor their family were ever seen again.

The King was known to take satisfaction from capturing and imprisoning people that were opposed to his leadership. It was also common knowledge that he had a harem at his beck and call, and that most of them were not there by choice. Noblemen who had visited the Shadow Palace for matters of the Crown would return to Olympia with a haunted look in their eyes, relaying how the King had young men and women, some no older than fifteen, chained to his throne, demonstrating sexual acts for all that cared to watch. Some had said that Aadhar would apparently be sitting on his throne, addressing a room full of people about Realm matters and how the relationship between

Olympia and Anka could be improved, whilst one of his chained slaves would be seated on his lap, making forced screams of ecstasy out of fear for their life, as he thrust deeply into them. The thought of this made me sick, and I prayed that I would never have to witness something like it one day.

CHAPTER FIVE

Thankfully, the rest of Sephere's class had passed without any extra attention on me. As Leena, Jaxon, and I exited, I excused myself from their presence, eager to visit the library to see if they had any rare tomes on the Gods that I hadn't managed to get my hands on growing up.

The Gods had always been my favourite subject to read about, as I often found the rivalry between the Flames and the Shades to be a captivating mystery, given that our two main gods, Nykus and Helin, were married. Nykus was the God of Night and Shadow, often depicted as a strikingly beautiful man with skin as pale as the moon, and hair as black as the sky in the depths of night. Helin was the God of Sun and Fire, characterised by her bronzed skin and hair the colour of sunlight, not too dissimilar from my own. She was often shown in a luminous chariot drawn by a magnificent white horse with wings made of amber flame.

Nanny Rosie often told me that her white-winged stallion was named 'Phaethon', but I was yet to find a reliable source that confirmed that.

It was believed that Helin led many battles at the inception of this world, and older murals depicted her in her golden war chariot, drawn by two winged horses, instead of one. The first was Phaethon, but the other was a stunning black stallion whose wings flickered with silver flames, a beautiful contrast against Phaethon's white coat and amber wings. Many people believed that the black horse represented Nykus before he took on an alternate form during battle, as it was rumoured that he could use his shadows to take any shape. This theory led to a variety of statues and altars being erected across the Continent in homage to the Dark God, ranging from the black-winged stallion to a black crow perched on Helin's shoulder.

As I passed through the archway that Leena had previously indicated led to the library, I stopped dead in my tracks, awestruck by the sight before me. Much like the grand hall, the ceiling was a magnificent dome, intricately painted with celestial motifs, and a vast floor-to-ceiling-stained glass window dominated the far wall, its colours shimmering in the afternoon light. The glass depicted scenes of the Gods, their forms captured in vibrant hues of deep greens and rich reds, transforming sunlight into a kaleidoscope of colours that danced across the room.

The walls on either side of me towered at least twenty feet high, lined with bookcases crammed to the brim with tomes of every shape and size, not a single space left empty. Rows upon rows of books seemed to stare back at me, their spines whispering tales of ancient lore and forgotten histories. Some were bound in cracked leather, while others glimmered with gold leaf, hinting at the secrets they held within.

Taking in more of the space, I noticed how the light filtering through the stained glass was muted yet warm, casting a cozy glow that enveloped the room and made it feel like a sanctuary away from the relentless Olympian sun.

Multiple rugs in similar hues adorned the floor, and large mahogany tables were scattered throughout the space, each accompanied by comfortable-looking armchairs tucked beneath them. Fire-lamps flickered atop the desks, adding to the warm glow from the window. When I raised my gaze back to the domed ceiling, a lump formed in my throat as I noticed hundreds of small orbs emitting a soft, ethereal light. They floated in mid-air, bobbing gently like lanterns dancing on the surface of a tranquil lake, their glow illuminating the intricate patterns painted on the ceiling. The sight was breathtakingly beautiful, and I found myself getting lost in them for several moments.

I had no idea what kind of magic was at play, but the orbs remained suspended above me, reminding me of the tapestry of stars that I often admired whenever I couldn't sleep, finding myself constantly entranced by the night sky.

Finally managing to tear my eyes away from the mesmerising orbs, I noticed a gracefully curved staircase at the back of the room, nestled to the right of the magnificent window. The staircase spiralled upward, its polished wooden banister gleaming softly in the warm light. I couldn't see much of the second floor from where I stood, but I imagined there were likely just as many books waiting to be discovered up there.

Underneath the staircase caught my attention. It was furnished with large, plush cushions in rich, earthy tones, scattered across the floor like oversized pillows; a perfect spot for lounging and losing myself in a book. Soft fur throws were draped over the edges of them, adding a touch of luxury and warmth, while the gentle glow of fire-lamps hanging from the underside of the staircase created an intimate ambiance that felt almost magical.

As the hours ticked by, the library grew darker, signalling that evening was approaching. I had combed through every inch of the shelves, selecting at least forty books that I wanted to read — ranging from

Histories of War, to Royal Family trees, accounts of extinct mystical creatures, and even a couple of books on Helin and Nykus' descendants that I hadn't encountered before. Weirdly, I appeared to have had the library to myself all afternoon. Surely a space as wondrous as this would have been highly sought after?

"Are you lost, child?" a croaking voice suddenly sounded from my left.

My heart nearly burst from my chest; I hadn't noticed anyone approaching while I was absorbed in examining the spines of the nearest shelf. I swivelled quickly on the balls of my feet, my eyes widening as they took in the figure standing next to me. Within a couple of heartbeats, I understood why no one else was in the library.

I wasn't sure whether the face I was staring at belonged to a male or female, but it possessed the palest complexion I had ever seen on a person. The figure's skin was so white that it was almost translucent, revealing a network of blue and green veins beneath the surface, and I swore I could see them pulsing faintly in the lamplight.

There was no hair on its head, save for a few long, wispy strands that clung precariously above its ears, as if they were remnants of a forgotten life. The creature's face appeared sunken and grey, with hollow cheeks that gave it an almost skeletal appearance, and its lips were drawn tight, as if never to smile again.

The most unsettling feature of all, though, was its eyes. They were nearly entirely white, clouded over like a foggy winter sky, and yet somehow, they seemed to bore into me with an unsettling intensity. It surely must have been blind, yet there was an eerie awareness in its gaze, as if it could see into the depths of my very soul. Light, stained robes hung from its bony body like a damp cloth. The creature was so thin that I was fairly certain a strong breeze could lift it from the floor and blow it away like a feather on the wind.

A chill ran down my arms, making my hair stand on end. This individual was, without a shadow of a doubt, the most unattractive being I had ever encountered. The air around it felt heavier, charged with a strange energy that made it hard to breathe, as if the very atmosphere recoiled from its presence.

I gulped, recalling it had asked me a question.

"Um, no… t..t..thank you. I was actually hoping to find my way to the food hall for supper. You have such a wonderful collection of books here that I hadn't noticed how late it was."

I stumbled over my words, my tongue tripping over itself as the unsettling figure edged closer to me. There was a long pause as it processed my statement, and much to my horror, it began leaning in even closer. I wasn't particularly tall — Nathaniel could rest his chin on my head — but this creature was small, only an inch or so taller than me, so when it leaned forward, its nose was practically an inch from mine. Without warning, a gnarled hand shot out and grasped my chin faster than my eyes could follow, twisting my head to the side, it brought my cheek close to its nose. The icy touch sent a shiver down my spine, leaving me frozen in place. It inhaled deeply, and I realised a moment too late what it was doing.

It was sniffing me.

Actually *sniffing* me.

Who in the Realm did that to someone they had just met?! At least buy a girl a tankard of ale first. Summoning all my courage, I took a step back, yanking my head free from its grasp.

"What in all of Olympia do you think you're doing?!" I whisper-shouted, adrenaline spiking through my veins like wildfire.

A surge of pride coursed through me; it wasn't in my nature to be confrontational, but the sudden rush of fear had clearly ignited a spark of bravery. The mist in the creature's eyes appeared to swirl and dance for a moment, like smoke dissipating into the air, before settling once more into an unnerving stillness.

"Hmmmm, I do believe you are lost, little Ember. You seem to be a long way from home…" It rasped, a forked tongue darting out to flick across its dry, chapped lips, much like a serpent scenting a mouse.

"W…w…what did you just call me?" More fear surged through me; only Nanny Rosie called me that, and there was no way this creature could know that. *Should* know that. "Who are you?" I croaked, tears prickling at the corners of my eyes, blending fear with an inexplicable sense of vulnerability.

"I am a person of many names, little Ember, but you may call me Az, for we are friends after all, you and I." It paused, cocking its head slightly as if listening to something. "Run along, child; someone is searching for you. But come and see me again when you are ready for some answers, and I will ensure I have the right book waiting for you."

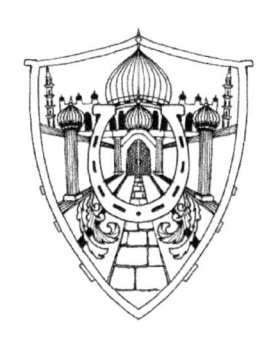

CHAPTER SIX

I fled from the library as quickly as my little legs could carry me, not daring a glance back at the skeletal figure. I thought Leena's nickname for me earlier, *'creepy little ghost',* was much more appropriate for Az rather than myself. As I raced through the library's archway, I collided with a hard body as I turned the corner, letting out a small yelp as I stumbled back.

"Aela?!" Nathaniel said as he looked down at me, his brows furrowing with concern as he instinctively grabbed onto my shoulders to prevent me from falling. His grip was firm yet reassuring, grounding me in the midst of my panic. Once I had caught my balance, he pushed me back slightly, his intense gaze searching mine, trying to read the storm of emotions swirling within my wide eyes and bloodless face. "I've been looking for you everywhere… what's wrong?!" His voice was a mix of urgency and care, and I could see his eyes quickly scanning the space behind me, searching for any looming threat.

I could hear my heart pounding loudly in my ears, each beat echoing the dread that Az's words had ignited in my mind. How could he have known Nathaniel had been searching for me? The thought sent a shiver down my already chilled spine.

Nathaniel took in my face once more and his expression softened when he realised there was no looming threat behind me. After a brief moment, he glanced back towards the way I had come, letting out a long sigh that seemed to exhale the tension from the air. A crooked smile crept onto his lips, a mixture of relief and mischief dancing in his eyes.

"Something tells me you may have just met our friendly resident librarian."

"Friendly?" I squeaked, disbelief colouring my voice. Then, a small, ragged laugh escaped my lips, breaking the fragile silence. My hands trembled as I balled them into tight fists against Nathaniel's shirt, a desperate attempt to steady my racing heart while I focused on taking deep, calming breaths.

Nathaniel's face relaxed, and his crooked smile turned into something softer.

"His name is Azrael; he likes to make somewhat of a memorable first impression."

"It's a man?!" My voice was incredulous, a mixture of shock and disbelief.

"Yeah, well, we think so. He used to be one, anyway." Nathaniel turned and put one of his arms around my shoulders, leading me toward the other side of the mezzanine. "There are a lot of rumours about him. Some say that he is descended from a long line of seers because of the scary eyes and his ability to always know what's going on. Others say he can talk to the dead. Leena likes to taunt Jaxon - who is petrified of him by the way - by saying that Azrael used to help Ouran by transporting the souls of the dead. But Ouran got so pissed off with his cryptic nonsense that he decided to leave Azrael here. I personally think it's all a load of shit and that he's just a Shadow Whisperer with an iron deficiency."

I could sense Nathaniel's light-heartedness was intended to soothe me, and as we walked, I felt some of the tension ebbing away. Nathaniel was my safety, my home, and just being near him eased my pulse back to a steadier rhythm.

We walked through the archway of the food hall on the other side of the mezzanine, and the smell of roasted meats hit me like a slap to the face. My stomach growled in response, reminding me that I hadn't eaten all day, save for a pear I had hastily snacked on in the cart before arriving. How had it only been a few hours since I stepped into this world?

The cafeteria was a stark contrast to the intricate décor of the library. The ceiling, predictably domed, loomed above us, but the room itself was square and utilitarian. At least forty tables lined the space, each with benches flanking either side, most occupied by about ten people or so. A door at the far end of the room swung open and shut with a rhythmic cadence, revealing figures clad in white aprons darting in and out, transporting steaming dishes from the kitchen to the hungry Cadets eagerly awaiting their supper.

"Nath! Aela! Over here!" Leena called to us, her elegant arm waving frantically in the air to catch our attention. We made our way over to where she sat with Jaxon and another auburn-haired man. He looked a lot like Jaxon; however, his cheekbones were more pronounced, his skin slightly darker, and his hair much longer and curlier. He was also much leaner than Jaxon, but it was clear he was firm with muscle.

"This is my brother Ollie, the uglier of the two of us. Unfortunately for him, he's only ten months older than me, so we were in all the same classes last year." Jaxon beamed, nudging his brother with an elbow. Ollie rolled his eyes while lifting a goblet of water to his mouth. Ollie and I made eye contact, and he offered me a small nod in greeting; I offered a coy smile in return. Apparently, he wasn't one for small talk either — my kind of guy.

Nathaniel and I set down our satchels and lifted our legs over the low bench in front of us. Nathaniel rested a hand on my shoulder to steady me as I lowered into a sitting position, clearly noticing that I was still a little shaken.

"How was the library?" Leena asked in my direction.

"She met Azrael," Nathaniel answered for me.

"How many times have I told you not to bring his name up in my presence, Everflame?" Jaxon said, visibly shuddering before he took a mouthful of gravy-covered vegetables.

"Stop being such a baby about it, Jax, just because he stroked your hair that one time," Leena rolled her eyes as she filled her mouth with a forkful of meat.

"He didn't just stroke my hair, and you know it!"

"What else did he do?" I asked, realising that getting sniffed by a half-dead-looking man was clearly classified as a normal occurrence here.

"He whispered in my ear! My *ear*!! He also told me not to be 'scared of the storm', whatever the fuck that means," Jaxon shrugged, "either way, I'll never forget how his cold lips felt as they grazed my earlobe." He shuddered again. "It's ruined sex for me ever since. Whenever someone leans too close to my neck, I freak out and shove them away from me."

Leena laughed at this. "My favourite memory from last year was seeing you running from Lex's room, stark naked and squealing like a little pig." Ollie and Nathaniel also snickered at this.

My eyes widened.

"Lex?!" I questioned.

"They're always on again, off again," Leena answered, waving her fork in the air at the statement. "I have no idea why she keeps going back to him with the amount of rubbish that comes out of his mouth; she doesn't strike me as someone who has a lot of patience."

"It's not my words she's interested in, my friends," Jaxon said, waggling his eyebrows and pointing his fork to his crotch. The entire table rolled their eyes at this.

"Wait," I scrunched my face in disgust, piecing things together. "Was that you I heard with her this morning?"

Jaxon winked. "Impressed with what you heard, Blondie?"

. . .

Nathaniel walked me back to my room as the blanket of night settled across Solarus, both of us full of roasted pork, vegetables, and potatoes. As we strolled down the dimly lit corridors, I couldn't help but steal glances at Nathaniel. He seemed more animated than I'd seen him in a long time, his laughter still echoing in my ears from the camaraderie shared with his friends. Their banter had been lively, filled with playful jabs and shared memories from the last year; one joke even made Ollie roar with laughter, infectious as it mingled with the others. It was nice to witness their closeness, a reminder that Nathaniel had made a life for himself here, full of connection and warmth.

I had never met his friends on the few occasions I had visited Nathaniel over the last year. He had always been protective of our time together, eager to ensure that we made the most of every minute. Perhaps because I never stayed longer than a day, with it being nearly a week's round trip to Thellas, I always felt guilty for leaving the children for too long.

A sudden pang of sadness shot through me as I thought of the children at the orphanage, knowing I wouldn't see them for what felt like an eternity. The thought of their laughter, their innocent joy, and the warmth of Nanny Rosie's comforting embrace left an ache that settled deep within. I quickened my pace, driven by a mix of nostalgia and longing, as well as an overwhelming feeling of fatigue and craving for my bed.

"You okay?" Nathaniel asked once inside my dorm, sitting at the end of my bed, watching me as I took off my shoes to climb under the covers.

"Yeah," I sighed. "I was just thinking about the children and Nanny Rosie, about how I'm not going to see anyone from back home for a while." I waved my hand in front of me, as if that gesture would signify the meaning of my statement.

Nathaniel nodded, thankfully understanding.

"I thought of Thellas all the time when I first got here last year. This place is a big adjustment, and it can sometimes feel like you're cut off from the rest of the world," he looked into my eyes as a shy smile graced his lips, "I thought about you most of all, though."

I smiled back at him as I sat next to him on my bed, my hand automatically going to the glass stone that hung from a leather strap around my neck. Nathaniel caught the movement and placed his hand atop mine.

"I can't believe you still wear that," he smiled, looking at our joined hands.

"I'll never take it off," I replied softly.

When Nathaniel was six, he had been playing in one of the sand pits in the orphanage's gardens, a makeshift playground as resources were too scarce to grow any plants, with water being so expensive in Thellas due to the constant droughts throughout the seasons.

I had been playing inside with Nanny Rosie at the time, when suddenly the door from outside swung open with a loud bang, and in burst a young Nathaniel, a whirlwind of energy, his wild chestnut hair tousled and his eyes alight with triumph. Behind him trailed several nannies, their expressions a mix of exasperation and concern as they tried to catch up to the long-limbed menace. Upon seeing Rosie and me, he victoriously held up a perfectly spherical, smooth piece of glass.

One of the nannies who had been watching him at the time, still breathless from the chase, had explained to Rosie how she had witnessed Nathaniel grab a handful of sand, only for flames to then spontaneously erupt from his palm, transforming the grains into a solid ball of glass with a tiny hole at the top.

It was the first time his powers had manifested, and Nathaniel had demanded that Rosie help him turn it into a necklace for me; a token of our friendship and a reminder of that fateful day.

That was nearly fourteen years ago, and I hadn't taken it off for a single second since. The smooth stone now hung several inches below my collarbone, a constant reminder of our shared past.

"It makes me smile knowing a piece of me is always so close to your heart."

I rolled my eyes at his statement and pushed his shoulder lightly.

"Quit being so soppy," I laughed, finally clambering into my bed and tucking my legs under the blankets, watching Nathaniel as he moved to stand from the end of my bed.

He leaned over me and ruffled my hair.

"You better get some sleep; you've had a big day today, and you're going to have an even bigger one tomorrow with Commander Bellum."

I let out a frustrated groan at his words as I slid down the bed, aligning my head with the pillow, my toes wriggling against one another beneath the sheets as I found a comfortable position

"I'm dreading it; they're all going to laugh at me."

"It can't be as bad as when you hit yourself in the face with a stick instead of my arm when we were younger in front of all of our friends." He responded, a teasing glint appearing in his eyes.

"Out!" I pointed to the door.

He chuckled as he headed for the door but then quickly spun around and returned to press a kiss on my forehead.

"Proud of you," he whispered against my hair before he pulled away.

"Proud of me, too." I smiled up at him.

Another soft chuckle escaped him, and this time he did make it all the way to the door. With a flick of his wrist, he extinguished the few fire-lamps that lit my small room.

"Show off!" I shouted at him as the door clicked shut behind him.

I could hear him laughing quietly to himself as he walked down the corridor away from my room. I closed my eyes, and the world quickly disappeared.

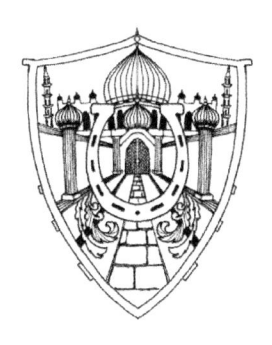

CHAPTER SEVEN

I woke to the sound of rustling in my room, a soft, shuffling sound that pulled me from the depths of sleep. As I opened my eyes and blinked away the lingering drowsiness, I noticed that dawn had crept in through the window, casting a bluish hue across the stone in front of me. The cool morning light illuminated rough, grey stone, their jagged edges and uneven surfaces prominent in the morning light. For a moment, confusion clouded my mind as I took in my surroundings, unsure of where I was. A couple of seconds passed, and then the memories from the last twenty-four hours flooded back — I was not in my bedroom at the orphanage, I was in Solarus.

I rolled away from the wall I had been facing and my eyes landed on Lex at the foot of her bed. She was fully dressed, clad from head to toe in second-year fighting leathers that clung to her, accentuating her trim and toned physique. The leather gleamed dully in the morning light, each piece meticulously worn in and scuffed from countless training sessions. She was packing some belongings into her bag, her movements quick and purposeful. A wooden sword was strapped to her side, the hilt slightly worn, hinting at her skill with it.

As she turned, flinging the strap of her bag over her head so she could wear it across her body, her sharp eyes caught mine.

"You have ten minutes until you're late for Commander Bellum." She said dryly, her voice carrying a hint of annoyance.

I bolted upright, panic rising in my chest — I must have missed breakfast. The realisation twisted my stomach. Lex spotted the frantic look in my eyes, sighed, and pulled something from her pack.

"Here," she said, extending her arm toward me; a small, round apple resting in her palm.

I eyed her suspiciously as I took the fruit, its skin glossy and red, the sweet scent wafting up to me. Well, this was an entirely different interaction from yesterday.

"Why are you being nice to me? Is this poisoned or something?" I asked, lifting my eyebrows in shock at the offering, half-expecting it to be a trap as I remembered a fairytale Rosie had told me when I was younger, where the princess had been tricked by an old witch with a poisoned apple.

"Oh, little mouse, this isn't me being nice," she let out a sarcastic laugh that seemed to echo off the stone walls. "I'm still annoyed that I have to spend the next year with you in this shitty little room, but I simply don't have enough daggers to throw at you every time you annoy me."

She sighed once more, the sound heavy with exasperation, and took a couple of steps toward the door; turning back to me, she continued, "Within these four walls, I will try to be civil. Let's call it a *'truce'* for now. You keep your mouth shut, which shouldn't be hard for you, and we will each stick to our sides of the room. Succeed, and I won't try to kill you. But out there," she pointed a thumb over her shoulder toward the door, her expression turning serious, "all bets are off. You are a Flame, and I am a Shade. We will never be friends."

With that, she opened the door and stepped into the dimly lit hall, the sounds of the morning bustle filtering in. "I'm only giving you a warning because if you're late and Bellum finds out that I am sharing a room with you, he'll pin some of the blame on me, since I know the schedule and should've woken you up," she took in my rumpled appearance and the fact that I still hadn't moved from my bed, "you look like crap so get out of bed and get your shit together. You also have the body of a starving child, so eat the damn apple. I'm not going to look after you if you pass out, face down, arse up."

She slammed the door, and I listened to her steps as they disappeared down the corridor, leaving me in a silence that felt heavy with unspoken tension, the apple still resting in my hand.

"Well, good morning to you too," I mumbled under my breath. My encounters with Lex seemed to be going from strength to strength.

I heaved myself up from the cocoon of my warm bed and pulled myself to my feet. I looked down at the clothing I was still wearing from yesterday—wrinkled, rumpled fabric clung uncomfortably to my skin, a reminder of my exhaustion that had prevented me from changing before I fell asleep. I dared to smell my armpits, and my nose crinkled in disgust at the sour odour that wafted up. I smelled terrible, a pungent mix of sweat and stale fabric. I hadn't washed since I left Thellas, and that had been four long days ago.

With no time to bathe properly, I stripped off my soiled clothes and moved to the small basin in the corner of the room, marvelling at the luxury of running water — a rarity I hadn't experienced in Thellas. I made quick work of flannelling the most crucial areas of my body, the cloth refreshing against my skin. I then brushed my teeth with mint paste, the cool flavour a brief comfort against my rising nervousness for the day.

I took a few steps toward the mahogany chest at the end of my small bed and pulled out some dark slacks and a black short-sleeved tunic, the unspoken uniform for the first-years of the college. Moving over to the dressing table that I hadn't initially noticed tucked next to the doorway; I finally faced my reflection in the small mirror above it. My long waves were a tangled mess, frizzy and wild, the result of a night spent tossing and turning. The strands against my neck curled more than the rest, likely from sweating throughout the night, and they were sticking uncomfortably to my skin. I grimaced at the sight; well didn't I look just *lovely*. The dark circles under my eyes and the dishevelled state of my hair painted a picture of the exhaustion I felt.

I pulled open the top drawer of the armoire and retrieved my hairbrush. Running it under some water for several seconds, I proceeded to tug the damp bristles through my long strands in hasty and jerky movements, wary of how quickly the minutes were ticking by. After detangling as much as possible, I gave up and tied my hair into a knot at the nape of my neck. I used the last precious seconds to splash my face and slap myself a couple of times to get some colour into my cheeks to appear slightly more alive. Grabbing my leather satchel from the floor and throwing the apple inside, I cast a final, quick glance in the mirror. I looked slightly better, but my slicked-back bun was a little too flat for my liking, and I now resembled a hard-boiled egg. *Wonderful.*

The campus was quiet, *too* quiet, and I quickly understood that I was now, in fact, definitely late. I hurried up the grand staircase of the main hall and took a left at the top when I reached the mezzanine level. I strode past the dining hall and into the spire at the end of the hallway, just as Leena had instructed the day before.

Once inside, I realised it was very similar to the one I had been in yesterday for Sephere's class, though this one lacked the tiered seating. Without it, the space felt open and airy; the impossibly high ceiling and circular design making it feel almost sacred. I spotted a few steps to the right that led up to an open archway, presumably leading to the roof terrace, where I could already hear the chatter of the assembled Cadets.

Racing up the steps, I prayed that no one would notice my late arrival. Some of the voices quieted as I stepped through the spire's archway, and several sets of eyes turned toward me. There were even more people here than there had been in Sephere's class yesterday — at least three hundred.

I could feel my face already turning red, the warmth creeping up my cheeks as I realised I was clearly much later than I had first thought. My pulse quickened with embarrassment, and I fought the urge to duck my head and hide. I needed to find someone I recognised; that was the logical thing to do — I just needed to blend into the crowd somehow.

Through the sea of faces, I finally spotted Nathaniel and Leena toward the back of the congregation. Nathaniel was trying to hold back a grin, amusement dancing in his eyes as he watched me awkwardly scan the crowd. I narrowed my eyes at him and sent him a glare that conveyed *{don't you dare make this worse for me}*.

If I were to try and reach them, I would have to make my way through the entire class and force people out of my way. Deciding that option wasn't exactly going to help me blend in, I sidled up to the group nearest me and acted as if I had been there all along. *{Nothing to see here, folks.}*

"You're late, Cadet!" I heard a stern voice call from my left.

Ah, shit. Turns out I wasn't very good at blending in after all.

Although the voice was sharp, it had a nice lilt to it, reminding me of smooth whiskey by a crackling fire. I turned my head and saw a tall gentleman step forward, clad in worn fighting leathers that had clearly seen many battles. He had dark, sun-tanned skin that had started to wrinkle with age; lines were etched around his eyes that hinted at both wisdom and the weight of experience. I would have guessed he was in his fifth decade. The lighter shades in his salt-and-pepper hair glinted in the morning light, catching the sun's rays and adding an almost other-worldly quality to his presence. He exuded a rugged handsomeness, and I had no doubt he would have had a line of suitors in his prime, drawn to his confident demeanour and the aura of authority that surrounded him. He stopped in place once he was several feet in front of me and tucked his arms behind his back, his posture straighter than an arrow. He looked down his bent nose at me, and I noticed a pale white scar running through his left eyebrow. A *warrior.*

"Commander Bellum?" I questioned in a small voice, my face now fully flushed with embarrassment as I noticed the whole assembly was watching our interaction. It turned out I hadn't needed to slap my cheeks that morning after all. He dipped his head in confirmation. "I'm sorry, sir, I took a wrong turn and got lost." It was a complete lie, but I would have tried to convince him I was a piece of broccoli if that's what spared me from Lex's wrath.

"A noble effort, girl; however, I suspect that if you had woken up on time, you would have seen everyone heading this way and would have known exactly where you were meant to be going." He tutted and raised his scarred eyebrow at me, clearly seeing right through my excuse.

Not knowing how to respond, I stayed silent, curling my trembling hands around my satchel strap so he couldn't see that I was absolutely terrified of him, as well as all the eyes that were still on me.

"You're on clean-up duty once we're done here Cadet, but I appreciate the loyalty to whomever your second-year dormmate is, who should have known better than to let you sleep in."

The Commander turned to a group behind him, and I noticed that Lex was standing directly in the centre of them, arms crossed and glaring at me with a severity that promised violence. Clearly, Bellum already knew who I was sharing a room with. Did he stay up late revising the induction schedule or something?!

Commander Bellum half-turned away from me, then paused, glancing over his shoulder as he said, "But for lying to me, Cadet, you can start off the target practice demonstrations."

...

Now standing in front of a row of targets, all varying in size and distance, my whole body trembled with trepidation and mortification. Nathaniel, Leena, and Jaxon were lined up behind me, forming a makeshift barrier of moral support against the sea of onlookers, who now surrounded me in a semi-circle, their eyes gleaming with curiosity and judgment. I searched the ground around me, desperate to spot a bow and quiver or some throwing daggers, but my efforts came up empty. Anxiety coiled in my stomach like a python, squeezing tighter with every passing second.

"What are you waiting for, Cadet? Call on your magic!" Bellum boomed from my right, his voice cutting through the murmurs of the crowd like a whip. My heart sank, a sense of dread washing over me.

{No, no, no, no.}

I closed my eyes tightly, sending a silent prayer up to the Gods, surely, I had suffered through enough embarrassment in the last twenty-four hours to warrant a break. *Surely.*

"You've got this, Aela!" Leena whispered from behind me. "Just aim for the largest and nearest one on the left; it's only about twelve feet away." I looked over my shoulder at her, and she gave me a supportive thumbs-up. I darted my eyes to Nathaniel, who stood to her right. His face was an unreadable mask, but I could see the pity in his eyes; he knew all too well how this was going to go for me.

As I turned back to the targets, I steeled myself and drew in a long, ragged breath. I closed my eyes once more, diving deep within myself to search for the small ember that resided in my chest. It pulsed within me like a distant star. I found that envisioning it flickering inside the darkness within me, attached to a long, invisible string, was the best way to locate it.

After several attempts that left me feeling more frustrated than focused, I finally located that inner string and gave it a firm and desperate tug. The ember rose to my call, as if it finally decided to put me out of my misery. As I coaxed it toward me, I focused on channelling it down the invisible thread of my arm to my right palm. Opening my eyes, I raised my arm, palm up, and a small flame flickered to life in the centre of my outstretched hand.

I smiled slightly but my expression scrunched in determination as I concentrated on the shape I wanted it to take in my mind. After a couple of breaths, the flame grew, swelling and morphing into a small, partially solid sphere in my hand, warming my face.

Exhaling slowly to steady my nerves, I planted my feet shoulder-width apart, feeling the solid earth beneath me, and raised my eyes to the target that Leena had told me to aim for. The moment felt electric, every heartbeat resonating in my ears. Concentrating on maintaining the flow of power to my flame, I pulled my arm back behind my head, grasping the ball of flame tightly. I exhaled deeply, then threw.

I watched it soar through the air; one foot… two, three… four… five….

It reached halfway, and a grin began to spread across my face. It was going to make it. It was *actually* going to make it.

But as if the Gods themselves heard my inner monologue, my ball of flame fizzled and turned to smoke around the eight-foot mark. It was as if someone had thrown a bucket of water over it mid-flight. My shoulders drooped in defeat, and I hung my head in shame, the laughter of the crowd filling my ears as my bottom lip started to tremble.

CHAPTER EIGHT

Commander Bellum insisted I keep trying to hit the nearest target, but with each attempt, my shots seemed to get progressively worse — if that was even possible. By the fifth try, my magic was entirely drained, leaving me swaying unsteadily on my feet, my limbs heavy and unresponsive. The sun hung high in the sky as mid-morning approached, casting harsh shadows across the training grounds, and I felt as if the weight of the world was pressing down on my shoulders.

The hours passed in a blur of muted voices and distant laughter as I sat on a low stone wall near the edge of the roof terrace, sweat rolling down my neck. A rare, cool breeze fluttered around me, a stark contrast to the heat that radiated from my flushed skin. I was wedged between Jaxon and Nathaniel,

Nathaniel's familiar presence and Jaxon's inappropriate but light-hearted jokes providing a sliver of comfort amidst my humiliation.

Each of the first years had taken part in the same challenge as me, while the second years lurked like hawks nearby, taking in their new competition. It was their turn after lunch, Bellum's attempt to showcase where we could be this time next year.

From what I had witnessed, there was a staggering range in the strength of abilities among the new Cadets; some exhibiting raw and uncontrolled power that crackled in their veins, whilst others had struggled to call on their magic almost as much as me. However, every single one of them had managed to hit the nearest target… apart from me.

Out of just shy of two hundred new students, only about twenty percent of them were Shades, most of which weren't powerful enough to wield their shadows into tangible weapons yet, but a few, with their dark eyes gleaming and movements fluid, had the potential to do so.

A woman named Mei stood out to me most of all. She was petite and of a similar height to me, yet there was an undeniable strength in her presence. Her black silken hair cascaded down her back like an onyx waterfall, gleaming under the sunlight. Her pointed oval eyes hinted to a lineage from Shangnon, the most northern sector of the Shadow Lands — a village nestled at the base of the imposing Ankan mountain range.

Even though it was evident she hadn't mastered complete control over her abilities, Mei struck with remarkable precision, hitting six of the targets with her shadows—more than anyone else. Her shadows streamed out from both of her hands like black ribbons caught in the wind. They twisted and twirled around her, dancing in the air with an elegance that captivated everyone watching. There was a fluidity to her movements, as if the shadows were an extension of herself, weaving together in a mesmerising display.

Once she finished, she had simply strolled away to join the rest of the crowd, her expression calm and composed, as though she hadn't just performed a feat that left everyone else in awe. She barely broke a sweat, her skin only glistening slightly in the sun, a testament to her effortless grace. Part of me wondered whether she had been holding back, deliberately tempering her power so she wouldn't draw too much attention to herself. Yet, the glances she received throughout the rest of the morning—some admiring, others envious—indicated that she had failed to avoid notice if that had indeed been her plan.

"You weren't that bad!" Leena said around a mouthful of bread at lunch. "At least you got your magic to take shape; that's a great start!"

"She was terrible, Du Preez, and you know it." Lex drawled from the end of the bench. To my horror, and Jax's delight, she had sat with us for our midday meal, clearly her relationship with Jaxon '*on*' again today.

After lunch, my group of merry bandits and I made our way back up the steps of the Fire Spire for the afternoon session of Combat Studies. Nathaniel tugged on my arm and pulled me back, away from the rest of the group as they continued ahead of us.

"How are you doing?" he asked, his voice low and concerned. We hadn't really spoken much since my memorable performance earlier; he had probably sensed that I needed a bit of space to gather my thoughts, and I appreciated his quiet understanding.

"Disheartened," I replied, letting out a weary sigh that felt like it came from deep within my soul. I looked up into his eyes, which today glinted with an undertone of warm amber, a contrast to the usual deep green.

"Try not to be. It's your first day. It can only get better from here," he said softly, his voice laced with encouragement as he squeezed my hand gently, his grip warm and reassuring. I could feel the spark of energy in his fingers, a reminder of his own steady power.

"Easy for you to say," I rolled my eyes, a mix of frustration and despair bubbling to the surface. My voice rose an octave. "You don't know what this feels like—to feel useless, powerless, angry with yourself and everyone else at the same time. Your magic never drains, and you've certainly never had a group of nearly three or four hundred people laugh at you for something that you can't control. It's just like when we were kids. I can't help the fact that I don't have a lot of magic. Believe me, I've tried for years, constantly practising in my room when everyone else had gone to bed, trying to push myself to find just that little bit more. But this is all I have, Nathaniel!"

My focus flicked to the floor, the polished stone beneath my feet suddenly captivating as I awkwardly kicked the ground in irritation. I pulled my hand from his as if to shield myself from further scrutiny, embarrassed by my little outburst. "Lex was right; I was terrible earlier, but it's all I have," I repeated, so quietly I wasn't sure he heard me.

"You're right, I don't know how it feels," he replied, unabashed, his expression steady and sincere. "But someone could have all the power in the world, and yet it doesn't necessarily mean they'll win the war. Sometimes it's the smartest that come out on top." He tucked a finger under my chin, raising my face so our gazes locked once more. His touch was gentle but firm, his voice softening as he continued, "And you are the smartest person I know, Aela. My advice: take in what Leena does when it's her turn. Her magic isn't the most powerful, but she is clever in how she uses it.

She'll be a formidable warrior one day, and so will you."

I nodded, looking away from his intense stare as I cleared my throat. His words lingered in the air between us. I didn't believe him, but I was done talking about it, aware that this feeling wouldn't vanish after just one conversation. He returned my nod with a subtle understanding, and we resumed our ascent of the spire steps.

The sound of our footsteps echoed against the stone walls, creating a steady rhythm that filled the air. Once we passed through the archway, we quickened our pace to rejoin the others, who had already pushed their way to the front of the gathering crowd. Their voices blended into the lively chorus of excitement in anticipation of the afternoon show.

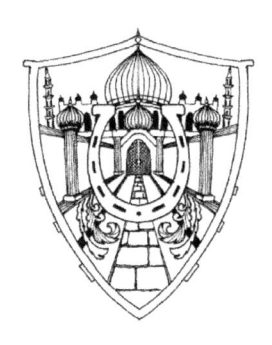

CHAPTER NINE

"Second years, it's your time to shine." Bellum raised his voice to settle the crowd, which was abuzz with excitement.

Unsurprisingly, the atmosphere was a lot more relaxed than that morning. Bellum carved a line in the ground with a long stick to indicate where the second-years should stand for their demonstrations. The nearest target was now at least fifty feet away, with the smallest, most difficult target being at least twice as far. A short, weaselly man stepped up first, wearing fighting leathers that were at least two sizes too big for him. The poor guy was probably in denial, hoping he would have a final growth spurt. He was a Shade, and his shadows successfully met ten of the twelve targets. They weren't as unruly as Mei's, instead coming from his palms in straight lines. It was a great demonstration of control, but for some reason, they didn't seem as powerful or as impressive as Mei's.

As the hours passed, I started to feel restless. It was very clear that Bellum had a certain way of training his Cadets, as both second-year Flames and Shades directed their magic in accurate, straight lines towards the centre of each target. Every second-year hit at least eight out of the twelve targets. Ollie, however, was surprisingly impressive; he was able to hit all twelve with less than a second between each strike. He was graceful in his movements, and it was clear he had a lot of self-control, but I guessed he had to, growing up with a brother as relentlessly irritating as Jaxon.

"Alexis Blake, you're up next!" Bellum instructed.

Lex prowled up to the line like a jungle cat stalking its prey. She shook out her shoulders and hands, and I could see her visibly release the tension in her body. Raising both arms, two black, swirling daggers appeared in her hands, and I let out a gasp.

"She can summon shadow weapons..." I whispered in awe.

"Of course she can!" Jaxon beamed proudly. "Her cousin is the strongest Shade here. He's a third-year, and they've been training since they were children. His father, Lex's uncle by marriage, is one of Aadhar's inner circle. Very powerful." I blinked at Jaxon's statement in disbelief at the fact that Lex had a direct link to the King. Gods, she probably knew him. I tucked that revelation to the back of my mind for later.

Lex flicked her wrists. Her daggers sliced through the air, like arrows released from a bowstring, before embedding themselves with a sharp thunk into the two closest targets, the sound reminiscent of our first encounter. Each dagger struck true. She repeated this action five more times until all twelve targets had her daggers sunk into them to their hilts, directly through the black circle that marked the centre.

With a final decisive flick of her wrist, Lex summoned the shadows back. I watched, breathless, as the daggers transformed into swirling tendrils of black smoke, the shadows coiling and intertwining like living creatures. They dissolved seamlessly into the air, disappearing as if they had never existed. A soft breeze whispered through, carrying away the last remnants of her magic and leaving behind an electrifying stillness that hung in the air, a testament to her power and control.

"She'd be a great assassin," Jaxon said, a hungry look in his eyes as he watched Lex walk back towards us, her hips swaying and a smug expression plastered on her face.

"I thought you said you didn't have enough daggers to throw at me every time I annoyed you?" I said to her as she joined us. I wasn't sure why I said this; perhaps

I was in shock. Fortunately, she ignored my statement and turned around to watch the next spectacle.

"Leena Du Preez, get your arse up here!" Bellum boomed to our group, making Leena jump. She had been speaking softly with Nathaniel just behind me, but I hadn't been paying enough attention to hear what they were discussing. She strode confidently past me, bumping my shoulder as she went and flashed me a quick smile.

"Watch what I do; if you like what you see, I'll teach you," she whispered to me as she passed. A small glow of appreciation warmed in my chest at her words.

As Leena stood in front of the target line, she adopted a stance like the one I had taken earlier, her feet shoulder-width apart and her back straight, exuding a quiet confidence. She raised both arms in front of her, palms facing each other, as if cradling an invisible box of power. Her eyes fluttered shut, and she inhaled deeply.

Suddenly, flames flickered to life between her parallel palms, illuminating her determined expression with a soft glow. Within mere seconds, twelve flaming arrows took shape, each one crackling with energy and poised for flight. She glanced back and forth between her arrows and the targets ahead, ensuring they were perfectly aligned, her focus sharp and unwavering.

As she exhaled, she released them in a fluid motion. The arrows shot through the air with a speed that left a shimmering trail, striking the targets with a chorus of twelve solid thuds. All of them hit dead centre, except for the two furthest away; yet instead of dissipating, the flames spread across the cloth of each target, engulfing them in a mesmerising dance of fire.

Fortunately, the targets were magically warded and didn't disintegrate; yet, if this had been a battlefield, we would have been hearing the piercing screams of twelve people burning alive. I shuddered at the gruesome thought, but my attention remained fixed on Leena, filled with admiration. Not only did she exhibit impeccable control over her abilities, but she also demonstrated a strategic mind in how she wielded her magic, ensuring that she wouldn't drain herself too quickly. In that moment, I realised that she embodied everything I aspired to be... kind, smart, and ruthlessly effective.

As she made her way back to us, I lurched forward and wrapped my arms around her shoulders. She was still for a moment, clearly shocked by my sudden outburst of affection, but after a moment, she hugged me back tightly.

"Sorry!" I said as I pulled back, slightly embarrassed at how forward I had been; it was very unlike me. "It's just, you were amazing up there!"

"Thank you," she flushed and looked away from me as a slight colour rose to her beautiful brown cheeks.

"Did you mean what you said? Will you teach me how to do that?" I asked, hopefully not sounding as desperate as I felt. I knew for a fact that I wouldn't be able to achieve what Bellum had been teaching the other Flames; there was no way I could channel that much power, but watching Leena's performance filled me with hope that one day I might not be entirely useless.

She reached up and squeezed my shoulder. "It would be my honour," she replied gently. I flashed the brightest smile at her since my arrival at Solarus, and to my relief, her face mirrored mine.

"Are you ready to be amazed, Blondie?"

Jaxon said to me once Leena and I had finished cooing over each other. I rolled my eyes.

"There's no way you can top Leena and Lex." Lex heard my compliment and raised an eyebrow at me. I scrunched my nose in her direction. "You scare the Gods out of me, but I'm not afraid to admit that you're an impressive Shadow Summoner, Alexis," I said, emphasising the name that I knew she hated. I swear I had a death wish today. There must have been something in the soup at lunch that had made me lower my inhibitions. I heard Nathaniel let out a shocked snort from behind me. Even more surprising than my confidence, though, was that instead of biting my head off, Lex's lips quirked up at the edges, as if she were trying to hold back a smile. Before I could say anything more, she turned to watch Jaxon as he walked away.

The sight that greeted me next was by far the most harrowing thing I had ever witnessed, and that was coming from someone who had seen Azrael. Instead of raising his hands, Jaxon bent his body forward slightly behind the target line, adopting a strange, almost predatory stance, as if he were crouching to pick something up off the floor. His posture was unsettling, a hint of mischief flickering in his eyes. Without much ceremony, he opened his mouth wide, the gesture making me pause in confusion. I couldn't tell if he was attempting to catch flies or preparing to unleash a scream that would echo across the training grounds. My brows furrowed as I tried to decipher the peculiar expression on his face.

Then, as if some unseen force had passed through him, a shudder wracked his body. In an instant, the darkest of shadows erupted from his open lips, swirling and twisting like black flames that defied gravity. They danced and writhed, forming chaotic tendrils that looked like they were made of flames, yet devoid of heat. I heard him push out a breath, a deliberate exhalation that seemed to command the shadows to spring into action.

With a sudden, frantic energy, the shadows surged forward, racing towards each target in wild, uncontrolled waves, as if they were sentient beings driven by their own free will. The sight was both hypnotic and terrifying, a display of raw power that looked almost alive. The wave of black flame made contact with all twelve targets in a dramatic flourish, enveloping them so completely that they vanished from view.

Satisfied with his performance, Jaxon slowly inhaled, and his shadows calmed and pulled back, reminding me of receding mist atop a mountain. As they gathered closer to him, he breathed them back inside himself, as if they had never existed at all. The whole performance was over in under twenty seconds, but I knew for a fact this was going to haunt my dreams later that night.

"Like what you saw?" Jaxon directed towards me as he returned to my side after planting a loud kiss on Lex's mouth and wrapping an arm around her shoulder.

"Not even a little bit," I responded with a grimace on my face.

"No one ever likes what comes out of your mouth, Jax," Nathaniel said from behind me. Leena and, to my surprise, Ollie laughed at this; I hadn't even spotted he was standing on the other side of Leena, his silent presence going entirely unnoticed.

"I do." Lex crooned as she ran her fingers through Jaxon's auburn hair.

"Keep it in your pants, Alexis; I'm up next," Nathaniel said, breaking up Jaxon and Lex's embrace as he walked between them.

"Cock-block!" Jaxon shouted towards Nathaniel's back as he reached for Lex once more, and several laughs filled the air as Nathaniel flipped a vulgar gesture over his shoulder back at him.

I understood then why Bellum had left Nathaniel's demonstration until last and had asked everyone else to take several steps back before he began.

Nathaniel adopted a stance similar to Leena's and mine, but he needed hardly any preparation time at all. Within just a couple of heartbeats, an arc of fire flickered to life around him, casting an intense glow that danced in the air. The heat radiating from the flames was overwhelming, and beads of sweat sprang up on my forehead almost immediately, and I had to place a hand in front of my face to prevent permanent damage to my retinas. It became hard to breathe as his flames sucked the oxygen from the air, and a few coughs spluttered from my lips, the air feeling thick and stifling.

Nathaniel barely twitched his fingers, as if mere thought alone summoned the power within him. In an instant, two walls of solid fire surged forth, hurtling towards the twelve targets with alarming speed. The sound of crackling and hissing flames surrounded us, reminiscent of a forest fire roaring through the night, consuming everything in its trail. I strained my eyes to follow the path of his fire, desperate to locate the targets, but they vanished from sight, swallowed by the inferno. Confused, I turned to Leena, my expression mirroring my bewilderment. Before I could even form a question, she shouted over the roar of the flames, her voice a mix of awe and concern.

"Not even the wards can stop his magic!" she shouted over the sound of the popping and spitting flames. I jerked my head back, alarmed.

"That's impossible!" I said, also raising my voice so she could hear me.

She shrugged.

"Clearly not. He'll be Olympia's biggest weapon once he graduates."

I had always known that Nathaniel was powerful, but I never imagined it was to this extent. His abilities could scorch hundreds of soldiers in a single blast, effortlessly barrelling through their Mage-enchanted shields. In fact, it was possible that he could even dismantle the wards protecting both the King's and Queen's castles. Gods, he could likely wipe out entire villages if he chose to.

While I knew deep down that Nathaniel would never harm an innocent soul, as I drifted off to sleep that evening, a troubling thought lingered in my mind: what would happen if his immense power ever fell into the wrong hands?

CHAPTER TEN

The rest of my first week passed in a blur as I settled into a new routine. My mornings were spent with Commander Bellum, who patiently sought to understand each of the first-years' abilities. While I showed no real improvement—no surprise there—some of the others had managed to create a few straight lines with their flames and shadows. I found their performances somewhat lacklustre, but Bellum assured us that this was the best way to begin mastering the shape of our magic and maintaining a steady flow. After all, unpredictability could spell disaster on a battlefield.

Unsurprisingly, Mei was the first to master this, placing her at the top of Bellum's list of favourites. A delicate, bird-like man named Bartholomew, whose hands looked like they should have been playing an instrument instead of wielding flames, took the second spot. I noticed friendship groups starting to form, but no one bothered with me *(shocker)*, which suited me just fine. I remained on cleanup duty, spending each lunch break tidying away the targets, setting out the fighting mats for the second-years' afternoon sessions, and taking sweaty towels to the laundry room near the kitchens. Leena brought what she could from the food hall each day for me to wolf down before Sephere's afternoon class, which warmed my heart every time she did so.

Every evening after dinner, I joined Leena in her room to practice my magic. We had become inseparable over the last week, and I worried that I was starting to come across as a bit of a limpet. She had given me the task of forming a triangle with my flames, as this was the first step to creating an arrow tip. It was much harder than I had anticipated, and several times I had burst into tears out of frustration and fatigue. Each time this happened, Nathaniel would appear within moments, as if he had been listening behind the door. He'd join us on Leena's bed, wrap an arm around me, and begin recounting stories about what it had been like growing up together. He'd tell us about the tales Nanny Rosie used to share before we went to sleep as children. This small gesture always made my heart swell, as if a piece of home had followed me here. More than once, I had fallen asleep beside him, lulled into oblivion by the warmth of his side and the familiar stories. I'd only wake up the next morning to Leena prodding me, reminding me that I did indeed have my own bed in my own room—and that she didn't want to top-and-tale with me for the rest of the year.

Sephere's lessons had covered the most notable wars from Alinoura's reign, running through each outcome and the strategies documented in the manuscripts of Alinoura's second-in-command, General Bertrum, who we learned was Commander Bellum's great-great-grandfather. There were some battles I was completely unaware of, most significantly the War of Thalattas. This was the first battle between Alinoura and Aadhar, around two-hundred and ninety years ago, taking place on the Thalattas Sea. Anka attempted to invade Olympia through the port of Orouras; the Sector where Leena and Jaxon grew up.

Although Olympia succeeded in maintaining a united front along the coast, Bertrum's notes described how it seemed as if Aadhar knew the Queen's every move. It wasn't until Alinoura stepped back and allowed Bertrum to take charge, directing the Olympians and altering their strategy, that Anka finally retreated. The General's guidance made it impossible for the enemy to predict the formations of Olympia's defences. From that day forward, Alinoura insisted that Bertrum lead the army, treating her as just another soldier, for she feared she had become too predictable.

It was now Saturday morning, and I stood shoulder to shoulder with Leena in the middle of the food hall, while Nathaniel, Jaxon, and Ollie were lined up in the row ahead of us. The room was full of first, second, and third-years awaiting the upcoming Realm Announcement. I scanned the room and saw Lex several rows back from us, leaning against the rear wall.

"Who's Lex talking to?" I whispered to Leena, craning my neck for a better view.

"Her cousin," Leena replied with a weary exhale. "He's insufferable."

"What do you mean?"

"Y'know how powerful men are," she waved her hand dismissively, "obnoxious, entitled, looking right through you as if they don't even know you're there. Lex is the only person he speaks to, but even then, it's no more than a few words."

I frowned, recalling what Jaxon had said a few days earlier.

"How is he here if his dad is a member of Aadhar's Elite? Only residents of Olympia can attend Solarus."

Leena sighed again, already bored with the conversation.

"He moved to Monacus with Alexis' family when they were children. They're more like siblings than cousins." She turned from me, focusing on the back of

Nathaniel's head as if it were the most interesting thing in the Realm, clearly done with the conversation.

Someone behind me shifted, allowing for better viewing of Lex and her cousin. I inhaled sharply, my jaw dropping. Lex's cousin was massive. He was at least several inches taller than Nathaniel, who was well over six feet. His hair was a mass of dark curls, complemented by equally dark, thick eyebrows. Unlike most of the Cadets here, he was not clean-shaven and had several days' worth of stubble. He was just as broad as Jaxon; however, while Jax reminded me slightly of a gorilla, this man had the height to balance it out. I could tell he was related to Lex, as they shared the same cutting cheekbones and pronounced jawline. His fighting leathers hugged his body (I silently thanked the Gods and whatever tailor made them for him), and two steel swords were strapped behind his back, indicating that he was indeed a third-year.

"Close your mouth, you're starting to catch flies," Leena whispered, still with her eyes pinned forward.

I snapped my mouth shut, but was still too focused on the man behind us to feel embarrassed by Leena's observation. Lex was still talking to her cousin, but his eyes were surveying the room like a predator among its prey, seemingly paying her no mind. His roaming gaze edged closer to our group, so I quickly turned my head back to the front, hoping he hadn't caught me staring.

"I can practically hear your ovaries crying from here, Blondie," Jaxon announced, purposefully projecting his voice much louder than necessary. I groaned inwardly, realising he must have caught me ogling. Nathaniel let out a snort, and Ollie shook his head. "Ollie has first dibs on him, though." Jaxon finished, pointing at his brother.

Ollie was facing away from us, but I could see the back of his neck turning red with embarrassment. Same-sex relationships were accepted throughout both Realms; however, old prejudices often lingered behind false smiles, so many people chose to keep their feelings secret.

"I don't believe he would have any interest in me, little brother," Ollie said in his soft, gentle voice, which he rarely used. In fact, I could probably count on one hand how many times I'd heard him speak in the last week.

"Who knows which way Kieran Blake swings," Jaxon said, raising both arms in a questioning motion. "He doesn't speak to anyone. Not even Lex knows, and she grew up with the miserable fucker. Don't give up on your wish just yet." Jaxon said, turning back to face the front with a wink directed at his brother.

A hush fell over the room, thankfully halting Jaxon's outburst, and I noticed a woman was now stood at the front of the dining hall. She was tall with a straight, muscular build. A sword was attached to its sheath on her right hip, and she wore an Olympian Army uniform, (a black and silver tunic with leather breeches), which was adorned with more medals than I could count just below her left shoulder, above the patch of Olympia's royal crest. The Olympian crest was an image made up of a sword overlaying a flaming infinity symbol and a crown, an homage to Queen Elena's last name, 'Everflame.' The strong-looking woman had deep olive skin, large oval eyes, and luscious dark hair plaited over her shoulder.

"Who's that?" I whispered toward Leena. She met my inquiry with raised eyebrows, as if I should already know.

"That's General Zaneer…"

"Oh," I responded, staring at Zaneer in awe. I had heard many stories about her, we all had. She was formidable. Not only had she achieved her rank in less than fifteen years since graduating from Solarus, but she had done so with very little magic. It was said that she nearly dropped out of her first year here because she couldn't compete with her peers, but now, those very same peers reported to her.

Zaneer was the main reason I wanted to be part of the Olympian War Council one day, as she gave me hope that I had a future with the Olympians, even with my depleted abilities.

"Good morning, Cadets. Thank you all for being here on time," Zaneer addressed the room in a clipped, clear voice. The room was so still you could hear a pin drop. Thank the Gods I hadn't overslept again today. "I am pleased to report that the skirmish in Monacus mentioned in last week's update was no more than a misunderstanding between an inn owner and a couple of his guests. It was quickly resolved by one of my patrols." She paused, her eyes scanning over the sea of silent faces focused on her. "There have been no further reports from the Passageway, indicating that everything is running smoothly and that those entering Olympia are abiding by our laws."

I heard Leena release a small, relieved breath from my left. I realised that these announcements must be the only way she knew her mother was safe, being so far away from the wall and her home in Orouras. It would be at least a three-week ride for a messenger to get here on horseback, compared to the army's courier hawks that could travel the same distance in a matter of days. What a horrible way to find out if her mother was hurt—or worse, had been killed.

"That being said," Zaneer continued, "one of the hawks arrived this morning with a message that there was a suspected attack near our border at Thellas."

My heart plummeted. Nathaniel looked back at me, and I could see in his eyes that he was thinking the same thing. Our village in Thellas was just a few miles from the Solarus border; it had been built there to be close to the trade route running all the way from Mytos, through Solarus, and over to Orouras.

Zaneer continued, "The missive indicated that there were no casualties to report; however, there was some significant damage to several homes and the market. It is the Queen's intention to offer Thellas aide; however, my patrol has not long left Monacus and is still at least two weeks out. I spoke with Commander Bellum, and he informed me that he would be willing to part with a couple of the second and third-years who know the route to scope out what is needed so we can best utilise our Queen's resources. Nathaniel Everflame, Jaxon and Oliver Drago, Leena Du Preez, Alexis and Kieran Blake, please report to the War Room immediately. That will be all."

CHAPTER ELEVEN

Several hours passed, and I was now sat beneath the library staircase, my body nestled deep into one of the cozy floor cushions. It was the first time I had mustered up enough courage to return since my encounter with Azrael, and to my relief, he was nowhere to be seen. Thankfully, Bellum's classes didn't take place on Saturdays, and Sephere had cut his lesson short, as people were still riled up after the morning's announcement. Normally, I would have been disappointed by this, but the thought of Thellas being attacked had left me spiralling.

The dining hall had erupted into chaos after Zaneer departed; apparently, no one from the college had ever been assigned a scouting mission before. At most, a couple of people over the years had been sent to deliver messages to the smaller villages in Solarus—nothing more.

From the chatter that had surrounded me in the dining hall, it was no surprise that my friends (along with Lex and Kieran) were chosen for the mission. Somehow, I had aligned myself with the most skilled magic wielders currently attending Solarus, something I gave myself a small pat on the back for.

I had cornered Nathaniel and Leena after their meeting in the war room—not daring to get too close to Lex and Kieran as they walked past—and had hounded them with questions. To my relief, the attack had occurred in one of our neighbouring villages, Olos, not the village of Illius, where Nathaniel and I had grown up. Dread had since settled in my stomach, however, as I remembered that Nanny Rosie sometimes volunteered at Olos' orphanage when they were short-staffed.

Leena and Nathaniel said they hadn't been told much more information, except that they were to meet at the stables at first light, as Zaneer wanted them to leave early the next morning. They assured me they would be back before the next Realm Announcement in a week's time.

I decided I needed some time alone to process what had happened, so I went to the only place I knew few dared venture, the library.

Trying to ignore the worried thoughts swirling in my mind, I focused on the page in front of me. It was a book about the Gods, a dusty tome that I had read only once before, when I was much younger and still filled with naive wonder. Nykus and Helin, the powerful deities at the centre of the cosmos, had two children who were also Gods in their own right. The first was Ouran, revered as the 'God of all Worlds.' He held dominion over Elysium, the Underworld, and our world—Gaia—each Realm a reflection of his immense power and responsibility.

Ouran inherited his father's shadow manipulation abilities, a gift that allowed him to slip through the ethereal barriers of Elysium and the haunting depths of the Underworld undetected. He could weave through the fabric of these Realms, a ghost among the living and the dead, whenever he wished to avoid notice. It was believed he shared his father's black hair but had the bronze skin of his mother. Among the Shades, Ouran was the most celebrated God, second only to Nykus. Shades were convinced they were his direct descendants, believing he must have mated with mortals, creating his own bloodline, while visiting Gaia shortly after the inception of our world.

He was known to be ruthless in his ruling of the Underworld, keeping the unredeemable in line while allowing those with lesser offenses to govern themselves, appointing them as his 'Generals.' He even granted his favourites a second chance at life, allowing their souls to be reborn into a new body. My thoughts wandered to Nathaniel's statement about Azrael aiding Ouran in the transportation of souls, and I wondered if there was some truth to his words.

The second child was Kera, his younger sister, known as the 'God of Lightning and Storms,' or 'The Lost God.' I only knew what Nanny Rosie had told me about her, as all documented history of her had been wiped out, as if the Gods themselves sought to erase her from existence. Apparently, she had glowing porcelain skin that shimmered like the dawn, long flowing white hair that crackled with energy, and bright blue and gold eyes that seemed to reflect the very storms she commanded. She was as formidable as her mother in battle; legends spoke of her splitting the sky with a mere flick of her wrist, striking down her enemies from miles away before they even had a chance to scream. Her lightning could turn anything it touched to flame, scorching the earth and incinerating entire Sectors in a breathtaking display of power if she wished it.

However, her legacy was tragically short-lived. It was said she fell in love with a mortal man, Erobon, whose very humanity rendered her vulnerable to threats and control.

Nykus and Helin banished Kera from their homeland of Elysium, ignoring their son's protests to forgive his sister, believing she was foolish and reckless for engaging with a lesser being. It was said she lived out a mortal life with her lover, stripped of her powers and memories to ensure she could never return home. This was the origin of her title, 'The Lost God,' and to speak of her was forbidden, as it was seen as an insult to the other Gods who remained selfless and dedicated to protecting humanity. This small amount of information was all I had gathered from my seventeen years with Nanny Rosie, who would only loosen her lips about Kera after a few tankards of ale.

Kera's story always filled me with a deep sense of sadness, and I often found myself empathising with her. At the end of the day, we can't help who we fall in love with, and I'm sure that was the case for Kera.

Perhaps it was the orphan in me, but I could never understand how Helin and Nykus could disown their own child like that. Of course, I could never voice these thoughts, as they would be considered blasphemy, and people had been executed for less.

A rustling sound interrupted my musings, causing me to jump and drop my book. I readied myself for another sniff from Azrael.

"Sorry!" A delicate female voice called from the bottom of the staircase. I squinted to see who it was; the light was much dimmer now, clearly indicating I had been lost in thought much longer than I realised. My stomach growled in response, alerting me that I had likely missed the evening meal, and that Leena and Nathaniel were probably wondering where I was. A small figure approached me, a heavy fur still draped over my legs, making it impossible for me to stand.

"Mei?" I asked as she emerged from the shadows; her face becoming clearer in the lamplight. I had already recognised her several seconds prior purely from her posture and the way she carried herself, having studied her in Bellum's class for the past week, but I decided to keep that to myself to avoid sounding like a stalker. She bent to pick up my book.

"I made you lose your place," she said, seemingly embarrassed as she handed it back to me. Albeit faint, I could still hear her Shangonese accent when she spoke.

"Oh, it's fine. I wasn't really reading anyway; my mind is a bit all over the place today."

I looked down at the cover, toying with its corner, unsure why I had shared that information. When I glanced up, her head was cocked at an angle, a questioning expression on her face.

I sighed. "I'm from Thellas." I said, hoping that would suffice as an explanation. Mei didn't react for a moment, but her expression softened. I perceived she was actually very pretty—her face pale and smooth, making her look much younger than her eighteen years. She settled herself on the cushion next to me, clutching a book of her own to her chest. The spine read, *'Alethia: The Truth of the Unknown Lands.'*

"Are you going?" she asked delicately. Noticing my attention on her book, she rearranged her arms slightly to cover it, as if to hide it. Well, that was interesting.

"Going... where?" I replied, my brow furrowing in confusion as I raised my eyes to meet hers.

"With the others?" She questioned, as if it was obvious. It took me a moment to understand what she meant.

"Wait... to Thellas? To Olos?" I scoffed, assuming she couldn't be serious, but she nodded in response. Perplexed, I continued, "I can't fight; I don't really have any magic..."

"Can you ride a horse?" she cut me off.

"Yes..." I responded slowly.

"Then, you go," she said matter-of-factly, her accent appearing stronger, as if the decision was already made.

"But I can't..." I sputtered. "Only second and third-years are allowed, and I..."

"Where I come from," she interrupted again, "my culture teaches us that family is everything. We are taught to respect our elders and to create a safe place for our children to grow. If I heard that someone was possibly threatening my loved ones or attacking my home, nothing could stop me from stepping in to protect it. Are you saying you wouldn't do the same?"

∙ ∙ ∙

As I lay in bed that night, flipping from side to side in search of comfort, Mei's words replayed in my mind. She had left shortly after her speech about family, taking the mysterious book with her. Although I found her notion of going to Thellas with my friends ridiculous at the time, the more I thought about it, the more tempted I felt to join them.

True, I couldn't fight.

True, my magic was useless.

True, I had social anxiety and wouldn't add much entertainment to the journey.

However, I knew the area better than anyone else. Over the last few years, I had gone on several trips to help at Olos' orphanage with Nanny Rosie—something Nathaniel never did, as he worked at our village's tavern instead. I understood the layout of the village and could offer advice on what resources the Queen should send, guiding our patrol through shortcuts that would save hours on the journey. As I finally drifted off to sleep several hours later, I knew what I had to do.

CHAPTER TWELVE

I dreamt of a horse with a coat the same colour as the lightest sand of Olympia. It shimmered with an opalescent glow under the moonlight. As I ran through the winding mountain path, I quickened my pace as sweat started to run down my face. I pumped my arms as I tried to catch up, not wanting to lose sight of the animal amidst the blanket of the night's darkness. Its long white tail and mane flowed freely as the horse galloped ahead of me. The strands billowed in the wind like silken banners as the moon's rays caught them in its hold, making them sparkle with what looked like embers of the whitest flame.

A fork appeared in the mountain pass, and the horse paused, turning to gaze back at me with a patient, almost knowing expression. Down the centre of its face was a wide white stripe, an elegant mark that accentuated the striking bright blue eyes on either side — eyes that took my breath away. They seemed to hold an endless ocean of wisdom and mystery, reflecting the starlit sky above and pulling me into their depths.

I slowed my steps as I finally caught up to it. Extending my hand, I reached out, yearning to stroke its velvety muzzle. As my fingers grazed the tip of its smooth nose, a warm shiver ran through me. The horse leaned into my touch, its breath soft and warm against my palm; deep, intelligent eyes locked onto mine.

Suddenly, the horse broke our connection and shifted its focus, looking over my head to the vast expanse of the night sky above, as if sensing something beyond the horizon.

Intrigued, I turned also.

A large shape emerged in the distance, gliding effortlessly through the sky's darkness, its outline silhouetted against the canvas of stars that twinkled like scattered diamonds. I stood transfixed for several moments, adrenaline heightening my senses as I listened to the gentle breeze whistling through the narrow mountain path, the sound mingling with the soft rustle of leaves in the trees and the rhythmic breathing of the horse behind me. The night air was cool against my sweat-soaked skin, carrying with it the earthy scent of moss and pine.

As the shape drew closer, its outline became clearer, the moon casting a silvery glow over its majestic form. I could hear the steady, powerful flapping of its wings now, a sound that resonated like faraway thunder; each beat stirring the trees below as it closed the distance between us.

Now fully illuminated by the moon, which had finally decided to grant the creature centre stage, bright red scales shimmered in the moonlight, each one reminding me of a work of art. The beast rolled and moved with an elegant grace that shouldn't have been possible for its formidable size.

Nearly above us, the beast let out a deep, resonant roar that echoed and danced through the mountains, a sound that reached deep into my soul.

I should have been afraid, but in that moment, I felt no fear. Instead, an overwhelming sense of belonging enveloped me, as if my soul; my very essence, recognised this magnificent being. It was as though I had been waiting for this moment my entire life, and I knew that whatever was about to unfold, would change everything.

CHAPTER THIRTEEN

I bolted upright in bed, wiping my sweat-drenched hair from my face. I let out a long sigh, I had not slept well, unusual dreams had plagued my subconscious. I glanced out the window and saw that the sun had already crested the sky, and Lex's bed was empty. I must have overslept—how *very* unlike me.

Wobbling to my feet, I got ready as quickly as possible. Grabbing my satchel, I shook out my pencils and parchments onto my bed, replacing them with a change of clothes, one of my trusty flannels, three sets of undergarments, and four water skins. From the trunk at the end of my bed, I retrieved an apple and a bunch of bananas, stuffing them in as well, wincing slightly at the thought that the bananas would likely be in a much different shape by the time I pulled them out that evening. Animals were scarce for hunting in the hot climate of Solarus, and I didn't particularly fancy snacking on a lizard if I could avoid it.

After double- and triple-checking my bag, brushing my teeth, and treating myself to another luxurious flannel bath, I raced down the flight of stairs from my dormitory, through the main hall and entry arch, and circled around to the back of the Shadow Spire. Before Lex fell asleep the night prior, I had badgered her with questions until I finally learned where the stables were located. I suspected she might have guessed my intentions, but she had begrudgingly relented and provided the information after my tenth round of questioning. Then, with a dramatic roll onto her side to face the wall, she made it clear she wouldn't be sharing anything more.

Fortunately, it was a Sunday, and with no lessons today, the halls were mostly empty. It was still very early, and presumably most people would remain asleep for another couple of hours. I slowed my run as I neared the stables to appear more casual. *{Nothing to see here, people, just a girl wanting to stroke some horses}.*

The stables stood as a sturdy wooden structure; its roof painted white to reflect the sun. Both ends were open to let air circulate, a clever design suited to the climate, and I couldn't help but admire it for a few seconds. As I crept around the corner into the left opening of the stables, I caught my first glimpse inside; it was immaculate. Leena had mentioned that Bellum loved horses and spent a lot of time ensuring they were cared for, and it was clear that a military man had organised this space. Stalls lined both sides, with room for at least fifty horses. I listened intently for any signs of company, but all that greeted me were the soft sounds of braying and nickering. The stalls closest to me were empty, so I moved stealthily forward on light feet, keeping close to the gated stalls in case anyone passed by. In my admiration of the structure, I hadn't really thought of how easy it would be to get caught here.

Finally, I reached an occupied stall. On tiptoe, I curled my fingers over the top of the gate to hoist myself higher. My eyes locked on an enormous grey-dappled mare resting near the back wall. She noticed me peering in and slowly walked over to greet me with gentle grace, nudging her muzzle into my shoulder when she reached me.

"Hi, beautiful girl," I whispered, running my palm down the centre of her face as I stepped back down to the balls of my feet. "Are you in the mood for an adventure today?"

Less than ten minutes later, I had the mare, whom I decided to name Juniper, fully tacked and ready to go. Luckily, her saddle and bridle were attached to the wall next to her stall, allowing me to make quick work of getting her ready. {*Thank you for your organisation, Commander Bellum.*}

I stuffed my satchel into one of the saddlebags and found some more apples nearby, packing them into the other bag to ensure Juniper had something to eat on our journey—at least until we reached the grassier lands of Thellas. Wary that I was already a few hours behind my friends, I hurriedly led Juniper by her reins out of the stables onto the nearby path that directed us toward a cobblestone road. Luckily, cobblestone roads were the norm throughout Solarus, as it was one of the wealthier Sectors, only outranked by Mytos, where the Queen resided. Unfortunately, the closer we got to Thellas, the stone gave way to dry, loose dirt trails, which could slow our pace if there had been recent rainfall. Fortunately for Juniper and me, Olympia was currently several months into a drought, so the terrain shouldn't be an issue. I needed to push Juniper over the next few hours to catch up with the others, so I planned to make up ground by taking a shortcut across one of the dried riverbeds instead of following the ring road around it.

Juniper and I rode hard for the next few hours, and I had to hand it to her—she was incredibly fast. We galloped past traveling carts, their wheels creaking, and other riders. We weaved through the bustling streets of a nearby village without drawing too much attention. The streets were narrow and lined with colourful brick houses, their façades adorned with flowers that had wilted in the heat, all topped with warm terracotta roofs that gleamed under the sun. People bustled about, their voices mixing in a lively symphony, either heading to the temples for Sunday morning services or on their way to the weekend market, where the aroma of fresh produce and baked goods wafted through the air.

As Juniper was such a large horse, people eagerly moved out of our way to avoid being trampled, creating a mostly unobstructed route for us. A few bystanders swore at us, their expressions a mix of surprise and annoyance, while others raised a middle finger as we passed, clearly unimpressed by our speed. I caught the eye of a vendor selling bright fruits, who merely shook his head, a grin creeping onto his face at our reckless enthusiasm.

In the midst of the chaos, a small girl dropped her honey-flavoured snow cone—a delicacy perfected by the water-wielders over the last century—as her mother barely managed to pull her out of Juniper's path. The snow cone tumbled to the ground, the vibrant colours splattering onto the cobblestones. All I could do was yell a small "*Sorry!*" as we raced by, my heart racing with the thrill of the ride and a twinge of guilt for the girl's lost treat.

We took my planned shortcut and crossed the dried riverbed after leaving the village, carefully avoiding the jagged rocks in the centre of it. I had no doubt that Juniper squashed some unsuspecting geckos as we sprinted through, and I sent a silent prayer to the Gods on their behalf, hoping they wouldn't smite me for ruining the girl's treat and the lizards' lives.

Finally, as we approached the fourth hour, I spotted dust clouds rising in the distance. I let out a sigh of relief at the sight of my friends. They must have been riding at an almost equally brutal pace for me to have just caught up, even with the riverbed shortcut. I patted Juniper's sweat-drenched neck, promising her a drink from one of my water skins and an apple when we reached them. I squeezed my legs together, and she lurched forward into a hard gallop to close the final distance.

"What in the three Gods do you think you're doing here, Aela?!" Nathaniel shouted from atop his chestnut gelding when he spotted me joining the back of their group. Juniper was breathing hard now that we had slowed, and I reached down to retrieve one of the apples I had promised her from the saddlebag.

"Have you lost your mind, Blondie?" Jaxon chimed in, his face uncharacteristically serious.

"You're going to get in so much trouble when they realise you've joined us, Aela," Leena said softly, aligning her smaller bay mare next to Juniper to ride alongside me. Her horse was at least several hands shorter than Juniper, and it felt nice to be looking down on someone for once.

I released a long sigh and looked back at Nathaniel, who remained in his saddle but gripped the pommel with white-knuckled intensity, visibly shaking with the effort to contain himself. I could tell he wanted nothing more than to pull me down from my horse and give me a stern talking-to, but he was trying his best to restrain himself. He knew it would embarrass me, and he probably didn't have the energy to deal with me if I burst into tears right now.

Diverting my gaze from Nathaniel's simmering frustration, I took in the rest of the group. All my friends were wearing their fighting leathers and looked close to passing out; the sun had already turned Jaxon's and Oliver's pale skin an unsettling shade of red. I had opted for loose, light clothing, and to my surprise, so had Kieran and Lex, both of whom had material wrapped around their faces, heads, and shoulders to protect them from the sun and sand. The dark-haired cousins at the front of our group still hadn't bothered to look back, and I wondered whether that was because Lex had already gathered I was going to be joining them at some point.

Unsurprisingly, Kieran's blue roan gelding was significantly larger than all the others, making Juniper look mid-sized in comparison. Lex's black mare was completely dwarfed next to it, but her horse's body was lean with muscle, and I had no doubt she would outrun the rest of the herd on flat ground. I glanced at Jaxon's red roan-coloured mare, which seemed much too small for him, and I couldn't help but feel sorry for the poor creature. A part of me was tempted to suggest we swap, but I already felt attached to the large, beautiful grey creature I was astride. Jaxon and his steed had made it this far after all—what were a few more miles?

Oliver sat atop a stunning sand-coloured stallion with a long black mane and tail. It already seemed eager to break into another canter, and I had no doubt this horse was why the group had covered so much distance in such a short time. A small smile tugged at my lips as I compared Ollie's quiet demeanour to the energetic horse he had chosen.

"Are you even listening to anything I'm saying?" Nathaniel snapped from my right.

Ah, crap. He had been talking to me, and all I had been doing was staring at the horses. Come to think of it, I hadn't even said a word to explain my arrival.

I exhaled and finally looked back at my oldest friend.

"It's my home, Nathaniel. I wasn't going to sit around for a week waiting for you to come back to tell me what happened." I noticed him take in my expression. I wasn't sure what he saw there, but after several heartbeats, his shoulders drooped in defeat. He closed his eyes and pinched the bridge of his nose, taking several calming breaths as he did so. After a few more moments, he finally relented, the anger visibly draining from his body.

"Fine, but if we are ambushed, we need to protect ourselves with magic to keep them at a distance until we can escape. You need to stay in the centre of us as we ride, at *all* times, you hear me? And I mean it, Aela, no pissing about. When we reach Olos, you'll stay with the horses by the water troughs on the outskirts while we scout the area. The last thing we need is a group of thieves who are scouring the ruins to spot you, a small, *blonde* woman, and presume they could get a decent amount of drachmae selling what they believe is a powerful Flame to one of the underground Shades." I grimaced at his words, knowing that if that happened, whoever bought me would be sorely disappointed to discover that all I was good for was lighting a candle.

"Who the fuck made you in charge, Everflame?" Lex called from the front, finally acknowledging my presence. "Last time I checked, Kieran is the third-year here, so he outranks you." A smirk appeared on her face as she pointed to her cousin. All our eyes turned to Kieran, but instead of responding, he squeezed his horse's sides, and the gelding pulled away from the group with surprising grace. Lex let out a huff and quickly followed suit, leaving the rest of us coughing in their dust.

Jaxon chuckled.

"Well, I guess you better get in the middle, Blondie."

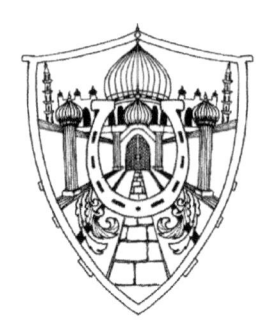

CHAPTER FOURTEEN

We reached the edge of Thellas the next day, just as the sun began to ascend to its highest point. Although the journey typically took three days by cart, the horses allowed us to cover the same distance in half the time. The atmosphere among the group had been tense since my unannounced arrival the morning before, but thankfully there hadn't been much opportunity for conversation at the speed we were traveling. The sandy, dehydrated terrain had started to give way the previous evening as we approached the milder climate of Thellas, revealing more familiar views of grass, sparse trees, and even some rolling hills. Just before the sun dipped below the horizon, I directed our group to a small cluster of trees and boulders that surrounded a shallow watering hole, a short distance from the dirt road we now travelled along. The stone roads of Solarus' inner sector were now far behind us.

It had been an excellent place to camp for the night, allowing us to wash the sweat from the horses and let them drink deeply after a long day's ride. We also freshened up and munched on the dried meat and fruit we had all packed that morning. I noted that once we had scouted the village, we would likely need to hunt for some wild game whilst we were in Thellas, as the return journey would probably be slower due to exhaustion and dwindling supplies.

Leena insisted that we practice my magic while we had the chance, and for the first time that week, I had almost managed to create the straight lines of a triangle before my power had sparked out. It was a small victory, but it was the only thing that had managed to lift my spirits since hearing about the attack on Olos. Nathaniel's mood toward me had also softened; he sat close to us, offering small words of encouragement and guidance whenever he could. Jaxon, surprisingly, was less irritating, keeping his crude jokes to himself as he chose to keep his quiet brother company instead. I noticed Ollie casting longing glances in Kieran's direction whenever he could get away with it.

Lex and Kieran remained slightly apart from the rest of the group, speaking too quietly amongst themselves for me to catch a single word. I still hadn't seen Kieran laugh, let alone smile, and I began to wonder if something was wrong with his facial muscles that prevented him from doing so.

In my haste that morning, I had forgotten to bring a bedroll, so I ended up lying on my side, squeezing behind Leena to try and fit on one between us. The temperatures dropped low in the middle of the night, so the body heat and our shared blanket was welcomed, although I wasn't sure Leena would agree.

"People are going to think we're a couple with the number of times we seem to share a bed." She mumbled to me not long before we fell asleep.

I awoke in the dead of night to the sound of repeated slapping. I sat up, heart racing, my eyes wide as I tried to make out any movement in the shadows, convinced we were under attack. To my horror, once my eyes adjusted to the darkness, I spotted Jaxon and Lex toward the edge of camp, and in that moment, I wished it were bandits I was hearing instead of what I had to witness. Lex's chest was pressed firmly against the rough bark of a tree, her lightweight slacks puddled around her ankles. Jaxon had removed his fighting leathers entirely, and I saw far too much of his skin as he thrust roughly into her from behind, his ogre-sized hands holding her in place. It seemed he might break her in half—a vision I longed to wipe from my memory entirely. I grimaced at the fact that they had been traveling all day and undoubtedly smelled like horse and sweat.

The unwelcomed interruption during the night, which lasted far longer than necessary, left me utterly exhausted the next morning. I glared holes into the back of Jaxon's head for the entire rest of the way to Thellas, wondering how a man of his size had the stamina to last an hour. However, what greeted us upon arrival washed away any lingering thoughts of the night before.

The architecture of Thellas differed significantly from the colourful brick and terracotta-roofed structures of Solarus. As Thellas was a small area located directly in the centre of the four other sectors in Olympia, it was historically served merely as a waypoint to break up longer journeys. For example, those crossing from Mytos to Orouras, or from Solarus to Monacus, often rested here, taking advantage of its strategic location. As a result, most of the village consisted of white-stone hut-like structures with dark grey cone-shaped roofs, known as 'trullis,' which were designed for easy dismantling and rebuilding, providing temporary shelter for passing travellers. It wasn't until several hundred years ago that people began to settle in Thellas, recognising it as an ideal hub for work and trade routes, facilitating the exchange of essential supplies such as food, clothing, and other materials. Over time, the villages flourished and became quite densely populated for such a small area. Aside from a few temples, bustling market stalls, and larger stone structures like the orphanages, most of the villages still featured the trullis, favoured for their affordability and practicality.

As we pulled our horses up to the water troughs at the periphery of the village, a heavy silence enveloped us. Olos, or what remained of it, lay almost completely destroyed. The attack had clearly been by fire, leaving the delicate structures of the trullis in ruins. The earth was scorched and blackened, and the acrid scent of smoke stung my eyes. I found it hard to believe Zaneer's claims that there were no casualties. No sound came from the derelict remains of Olos, and I prayed to Helin that it was because the village had been evacuated, not for some other gruesome reason.

"Stay with the horses," Nathaniel said to me, so quietly I almost didn't hear him.

"What?" I replied, my eyes still fixed forward. I wasn't sure if they were running from the smoke or if tears were actually streaming down my face.

"That was the deal, remember?" he responded curtly.

I nodded. My hands trembled around Juniper's reins, and I wasn't sure I could even move if I wanted to, my mind needing time to process what my eyes were taking in.

My friends, Lex and Kieran, dismounted their steeds and headed toward the village to investigate how far the damage had spread. Leena gave my thigh a quick squeeze as she walked past me, still seated atop Juniper—a small sign of support. I offered her a tight-lipped smile in return; a silent understanding passing between us that any shared words would be useless in that moment.

As the minutes ticked by, restlessness crept in. I dismounted Juniper to stretch my legs, but pacing back and forth in front of our line of mounts only deepened my anxiety. My gaze remained fixed on the boundary of Olos, but still, there were no signs of my group. The sparse trees surrounding the village rustled in the afternoon breeze, and I flinched at every noise. My heart pounded in my chest, quickening whenever a bird startled from its perch or when one of the horses stomped its hooves on the ground, the sound seeming to echo in the tense silence.

Glancing up at the sun, I noted it had dipped past its peak, casting ominous shadows across the ground that hinted we were well into the afternoon. My friends had been gone for at least three hours—far too long in a place like this. Scanning the bleak horizon, I felt the weight of uncertainty pressing down on me. Had something happened to them? I bit my lip, wrestling with the gnawing worry that twisted my stomach.

"What do you think, girl? Shall I go look for them?" I asked Juniper, absently stroking her muzzle. She snorted in my direction, but her big brown eyes seemed to look over my shoulder toward Olos. I took that as my cue. Turning on my heel, I steeled myself and marched toward the village ruins.

What in the Underworld was I doing? This was possibly the most foolish decision I had ever made. Walking through the narrow streets, the damage was far worse than I had initially realised. The stone of the trullis should have withstood most of the fire; however, some walls had crumbled, causing roofs to collapse in on themselves. It looked as if the Gods had taken a large sledgehammer to them.

I passed home after home, and it began to feel like a graveyard of memories. Peering through a gaping hole in one of the trullis' walls, I glimpsed a humble interior that lacked any luxuries, reminding me of the orphanage where I had grown up. I spotted a dining table in the centre of the space, with six wooden seats around it; plates, goblets, and cutlery still adorned its surface, indicating that the family living here had been about to sit down for a meal together, blissfully unaware of the devastation that was about to rain down on them. I whispered a small prayer to the Gods, hoping it hadn't been their last meal together, clinging to Zaneer's earlier assertion that no one had died.

I wandered the streets for what felt like hours, the ground beneath my boots crunching with every step. Dust lined my nostrils, causing me to sneeze and splutter, the sounds bouncing off of the abandoned buildings. I winced each time it happened; I might as well have been walking around shouting, *"I'm here! Helpless woman over here, come find me!"*

My throat felt tight, and I fought to hold back the coughing fits, the pressure building in my head like a storm ready to break.

As I turned a corner onto what felt like the hundredth street, I let out a small gasp. On one of the white stone walls of a destroyed home, painted in a red substance—one I prayed wasn't blood—was a lightning bolt symbol made up of three jagged lines. My breath almost caught in my throat.

"Kera's lightning…" I whispered to myself.

CHAPTER FIFTEEN

"You should know better than to speak her name, little bird."

I spun so quickly to the sound of the low, gravelled voice that came from between the trullis to my left, that I almost lost my balance. I stumbled backwards until my back hit the hard surface of the ramshackled home behind me.

"H-h-h-hello?" I managed to stammer out between the beats of my racing heart. The shade between the buildings that the sun created in the afternoon light made it almost impossible for me to decipher where the voice had come from. As my eyes darted around the space in front of me, I spotted movement next to the trullis with the lightning symbol. Finally, a foot stepped forward from the darkness, followed by a slim, long leg, and then a body.

The man was tall and reedy, dressed all in black with a cape that had a deep hood drawn low to cover his face. All I could make out was a straggly light brown beard framing thin lips. His mouth parted in what I could only describe as a twisted smile, and I noticed his teeth were chipped and yellow.

"Well, well, well, what do we have here then. Such a pretty, little bird aren't you, and what lovely hair you have, is that *blonde* I see?"

He raised his hand to run his fingers through his beard, revealing nails that were long and unclipped, lined with grime and dirt. He took a couple of steps closer to me on light, almost soundless, feet. My hackles instantly rose, and I realised very quickly that this man was not here to be my new best friend. Why did I not wear something around my head like Lex and Kieran to hide my hair?

{Stupid, stupid, stupid.}

Panic started to thrum through my veins, but I tried to ignore it. Panic lead to dumb decisions.

{Think, Aela.}

I didn't have any weapons, but it wouldn't have mattered if I did, I didn't know how to fight. My mind flashed back to a comment Nathaniel made earlier about my hair. Yes, that could work.

With all of the strength I could muster, I searched for that ember that resided deep within my chest and focused on bringing it to the surface. I kept my breathing even, not taking my eyes off the man for a heartbeat. To my relief, and my surprise, my power rushed through me in an unexpected surge. and I pulled a steady channel of magic to my palm, flames sparking to life. I raised my flaming hand in the man's direction.

"You see this?" I nodded my head towards my blazing palm, "If I were you, I would run if you want to live. I'm a powerful fire-wielder and I am not afraid to hurt you." My voice shook slightly as the lie tumbled from my lips, and I prayed he didn't notice. Hopefully, my blonde hair was enough of a deceptive façade to mask the true power of my magic.

The man cocked his head to the right and although I couldn't see his eyes, I could feel him drinking me in, as if weighing up his options.

We stared at one another for what felt like an eternity, though it could have been just a couple of seconds or a few minutes. Sweat trickled down my brow, and the heat of anxiety prickled my skin as I sensed the building pressure within me, a familiar warning that my magic was nearing its limit.

Seemingly out of nowhere, the man lunged for me, apparently coming to the decision he would rather risk his life and take his chances with me to earn a few coin. He startled me, but before I could think, my body responded on instinct, and my hands reached forward to stop him, releasing the fire from my right hand. To my shock, it made contact with his left shoulder. It probably wouldn't have reached him if he had remained where he was, but given that he was now only a few feet in front of me, my fire hit its mark.

The man hissed and looked down at himself, raising his hand to his flaming cloak.

"You little *bitch*!" He roared.

Once he extinguished the flames by patting himself down like a madman, I noticed my fire had burned away the material of his cloak. A small circle the size of a fist revealed red, weeping skin just below his collarbone—most likely a second-degree burn. He looked back at me, and I finally saw his face. His skin was marred with scars and craters, and his eyes were so dilated with rage that they appeared black.

Shit, it was time to run.

I cast a glance to my right but before I could move, the man lurched forward the last several feet; his hand wrapped around my neck as he pinned me to the wall. I writhed and strained beneath him, kicking my legs and flailing my arms as I did so to try and loosen his hold. I wrapped my fingers around his and tried to pry them loose, but his grip remained firm. I started to see stars as I struggled to pull enough oxygen into my lungs. Panic did threaten to overwhelm me this time and the temptation to just close my eyes and accept my fate almost got the better of me. In a last, desperate attempt, I removed my hands from where they were pulling on his and delved two of my fingers deep into the open wound on his burnt shoulder. The skin was hot as it squelched beneath my touch and a warm, wet substance coated my fingers. I almost threw up the apple I had for breakfast in revulsion at the sensation. The cloaked man let out a blood-curdling scream and released his grip on me as he pulled away from me, raising a hand to his shoulder once more, panting and closing his eyes against the pain that was undoubtedly searing through his body.

I fell to my knees as he released me, taking in deep gulps of air, trying to inhale as much as I could. No, there was no time.

{*Get up, Aela*} I said to myself.

"*Run,*" an ethereal voice whisper-shouted in my ear. The voice startled me, but I didn't hesitate to listen.

I got to my feet and darted past him, heart still racing. I ran as fast as I could back the way I came, adrenaline fuelling my every stride; if I could just reach the horses, I might have a chance to escape him. A fleeting thought for my friends' safety crossed my mind, but I quickly pushed it aside, knowing they could handle themselves; they wouldn't be on this mission if they couldn't. *{Which is precisely why you shouldn't be here}* my inner voice chided me, a mix of panic and self-recrimination swirling in my gut.

Panting and gasping, I turned several corners, black spots swirling in my vision as I glanced over my shoulder—he wasn't there. I continued running, scanning the buildings around frantically, my pulse pounding in my ears as I dashed through the narrow, winding streets like a lunatic. Shadows loomed around me, but he was nowhere to be seen. Relief began to swell within me, and my steps slowed slightly, though I didn't dare stop.

As I took a few more turns, the atmosphere shifted, and I noticed that I had reached the main street leading out of Olos. The sun glinted off the horses in the distance, their silhouettes almost glowing against the dusty ground. I let out a hysterical laugh; there was probably only about half a mile left until I reached Juniper.

A hand wrapped around my hair, jerking me backwards, the force of the movement making me bite my tongue, the taste of copper flooding my mouth. I was pulled against a hard chest, and the smell of body odour, old ale, and tobacco filled my nose.

"Trying to fly away, are you little bird? But we were only just starting to have fun."

I was dragged by my hair to a darkened alley in between a couple of the trullis, and the foul man proceeded to slam me face first into a wall. Blinding pain radiated from my nose as I heard a crunch that rattled my skull. Blood instantly poured down my chin and into my mouth, mixing with the blood already welling from my tongue. The man pressed his body flush against my back, so I was pinned between him and the wall. I started screaming as I tried to rotate my body from side to side with the aim to twist myself free. He groaned at the movement and pushed his hips into my back, gyrating against me as his breaths came quicker against my neck. I felt a hard length against the base of my spine, and I instantly stopped my struggling, realising that he was actually revelling in my fear and how he was managing to overpower me.

My mind distantly registered that my legs were wet, my bladder must have released in my fear, but I didn't care, too far gone within the swirling chaos of panic to feel any shame. I tried to take some calming breaths, but I only managed a few until he realised what I was doing and pressed his body into me further, crushing my ribs.

"I know someone who would pay a lot of money for a little blonde bird like you, but I want to try you out for myself first." He said against my neck. His stale breath danced across the skin of my cheek as he spoke, and a shudder of repulsion rolled through me.

He released his hand from my hair, and in a swift movement, he managed to raise both of my hands above my head. With one arm, he pinned them against the wall, and with his other, he reached for my slacks. My screams turned to whimpers as I realised what he intended to do. I had never been with a man before and this wasn't how I envisioned my first time happening.

"You can survive this. You can survive anything. Just breathe." The ethereal voice whispered to me again as tears streamed down my cheeks.

As the man pulled down my waistband to expose me fully, he felt the result of my bladder emptying several moments prior.

"If I had known you were going to be this wet for me birdy, I would've done this sooner." He chuckled darkly. Sobs racked my body so strongly now that my whole body began to tremble.

I heard him unzip his breeches and as he shifted behind me. Soft, hard skin pushed against my exposed rear and a rancid smell filled my bleeding nose from his lack of hygiene. I knew enough to understand that he was positioning himself for what came next. His arm was still pinning my hands against the wall, but I scraped my nails against the surface; they broke and splintered until my nailbeds started to bleed, my last desperate attempt to get away, to flee from the horrors that were about to unfold.

His breaths fluttered against my neck even quicker than before as he became increasingly more aroused, as if he was drunk on my fear, like a cat who had finally caught a mouse. My mind began to unravel, fraying like a worn tapestry, and I felt myself slipping into a dark, endless void. It was a chilling expanse that seemed to swallow all sense of time and reality. The coldness tried to envelop me, promising a numbness that whispered sweetly, assuring me I wouldn't feel anything here—no fear, no pain, just an endless, serene silence. It beckoned me deeper, a tempting escape from the chaos that surrounded me. *"You'll be safe here,"* it seemed to say.

The tip of his length pushed against my entrance, and I closed my eyes, readying myself for the pain.

A thud sounded from behind me, followed by a wet gurgling sound. The man went very still, and I braced myself for what would be coming any moment now. A few seconds passed…

Then ten…

Then twenty…

Nothing happened.

The weight behind me vanished, and I slid to the floor in a heap. Curling in on myself as small as I could. I rocked back and forth in a subconscious bid to self-soothe, my eyes vacantly staring at the wall in front of me. I didn't care that I lay in a dirty alley, most likely in my own urine; all that mattered was the quiet rhythm of my movement.

"Get up." A deep, rich voice came from behind me.

I was so lost within the dark, endless void that had cracked open in my mind that I didn't register the words. A tipped boot lightly kicked the base of my spine, not far from where the man had pressed himself against me only moments before, and I flinched.

"I said, get… the fuck… up."

Finally, I looked over my shoulder; Kieran and Lex were standing behind me. Kieran was clutching a dagger in his right hand, a dark brown liquid dripping from it. As he took in my bloodied face, soiled clothes, and wet, half-naked body, a pure look of repulsion swept across his face.

"Disgusting." He muttered under his breath. Shame instantly coloured my cheeks, and I felt bile rising in my throat. I turned to Lex, shocked to see concern etched across her face, her eyes lined with silver tears. Surely that couldn't be right? Before I had time to think on it further, nausea overtook me, and I vomited on the ground.

I raised my hand to wipe my mouth as I heard a set of footsteps receding from the alley, my nails smearing dirt and mud across my lips. The gritty texture made me wince, and I lay back down, accepting that they had chosen to leave me there. A soft hand touched my shoulder. I cowered away from it, letting out a small, startled cry.

"It's only me, little mouse," Lex said, her voice gentle. I heard her rustling behind me, the sound of fabric brushing against itself. "Can you stand?"

I could only manage a small nod in response. Lex grabbed one of my arms and pulled me to my feet, her grip steady and reassuring. I turned to face her and saw her visibly gulp as she took in the state of my appearance. My eyes flicked past her to a crumpled heap on the ground, and nausea surged through me once more.

"Don't look at him, look at me. Kieran will take care of it." Her voice held a firm resolve, anchoring me in the moment. She extended her hand to me, a bundle of material clutched within her fingers.

In those next few minutes, Lex showed me more kindness than I ever thought possible from her. She dampened the fabric of the wrap she had worn around her head, the coolness of it contrasting sharply with my shame-flushed skin, and began to clear the blood from my face and nails. When she handed the cloth to me, I took it with trembling fingers, using it to clean myself up before pulling on a spare pair of breeches she had pulled from her satchel. I left my slacks behind, wishing I had enough magic to burn them away.

Lex then wrapped one of my arms over her shoulder, wrapping one of her own around my waist to support my weight, her presence steadying me. We slowly hobbled back to the horses in sullen silence, the atmosphere charged with wordless comprehension.

CHAPTER SIXTEEN

I stared down at my hollow reflection in the water. We were back at the cluster of trees where we had gathered the night before. Nathaniel and Leena had been hysterical when they saw me limping back to the horses, draped over Lex's shoulder. Apparently, I had also twisted my ankle in the fight, which had led to my leg almost buckling when I pulled away from Lex to reach for Juniper's reins. I had tried to provide my friends with a brief overview of what had happened, but I struggled to convey the final details, flinching away from Nathaniel when he reached out to wrap me in a hug. Fortunately, Lex stepped in to fill in the gaps when it became clear I wasn't ready to share any more.

Now, as I stared back at myself, my cheeks gaunt and black circles appearing under my eyes from my broken nose, I felt... *nothing*. A deep part of me knew

I must be in shock, but I couldn't seem to care. My face was clean, but my light tunic was soaked in blood, the dark stains stark against the fabric. I was unaware of how long I had been sitting there by the watering hole, the cool water lapping at my fingers as I aimlessly scrubbed at my hands, as if I could wash away the memories of the day. Each ripple distorted my reflection, reminding me of how far I had fallen from the person I was that morning.

We hadn't ridden as hard on our way back to our designated campsite, which allowed for conversation among the group. They shared that several other cloaked men had been among the ruins of Olos, rifling through the abandoned homes and markets, looking for any discarded valuables that could earn them a quick coin.

One had tried to attack Leena at first but had swiftly met the fate of Jaxon's open mouth. At the sight of their comrade being torn apart by shadow fire, the rest of them had run. My group was on their way back to me when Lex and Kieran heard my screams and ordered the rest to continue while they found the source of the commotion. If I had only waited another ninety minutes, my whole ordeal could have been avoided.

I heard light footsteps crunching on the grass behind me, and I instantly knew it was Leena. She sat beside me, keeping a few inches between us so we didn't touch, which I was grateful for, but she was close enough that I could still feel her warmth seeping into me, easing some of the tension in my shoulders. We didn't say anything, but the silence spoke a thousand words. She was my friend. In that moment, I knew it, and I mentally swore to myself never to make her worry for me like this again.

Minutes turned into hours as we sat there in companionable silence. The sun started to kiss the horizon, and as the sky began to darken, Leena stood to make her way back to camp. Mindlessly, I followed to join her.

Once we were back at camp, she perched on a bedroll, and I noticed there were two closely positioned next to hers, with Lex already sprawled out on one. My brow furrowed.

"Kieran is going to keep watch tonight, just in case any of those cowards from Olos decide to pay us a visit while we are asleep, so there's a spare bedroll," Lex said in response to my expression, pointing at the one in between the two women. They had clearly positioned it in a bid to protect me, to assure me I was safe with them, that they would guard me from any more external horrors. A distant emotion flickered to life within me, something akin to gratitude for their unspoken support and concern. But just as quickly, the heavy blanket of nothingness that had settled deep inside me smothered that feeling, extinguishing it before it could fully form. It was as if I were trapped in a fog, unable to grasp at the light that was trying to reach for me, leaving me alone with my thoughts and the weight of my experiences.

...

I awoke several hours later to the sounds of braying and nickering, the horses clearly unsettled. Panic surged through me as I bolted upright, images of the afternoon flooding my mind and clouding my vision. I scanned the camp, heart racing as I searched for the group of bandits, but it seemed I was the only one disturbed. Lex and Leena had nestled even closer to me than when we had fallen asleep, their presence creating a cocoon that shielded me from the outside world.

Glancing across the smouldering embers of the small fire in the centre of the clearing, I spotted Jaxon, Oliver, and Nathaniel, all sleeping soundly, oblivious to my turmoil. I continued my search of the space, my gaze finally settling on a large figure in the distance. Not far from the horses by the water and trees, Kieran leaned against a boulder, his massive arms crossed over his chest. The moonlight cast a silvery glow over his chiselled features, highlighting the tension in his posture as he scanned the dark horizon like a bird of prey.

I pushed myself to my feet and carefully stepped over Leena's legs, moving as quietly as I could. Tiptoeing toward Kieran and the horses, when I got close, I made sure my feet crunched on the twigs and fallen leaves beneath me to avoid startling him. He didn't glance in my direction as I came to stand nearby, and I kept a cautious distance from him, several feet away—a safe buffer.

I followed his eyeline and squinted to try and decipher what he was staring at. Just ahead of the line of horses was a shape peeking through the foliage, its colour reminding me of the lightest sand of Olympia. I began to walk toward it, feeling an invisible pull guiding me closer. Kieran made no move to stop me; the stillness around us was almost palpable, not even the sound of his breathing reached my ears. As I edged closer to the bushels, passing Juniper and giving her a soft pat on her side, I stopped several steps before the shape. Bright blue eyes, either side of a white stripe, pierced the darkness.

I let out a gasp.

The horse from my dream.

My breath hitched as I reached out my hand to stroke its muzzle. As my palm made contact with the soft tip of its nose, a sudden pulse of electricity coursed through every part of my body, awakening every nerve. I froze for several moments, bracing for pain, but it never came. Instead, a profound warmth bloomed in my chest, a sense of belonging washing over me, as if I were finally… *home*. It was a feeling I had only ever experienced a few times before, during rare moments of connection when Nathaniel and I had touched, our energies intertwining in a way that felt both foreign and beautifully familiar.

"You have magic," I whispered to its beautiful face. The horse dipped its head subtly as if in answer. It took a step toward me and pushed its long face into the crook between my neck and shoulder, and I wrapped my arms around its neck. We stayed like that for several heartbeats, and I closed my eyes to relish the moment. Tears started to fill my eyes, and I realised that it was because I felt safe, understood, *loved*; such an unexpected feeling after everything that had happened.

I let out a small shaky laugh in disbelief as the thought crossed my mind, knowing that this must all be in my head, that maybe the events of today had driven me to madness. I was embracing a wild horse, for Gods' sake.

Much to my disappointment, the beautiful creature pulled away from me and turned to retreat into the dense brush once more, seemingly endless in the night's shadows.

"Wait…" I whispered. The horse paused and looked back over its shoulder toward me, as if in understanding. "Thank you," I said in a raspy voice, a tear silently rolling down my cheek. The horse slowly dipped its head in what I could only describe as a bow; {*you're welcome*} the gesture seemed to say.

More tears fell from my eyes as I watched the horse walk away, the deep-seated feeling of abandonment that I always carried threatening to well up inside me. Its beautiful cream coat shimmered in the moonlight, just like it had in my dream. Once it fully disappeared from my sight, I made my way back toward my bedroll, raw emotion making my legs tremble slightly.

I stopped next to Kieran before I passed him, who had watched the entirety of the bizarre exchange between the horse and me. Still revelling in the previous moment, I turned to him.

"Thank you for saving my life," I said on a whisper.

He turned to face me, and I realised it was the first time he had ever made eye contact with me. His eyes were a bright silver that seemed to glow with the same intensity as the moon, reminding me of something otherworldly. His stare trapped me in place, and I found myself holding my breath.

"Your naivety almost cost you your life today, and if things had gone differently, mine and Lex's could have been in danger too. Believe me, I am not prepared to die for a girl who acts like a child, running blindly into danger without a plan, any magic or any knowledge of how to protect herself. How stupid are you? You didn't even take a weapon with you."

He shook his head and looked away from me, releasing a scoff as he did so. Humiliation burned my cheeks at the truth of his words, and tears gathered in my eyes again; an entirely different feeling from the fleeting joy I had felt only moments before. I tried to reach inside myself for the numbness that I had been wearing like armour all afternoon, but it was no use, it's like the horse had opened a dam within me. Letting out a shaky breath, I stepped away from him, attempting to make my way back toward camp.

"Do yourself a favour," he cut me off mid-stride, "learn how to fight if you can't wield your magic. There are people out there who will make what you experienced today look like child's play. You can surround yourself with your ridiculous band of misfits all you want, but there will come a time when you have no choice but to fight your own battles, and I'm sure as fuck not running to your rescue again."

As I lay back on my bedroll, staring up at the stars of the night sky, tears rolled down the sides of my face into my hairline as I tried to contain my sobs, the reality of the day hitting me anew. Kieran's words rattled around in my head like a song on repeat, the truth of them drowning out any lingering feelings of peace from my embrace with the horse from my dream.

"He's not a monster," Lex whispered from my right, startling me. "He's just seen too many of them."

I nodded my head, unable to speak, hoping that was answer enough for her. She sighed and rolled away from me, accepting my response for what it was.

I continued to gaze upon the night sky, counting down the minutes until sleep claimed me, hoping the stars would offer me comfort like they had so many times before. I just wanted to get back to Solarus, to my bed, to change out of my soiled clothes, to take a proper bath, to wash myself free of everything that had happened.

Kieran was right; I needed to learn how to fight. I needed to protect myself and to not be a liability to Nathaniel and to those I was beginning to care for.

As my eyes grew heavy and I hovered between reality and my dreams, I vowed to myself that I never wanted to feel helpless again.

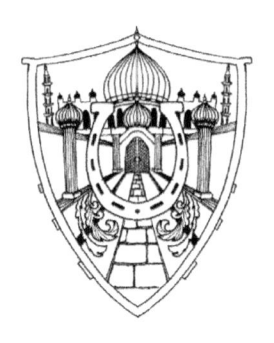

CHAPTER SEVENTEEN

Much to our dismay, Bellum had been waiting for our return outside the stables when we arrived at dawn four days later, arms crossed and jaw tense. I found myself wondering how long he had stood there, his eyes fixed on the horizon waiting for a group of seven riders to come into view. A small part of me had hoped he might not have noticed my absence, considering he was only just becoming familiar with the influx of first-years, but when his glare met mine as I rode into the stables atop Juniper, I knew I hadn't been so lucky.

To rub salt in the wound, I discovered that Juniper was actually Bellum's personal horse, whose true name was Stratus—a titbit of information the group had kept quiet until Solarus' War College had come into view. I personally thought '*Juniper*' suited her far better; she was too majestic for a name that literally meant '*grey cloud.*'

True to Nathaniel's and Leena's earlier statements, we returned just in time for the next Realm Announcement update. However, instead of joining the rest of the college in the bustling dining hall, we found ourselves confined to the War Council room, sitting in tense silence beneath Bellum's watchful gaze. Anxiety coiled in my stomach as we awaited Zaneer's arrival after she finished addressing our classmates.

The room was a plain, square space, no more than twenty feet wide, with a circular table in the centre surrounded by twelve chairs. Several maps of Olympia adorned the walls: one displaying the varied terrain across the Realm, another highlighting notable landmarks such as the wall, the college, and the Queen's palace. The final map was dotted with numerous pins, which I presumed marked the latest skirmishes throughout the Realm. I noticed multiple incidents in Monacus, the Sector located adjacent to the wall and Passageway, and several more at the docks of Orouras. A large red pin marked Olos, and I had to suppress a grimace as memories of the trip clawed at the edges of my mind. I focused intently on this map, trying to mentally catalogue as much information as possible for future reference.

An agonising hour later, Zaneer sat across from us, with Bellum standing rigidly to her right. He was as straight as a board, arms clasped behind his back. His face was flushed a plum shade, and a vein pulsed in his forehead, evidence of the fury simmering beneath the surface. Though he didn't meet my gaze directly, it was evident that he yearned to unleash a tirade upon us, restrained only by the presence of his General. Zaneer, in contrast, appeared somewhat more relaxed in her seat, one arm resting casually on the table with her hand propping up her chin. Yet, her eyes remained keen and vigilant, darting from one of us to the next, scrutinising each of our faces in quick succession. She was yet again clad in her refined uniform, adorned with medals and weapons, her silken locks plaited around her head like a crown this time, reminding me of a warrior princess.

"Can someone please explain to me what in the Gods' Realm happened, and why a first-year with no training in combat or magic ended up as part of this patrol?" Zaneer asked, her voice quiet but laced with authority.

"She snuck out to join them, General," Bellum responded for us.

My eyes remained glued to the wall above Zaneer's head as I frantically nibbled on my lower lip, guilt plastered across my face.

"She grew up in Thellas, General. It was killing her not knowing what had happened." Leena said, seated closely to my left. I reached beneath the table to squeeze her hand atop her thigh, an attempt to offer her a silent *{thank you}*.

"I gave her strict orders to remain at the centre of the group and not to enter Olos once we arrived. Unfortunately, she did not listen." Nathaniel added. We had agreed to keep my encounter in the village quiet for now, but his statement felt like he had thrown me under the cart a bit.

"Blondie just wanted to see it for herself, ma'am." Jaxon chimed in. I winced at his informal nickname for me, not to mention the fact that he called the high-ranking General of the Olympian Army '*ma'am*'.

Zaneer's eyes pierced through our group, taking in our sheepish faces and rigid postures. Turning to Kieran, she asked;

"Given that you were the highest-ranking officer of your patrol unit, why did you not order one of your riders to escort the first-year back to Solarus while the rest of you continued the mission?"

My temper flared unexpectedly. How *dare* they discuss me as if I weren't even in the room? My mouth opened before I had time to think.

"Tell me, General Zaneer, when you were a first-year, would someone have been able to stop you if you had heard there was an attack just a few miles from your home village? If you thought someone who had been a mother figure to you for most of your life might be in danger? Would you have waited a week for those deemed more powerful, more *worthy,* than you to return and give you the answer?" I met her gaze, feeling a surge of defiance instead of the usual embarrassment.

Silence fell over the room, stretching into what felt like an eternity. Eight pairs of eyes stared at me, and my skin prickled under the weight of their attention, my friends seemingly shocked by my audacity. Zaneer's dark brown stare was locked onto mine, an angry glint sparking within her irises. I could tell she was searching for a response, but I knew my question had struck a chord when the silence lingered.

"What is your name, Cadet?" she asked at last.

"Aela Everflame," I replied confidently, lifting my chin. I swore I caught a glimmer of recognition in her eyes, but it vanished as quickly as it had appeared.

"Leave us," she said sharply, waving her arm toward the door. I pushed my chair back, preparing to stand. "Not you." She added, directing her gaze at me. My brows furrowed in confusion, but I remained seated, unwilling to push my luck any further. The rest of my group, including Bellum, filed out, leaving me completely alone with Zaneer, the atmosphere taut between us. She let out a sigh and leaned back in her seat, rubbing her temple with two fingers—clearly, I was beginning to give her a headache.

"You are right; there is nothing that would have stopped me when I was a first-year. I would have run headfirst into a pit of vipers if I thought I was doing the right thing, but I was young and ignorant back then, much like you are now. You didn't think about the consequences of your actions, Cadet, not only for you, but for your fellow classmates also. I could expel all of you right now for ignoring a direct order from your General, slamming the door on all your hopes of enrolling in the Olympian Army one day."

My heart sank. I wasn't sure what my friends' goals were for the future, but the thought of my actions jeopardising Nathaniel's dream of serving Olympia on the front lines made a lump rise in my throat. I swallowed hard, trying to push it down.

Zaneer continued, "The only reason I won't do that is that Commander Bellum has personally vouched for each of your comrades. Their skills and power are unmatched; they are the most promising Cadets we've seen in the last decade. Expelling them would only hinder me when it comes to preparing my front lines in the years to come." My body sagged with relief at her words, but as I held her gaze, I sensed that she was still assessing me sharply, understanding dawned that she hadn't decided my fate yet. "You have no magic?" she asked after a moment of silence.

"Very little..." I admitted, glancing down at my hands resting in my lap, nervously fiddling with a loose piece of string from my tunic.

"And you can't fight…" she trailed off. It felt less like a question and more like a statement, but I shook my head anyway.

She stood abruptly, her chair nearly clattering to the floor behind her, as if a decision had been made. "The Commander will train you every morning before classes in hand-to-hand combat and military manoeuvres. We don't teach this to Cadets until their second year, as we prefer them to grasp their magic first. However, given that you would do very little damage with yours, I can't see this being a problem. Every Saturday, after the Realm Announcement, I will want a personal demonstration of your progress that week. If I so much as hear a *whisper* that you are falling behind in your other studies—whether in Realm History with Sephere, or in training what little magic you have with Commander Bellum—I will have no hesitation in expelling you from this academy and sending you back to where you came from. Do I make myself clear, Cadet Everflame?"

She was clear alright, and I had a sinking feeling that things were about to get much, much worse.

PART TWO

Though the body fades away,
The soul knows no end,
Adopting countless forms,
With many names to send.
A timeless journey weaves,

Where memories may blend,

If the Gods deem you worthy,
Of this life, you may transcend.

CHAPTER EIGHTEEN

To put it bluntly, the next few weeks were utterly awful. Bellum was relentless with his training, knocking on my bedroom door every morning before sunrise as if he were the world's most obnoxious rooster. Much to my annoyance, each time I swung open the door and cast my eyes over his bronzed face and salt-and-pepper hair, he had looked as fresh as a daisy, as if he had been up for hours. During that first week, he had me endure a gruelling exercise routine that seemed designed by a sadistic artist with a penchant for torture. He had explained that I needed to work on my muscle tone before I could even think about performing any fighting manoeuvres. I had initially felt frustrated, wanting to dive head-first into practicing with weapons, but after my first session left me gasping like a fish out of water when I couldn't even complete two push-ups, I knew he was probably right. One small blessing was that I hadn't actually sprained my ankle when I was attacked in Olos, it was merely bruised, so didn't particularly affect my progress.

Jaxon, with his typical charm, had repeatedly reminded me each morning over breakfast that I appeared so bedraggled, it looked like I had been up all night enjoying the company of a '*lover,*' though, as you can imagine, he hadn't used those exact words.

The first Saturday arrived, bringing with it the moment I had to showcase my progress to General Zaneer. I managed to complete two laps around the rooftop terrace, twenty sit-ups, three push-ups, and ten exercises that Bellum had ominously dubbed 'burpees.' I had never heard of them before, and a part of me was convinced he had concocted the agonising full-body exercise solely to make me question my life choices.

After finishing, I beamed with pride, even as I stood there drenched in sweat, my arms trembling like jelly and my legs shaking like a defecating dog. It was the most I had ever accomplished in one go, and to my surprise, it earned me a hearty clap on the shoulder from Bellum. The gesture felt monumental, like a knight bestowing a knighthood. Bellum was a man of few words, and I had really started to warm toward him. Not once had he scolded me for my actions in

Olos, nor had he belittled me when I struggled with one of his drills.

The General had been less than impressed with my feeble display of strength, but to his credit, Bellum had explained how much I had progressed in just a few days and believed I was ready to learn some basic fighting manoeuvres with a wooden sword.

Although the second week was more mentally draining, I began to appreciate the distraction it offered. Memories of the attack and the cloaked figure in the alley at Olos had plagued my dreams. Often, I would wake abruptly, jolted from the depths of those vivid nightmares by Lex shaking my shoulders, her voice cutting through the fog of terror as she tried to pull me back to reality. In those disorienting moments, between sleep and existence, I could swear I still smelled his breath and felt his coarse beard scraping against my cheek.

"He's dead, little mouse; he can never hurt you again." Lex had said each time, and it became a mantra that played over and over in my mind as I executed the choreography of footwork that Bellum had me learn. To my relief, my size and the fact that I was light on my feet meant that I picked this up quite quickly. The Commander had praised me several times for my speed, noting how I seemed to dance rather than fight. My downfall, however, had been trying to incorporate the movements with the practice sword. Bellum had opted to train me with a long, thin wooden

sword that was surprisingly light. He explained that this would mimic a 'rapier,' a weapon more suited to my build, offering the finesse needed for quick, precise strikes rather than the brute strength of the broadswords favoured by the Olympian Army.

I had initially pushed back against this notion, a small part of me wanting to prove I was just as capable as any other fighter. But Bellum remained steadfast, insisting it was the best option for my strength and size.

"With this, you can move swiftly, strike precisely," he had said, his tone unwavering. *"You'll wield it in one hand, leaving your other arm free for a shield."*

By the end of my second week, calluses had started to form on my right hand. When I performed what I secretly nicknamed my *'sword dance'* for General Zaneer that Saturday, which consisted of various sequences of footwork while thrusting and slicing my wooden rapier at an invisible opponent, she seemed relatively impressed with what she saw. Of course, she hadn't said anything of the sort, but I took the slight nod of her head in my direction as approval enough.

The third week was the hardest. Although the Commander had seemed impressed by how quickly I had picked up the initial formations of wielding a sword, he said that the toughest part about defending oneself was understanding the opposition's weaknesses and strengths, and essentially predicting their next move. Therefore, Bellum had decided it was time for me to learn how to attack and defend against an actual opponent, which to my horror, turned out to be him.

My smugness from the weekend before evaporated in mere moments as I tried to defend myself against Bellum's advances. I parried and feinted as much as possible; still, by the end of the first day, I was black and blue with bruises and welts from the hits he had successfully administered. At the end of our session, he had gleefully announced that I would have been dead forty-seven times.

By Tuesday, I was ready to burst into tears over how truly awful I was, I could hardly tell where one bruise ended and another began; it was like a grotesque patchwork quilt of my failures. At the end of the session, the Commander threw me a lifeline and decided that a change of pace was in order, suggesting that I would benefit from facing a different opponent the following day.

I was pretty much ready to throw myself off the roof terrace the next morning as I waited, for what I presumed would be an obnoxious third-year, to emerge from the Fire Spire, my muscles aching as my body begged and pleaded for more rest. Instead, I was relieved to see a petite figure with dark hair cross the roof terrace as the sun rose. Frustratingly, Mei looked just as alert as Bellum in the morning, in stark contrast to my rumpled appearance and puffy face. Was there something wrong with me, why did everyone look so fucking awake before the sun rose?

Since Mei was also a first-year, meaning she wasn't due to learn military fighting training until her second year, I had expected to have an advantage over her, given my success from the week before. However, my cockiness quickly dissipated after a few seconds of facing her. Much like her shadows, Mei moved with the grace and stealth of a cobra slithering through tall grass. Although we were similarly matched in size, Mei fought as if it were second nature, as if she had been born to do it. Frankly, I was in awe of her. Halfway through the session, Bellum insisted I observe them, as I was getting utterly pummelled by Mei and achieving nothing beyond adding more bruises to my ever-growing collection.

Mei and the Commander had completely different fighting styles. Where Bellum moved with precise, powerful movements, Mei was more fluid, using her size to her advantage. She understood that if Bellum—or at least someone of his skill and stature—were to gain the upper hand on a battlefield, she would be dead.

She was a blur, moving with the speed of a racing snake. She constantly danced away from his strikes, always one or two inches *just* out of reach of his wooden broadsword, but close enough to dart in, under an arm, from the side, and even from behind. Once, she had even flown through his legs on her knees, her spine bending so far backward it was as if she was a puppet being held up by an invisible string from her chest. She made countless small blows to Bellum's body, barely hard enough to earn a grunt from him; nevertheless, after about ten minutes, he raised his hand to stop their duel and informed me that if her sword had been steel and they were in a real combat situation, the number of cuts she had made would mean he would now be face down in the soil, bleeding out.

Mei joined our sessions for the rest of the week, and I greedily drank up every detail as I watched her. Observing both Bellum and Mei greatly enhanced my progress; I reminded myself it was just like learning in a classroom. I had always grasped concepts quickly when they were demonstrated, and with reading, I would pour over the words again and again, until I could visualise them, only putting them into action after analysing all the possible outcomes.

Mei had shared that all Shangonese households grew up learning two forms of fighting: one called 'wushu' and the other, 'jianshu'. 'Wushu' was a way of fighting that combined fluid kicking, jumping, punching, and slicing with one's hands. It was not only physical, but spiritual, a way of connecting to their ancestors, requiring a lot of mental discipline and patience. 'Jianshu' was a development of this fighting technique, incorporating a delicate but deadly straight sword, much like my rapier. Fortunately, the library had many books on Shangonese culture. I spent my nights nestled under the staircase in the library, pouring over the detailed descriptions and history of this fighting style, colloquially referred to as 'martial arts'. Mei joined me each night without me having to ask, silently reading next to me, offering insights whenever I had questions, or demonstrating a sequence for me when I couldn't quite envision it from the page.

That Saturday, General Zaneer had offered the faintest of smiles with her nod of approval and insisted that I continue training with Bellum and Mei, saying I should get all the help I could get. I had been practically giddy from her praise for the next few days.

It was now the Wednesday of the fourth week, and Mei and I had taken our usual positions under the library staircase that evening. I had been trying to focus on the page in front of me, which was a detailed account of the first ever recorded battle involving martial arts, but my eyes were growing heavy. I looked to my right, toward Mei, who was nestled so deeply into one of the large bean-bag cushions that I could barely make her out in the dim light.

"What are you reading?" I asked, noticing that her face was so close to the pages of the book in front of her that I couldn't understand how she could see anything at all.

"It's a book on the lineage of the Gods, and I think this page hints at Kera's existence."

I let out a gasp at how casually she spoke of her name but also made a mental note of the title, *'Celestial Ancestries, Vol II',* for later.

"You can't speak her name, Mei; you know that!" I hissed back on an urgent whisper, my eyes darting around the dark space to see if anyone was nearby.

Mei let out a weary sigh, finally pulling the pages away from her nose to look in my direction, offering a small nonchalant shrug.

"We're the only ones here; we're *always* the only ones here. Stop getting your breeches in a twist." She waved a hand dismissively and reached for her book once more.

"Azrael is always lurking in the shadows somewhere, you know that, and he could report you to Bellum, or Sephere, or even the General. Only the Gods know what would happen if he did!" I spat back, my words tumbling out quickly as annoyance grew at her indifference.

Mei scoffed, and I only just managed to see her roll her eyes at me in the darkness.

"Oh please, that creep probably has a little shrine set up to her in whatever cave he sleeps in at night," she waved her hand dismissively again. "Besides, I know a lot of people who've spoken about her, and nothing has ever happened to them. There's even a secret market back in Shangnon where vendors sell all kinds of junk meant to honour her, from little trinkets shaped like lightning bolts to ten-foot tapestries showing a silver-haired woman riding into battle, and they still show up every week without a scratch on them."

I was shocked by Mei's anecdote, but growing up, I often spotted symbols of lightning bolts painted between buildings or on the sides of taverns, much like the one I had seen in Olos a month ago. When I asked Nanny Rosie what they were, she said they were painted by those who prayed to her in secret, believing she still lived among us and was the rightful ruler of the Continent, of both Anka and Olympia. These symbols were always swiftly washed away the next morning, as village-folk were nervous it would only fuel the uprising against the two Crowns. I personally believed it was probably just some adolescents who had drunk too much ale, trying to bring excitement to their dreary lives, but what did I know?

"Either way, Mei, we aren't in Anka anymore, and you've been here long enough to know that speaking of her is strictly forbidden in Olympia." I began to pack my things away into my leather satchel, my actions jerky with annoyance. Abruptly, I stood and flung my bag over my shoulder. The movement was so rough that a few pencils and parchments slipped free from my satchel and clattered to the floor. Grunting in further annoyance, I bent down to pick them up.

"What's that?" Mei asked from my left. I looked over to see her pointing at me.

"What's… what?" I asked, trying to understand what she was referring to.

"What's that hanging from your neck? I've never seen it before."

I looked down to see that my stone necklace had come free when I bent down to retrieve my belongings, peeking out from where I normally tucked it beneath the collar of my tunic.

"Oh…" I said, a small smile appearing on my face and my cheeks reddening as I straightened. I tucked the necklace back to its normal resting place against my skin, just above my heart. "It's a necklace Nathaniel made from his magic when we were young. He grabbed a ball of sand, and his flames turned it into glass. It's nothing fancy, but it has a lot of sentimental value. It reminds me of when we were kids."

Mei stood, flinging her own satchel over her shoulder, and took several steps toward me, frowning.

"It looks a lot like the enchanted necklaces from the stories my Yeh-yeh told me when I was growing up." She reached out as if to touch the leather strap around my neck to expose the stone once more, but I pulled away, turning toward the library exit.

"Well, like you said, they are just your grandfather's stories. It's nothing more than simple glass. I wear it because it reminds me of Nathaniel and where we grew up, nothing more."

We made our way through the library's amber glow toward the exit archway, and when we were only a few feet from the hall, we heard a rustling.

"Ah, well isn't it the little lost girl and the sword of grace from Shangnon. You're leaving earlier than normal this evening; have you somewhere to be?" A voice that sounded like sandpaper rubbing against metal came from behind us, sending chills down my spine.

Turning, we were greeted by the skeletal figure and milky white eyes of our wonderful librarian, Azrael.

"We've had a long week, Azrael, and we want to get some rest before we have another early start tomorrow," I responded, my voice surprisingly neutral despite the churning of my insides, as I took in his appearance. He looked just as harrowing as I remembered, and if possible, he seemed even thinner; the scraps of rags he tried to pass off as clothing hanging off him even more than before. His white skin had taken on an even greyer hue, and his cheeks were so sunken that I swore I could see the outlines of his teeth beneath the flesh, if that was even possible.

"Oh, come now, lost girl. I told you, you are my friend, so you must call me Az." Azrael attempted a friendly smile, but his dry, thin lips parted to reveal pointed yellow teeth, and the expression seemed far more menacing than he probably intended. He took a few steps toward us, and I had to lock my muscles to avoid stepping back.

"What do you want, old man?" Mei asked, sounding bored by Azrael's antics. Was she not as disturbed by his presence as I was?

Azrael's milky eyes flitted to hers, but then quickly returned to me, as if Mei were no more than a fly buzzing around his ear—an annoyance he was trying to ignore.

"You should be cautious with your words around the shadows, my young warriors. Their whispers slither through the air, reaching ears that hunger for secrets. I sense that someone not of this place may already be lurking, having gleaned all they desire. If you value your safety, steer clear of the main hallway tonight."

CHAPTER NINETEEN

As Mei and I made a hurried exit out of the library archway, we turned the corner to the mezzanine hallway so quickly that I slammed face-first into a solid chest, *again*. Letting out a low "oomph," I took several steps back and looked up at the figure in front of me. Why did this keep happening whenever I ran from Azrael? My stomach did a little somersault as I took in the handsome face before me. Nathaniel's golden chestnut hair had grown since I first joined the college, now dancing over his shirt collar and giving his sun-bronzed features a softer edge. His darker skin, a testament to the countless hours spent training on the roof terrace, accentuated the varying hues of his moss-green eyes and I swore I got lost in them for several moments; the world falling away.

The gruelling schedule of my training with Bellum, my classes, and late nights in the library with Mei meant that we had barely seen each other over the last month. Nathaniel wore his standard black breeches, but instead of the usual black tunic, he opted for a fitted linen shirt rolled up to his elbows. He had somehow become even more muscular; gone was the boy I grew up with, the one I used to play with in the sandpits of the orphanage. Instead, before me stood a future leader of the Olympian Army.

"Are you done checking me out?" Nathaniel asked, one eyebrow quirked, his voice laced with smugness.

"I wasn't!" I responded much too quickly, my voice reaching an unnaturally high octave as heat rose to my cheeks.

Nathaniel rolled his eyes at me, but I noticed a small upturn of his lips. Safe to say, he knew I was lying.

"Here, you missed dinner... yet again," He passed me a brown paper bag that I had failed to notice tucked under his arm. "Mei, I think Oliver grabbed you something to eat too. He said he'd leave it by your door on his way back to the dorms. You better hurry before someone helps themselves before you get there."

Mei excused herself with a brief nod in our direction. She was always quiet around Nathaniel, most likely due to his reputation, but he was always kind to her, which I appreciated. I opened the paper bag Nathaniel had handed to me, and the smell of roasted chicken and gravy filled my nose. My stomach growled in recognition, and I let out a weary but contented sigh. Small gestures like this reminded me how grateful I was to have Nathaniel here with me.

"It's like you always know what I'm feeling," I said softly, still gazing into the bag, tempted to tear into it like a starved animal in the hallway.

"You need to look after yourself more. You're burning the candle at both ends. You can't strengthen your muscles properly if you aren't eating enough. I worry about you enough as it is." Nathaniel replied bluntly, a hint of annoyance in his voice. I looked up at him, expecting to see the light-hearted expression he usually wore when he spoke to me, but instead, I was met with a serious, stony gaze. I sighed, crumpling the top of the bag to keep the heat in until I got to my dorm.

"I know, I know, you're right, but my mind has been… elsewhere, recently. There has been a lot going on. Sometimes I lose track of time, and sometimes I just forget to eat." I raised one shoulder in a half-shrug, trying to lighten the moment.

We started toward the staircase to the main domed entryway, and Nathaniel slipped an arm around my shoulder. I nestled into his warmth, his familiar scent reminding me so much of home as our steps fell into rhythm.

"You could have died out there, Aela. It's a miracle you didn't. I don't know how I would have survived without you."

I gave him a comforting squeeze, my arm wrapped around his waist.

"But I'm fine; I'm here, with you, and nothing bad can happen to me here," I replied softly, forcing a smile onto my face for his benefit.

"No, you're not fine. You're using Bellum's lessons as a distraction rather than facing what happened to you. I've barely seen you over the last few weeks, and I can't help but think you're avoiding me. I don't know if it's because you're worried I'll see right through your façade or if you blame me for what happened…"

I cut him off as we reached the bottom of the marble stairs, pulling away from him to stand directly in front of him. Placing my hands on my hips, the bag still crumpled in one of them, I frowned up at him.

"Why in all of Gaia would you think I blamed you for what happened, Nathaniel Everflame? You told me it was going to be dangerous; did I listen? No. You told me to stay with the horses; did I listen then? No. Did you tell that man to attack me? No. How is any of this your fault?" I threw my hands up in exasperation, almost launching the bag of food away from me. My voice came out louder than I intended, drawing several looks from people making their way to their dorms for the night.

Nathaniel's shoulders visibly slumped.

"It should've been me that stopped him, not that arsehole, Kieran *Blake*." He spat his last name like it was cursed.

My anger dissipated as if all the air had been pulled from me, and I tucked myself back under his arm once more. He wasn't angry, he just felt guilty; guilty that he wasn't the one who saved me, guilty that he wasn't there to protect me.

"You can't be there to protect me every time something bad happens to me, it's impossible; you can't split yourself in two, you have your own life. Besides, the reason I am so focused on this training is because I don't *want* to rely on anyone for protection. We won't always be together, Nathaniel. I need to learn to stand on my own two feet... sometimes literally, in my case." I let out a light chuckle, but I felt him tense at my statement. I continued before he had a chance to comment. "I don't want to sit around and talk about what happened, Nathaniel. That's not who I am, that's not how I process things. Instead, I want to find a solution to the problem so it never happens again," I gave him another squeeze around the waist, "But I'll never turn down my handsome best friend fighting by my side in the future if that's what it takes to keep you happy." A genuine smile did grace my face then as I felt Nathaniel relax against me, and I heard a small laugh rumble from his chest.

"*Handsome*, huh? I knew you were checking me out."

I pulled away from him to give him a light shove, rolling my eyes to cover the blush creeping onto my cheeks.

We made our way back to my dorm in companionable silence, our hands brushing against each other every now and then, tiny pulses of electricity zinging up my arm each time we did. I barely noticed the feeling anymore; it had first started when my powers manifested when I was young, not long after Nathaniel's had.

Once I reached my room, I flung the door open and plonked myself down on my bed, tearing open the brown paper bag and diving into the chicken thigh without hesitation. After several moments, I realised I still had company, pausing my fevered attack on the meat to look over at Nathaniel. He leaned against the doorframe, one leg crossed over the other, a small, fond smile on his face.

"Your grace never fails to amaze me." He said.

I raised a middle finger in his direction and patted the empty space on my bed next to me, careful not to cover my sheets with gravy and chicken juices.

We sat together like that for the next thirty minutes, Nathaniel catching me up on the latest moves he had learned in Combat Studies with Bellum. A month ago, I would have zoned out during these conversations, but now, I listened intently. I mentally pictured each sequence he explained, envisioning myself executing each thrust, feint, and block on a battlefield. Those visions often shifted from a bloody battlefield to a dark, crumbling alleyway, and instead of a faceless warrior, I saw the hooded, bearded man from my nightmares.

"You okay?" Nathaniel asked softly, bumping my shoulder when he realised my eyes had gone distant, and I was no longer listening. I shook off the memory and wiped my greasy hands on my breeches, now finished with my supper. Rising to my feet, I stretched to loosen my limbs.

"Just lost in some memories; I'm fine."

He remained seated on my bed, his long torso bringing us nearly to eye level as he drew me closer. The proximity made my heart race, each breath we took blending together in the charged air around us. He looked at me with an intensity I barely recognised.

"You know, I would rip apart anyone who threatened to take you from me, Aela. I wouldn't be the man I am today if it weren't for you." His low voice rumbled through my chest, the air thick and heavy, as if it carried the weight of all the unspoken fears and lingering doubts between us. I felt an instinctual urge to recoil, as if alarm bells should have been ringing in my mind, but instead, a strange thrill coursed through me at the severity of his words, blurring the line between danger and desire. A slow heat began to burn in the pit of my stomach. I licked my lips, and his eyes caught the movement, lingering on my mouth for several beats longer than normal. The tension grew taut between us, and I swore I could hear the energy now crackling in the air around us. I found my face moving toward his, as if my body were being controlled by an invisible thread, with no way to resist. His warm breath skated over my mouth as I edged closer, causing hot shivers to ripple across my skin. We were so close now that our noses almost touched.

"What are you doing, Aela?" Nathaniel asked in a low, raspy voice I had never heard from before.

"I don't know; I just want to… feel something," I answered back, my voice husky and sounding very much unlike my own. I had tried to act normal since the attack on Olos, since the man in the alleyway, but I constantly felt like I was watching myself from behind a frosted window, as if I was a spectator to my own life. Nathaniel's hands moved from my waist and made their way down towards the outsides of my thighs, just below my hips. The action, although innocent enough, felt indecent. The heat that had started in my stomach, spread, moving lower, and a desperate ache started to form between my legs. I pushed myself further forward, nestling deeper into the space between Nathaniel's spread thighs. The entire length of my upper body was now flush against his, my heart pounding at a racing rate. As I laid a palm flat against

Nathaniel's chest, I swore I could feel his following the same kind of tempo as my own. Our eyes locked and I got lost in the hue of them for the second time that night. They reminded me of the meadows in Thellas, so much of Nathaniel forever feeling like home. We were so close that our lips lightly grazed as I took a ragged inhale, the familiar jolt of electricity sparking across my mouth, and it took everything in me to suppress a moan. How could such a small touch feel so good, so *right*? It was as if some part of me recognised him, was yearning to claim him, to take what was *mine*.

We stayed like that for several seconds, and it took all my willpower to remain still, fighting the urge to press my mouth against his finally; to kick down the door that we had never dared open. It was a moment suspended in time, fraught with unspoken words and desires — I was afraid to move, afraid to break the spell we had woven around ourselves.

"If we cross this line, I don't know if I will be able to stop, Aela," Nathaniel said against my lips.

"What if I don't want you to stop?" I replied quietly, my voice even huskier than before.

"You might look back one day and wish it never happened."

"Never," I whispered back. Nathaniel raised one of his hands to the nape of my neck, his fingers threading gently through my hair, sending a warm tingle across my skin. He tugged softly, drawing me closer until our foreheads touched, my whole face now tingling with electric intensity. I closed my eyes to savour the moment, breathing in the scent of him—warmth, musk and something earthy. I felt Nathaniel do the same, our breaths mingling in the space between us, each inhale and exhale getting quicker.

"Good *Gods,* this is painful to watch."

CHAPTER TWENTY

I flung myself out of Nathaniel's grasp as if he were on fire, panting quickly as the aching heat from moments before gave way to fright, then to mortification.

Standing in the now very wide-open doorway were Lex and Jaxon. In our distracted state, Nathaniel and I had completely missed the soft click of the door latch, and the creak of the hinges as it swung open. I didn't dare think how long Jaxon and Lex had been watching our exchange.

Lex, who had been the one to interrupt us, glared at Nathaniel, her mouth twisted into a sneer as if a fisherman's hook had snagged her lip. Jaxon, on the other hand, wore the widest grin I had ever seen on him, his oceanic eyes sparkling with mischief as he looked between Nathaniel and me, who were now a conservative four feet apart.

"Nothing happened!" I shrieked back at them, my voice shrill with embarrassment.

"Only 'cause Lexy interrupted you, Blondie! You were about to jump his bones!" Jaxon taunted, shouldering his way past Lex toward Nathaniel, who was now edging toward the doorway, clearly wanting to make a speedy exit. He gave Nathaniel a light pat on the back; a gesture that I presumed was meant to mean *{good for you, about time}*.

"This is just a recipe for disaster," I heard Lex mutter under her breath. Louder, she continued, "Get out of here, Everflame. I'm sure you have somewhere else to be."

Nathaniel glanced back at me, and as our eyes met, I saw a whirlwind of emotions flash through his expression—anxiousness, frustration, disappointment, longing—and I was almost certain mine mirrored his

. . .

BOOM. BOOM. BOOM. BOOM.
BOOM. BOOM. BOOM. BOOM.

"What the fuck is that?" Lex's muffled voice sounded from her bed beside mine, dragging out the last word in an annoyed moan.

BOOM. BOOM. BOOM. BOOM.

"Fuck off!" She shouted louder, "For Gods' sake, it's the middle of the night, whatever it is, IT CAN WAIT UNTIL TOMORROW!"

I creaked my eyes open as I heard sheets rustling. Through the darkness, I could just make out Lex putting her pillow over her head to block out the noise. Last night, she had swiftly ushered Jaxon and Nathaniel out of the room, and in response, I had jumped straight into bed, fully clothed, hiding under the covers until she turned off the lamplights and settled in herself. I had convinced myself that shame could not find me under the safety of my duvet, nor could her questions.

BOOM. BOOM. BOOM. BOOM.

"I think someone's banging on our door." I croaked in her direction, my voice thick with sleep

"No shit, little mouse."

I rolled my eyes at Lex, a mix of annoyance and sleepiness tugging at me as I pulled myself free from the safe-haven of my blankets. Stumbling toward the door, I fumbled for the small fire-lamp perched atop the dresser to its right as I searched for the doorknob. I heard a hiss from Lex as the light flickered to life.

"Oh, shut up, your face is covered with a pillow, it's not exactly blinding you, is it?!" I snapped back at her, to which she wrestled a hand free from under her bedsheet to show me a middle finger.

Charming.

Swinging the door open toward me, I saw Jaxon standing there, his fist raised as if poised to unleash another assault on our eardrums. The moment he spotted me, an audible sigh of relief escaped his lips, and his shoulders slumped as he lowered his fist back to his side.

"Blondie, you're okay." He wiped one of his calloused gorilla paws over his face in an agitated motion. "Is Lexy in there with you? Is she okay?"

I frowned at his questions but stepped back to allow him into our room. His auburn hair was ruffled, as if he had been frantically tugging at it, and his skin looked deathly pale with worry, making his bright blue eyes stand out even more, a striking contrast against his white complexion.

"Are you... okay, Jaxon?" I asked slowly, taking in his rumpled nightwear and bare feet. It was clear he had also just pulled himself from bed.

Jaxon moved quickly toward Lex's bed, where she was now sat up, watching him with a perplexed expression as he rushed toward her. He placed both hands on her face when he reached her and planted a swift kiss on her mouth, as if needing reassurance that she was really there. It was an incredibly sweet moment, given the bizarre circumstances.

"Jaxon, what is going on?" I bit out, my tiredness beginning to lead to frustration. I was exhausted, having barely slept the past month. The last thing I needed was a hulking brute trying to break down the door when I was finally getting a bit of much-needed sleep.

"I heard someone screaming," Jaxon said, standing back up straight to face me, "a girl, a woman. I don't know how to explain it, but something in my gut told me something was not right. So, I instantly came to check on you both, given that I am only next door. But thinking about it now, it sounded like it was further away..." He looked between Lex and I, confusion and worry creasing his features.

"Leena." I said on a whisper. Jaxon nodded, already moving back the way he came.

The next moments became a flurry of motion. Lex jumped out of bed to throw on her fighting leathers while I pulled on my boots, tied my hair back from my face, and grabbed my wooden rapier from the end of my bed. Jaxon returned from his room in less than two minutes, fully dressed in the standard-issue black breeches and tunic that I was also wearing, though his looked somewhat less wrinkled than mine—seeing as I'd chosen to wear mine to bed.

As we made our way into the hallway, we noticed other Cadets emerging from their rooms, all in various stages of undress, reacting to either the screams Jaxon had heard or the commotion he had caused by banging on our door.

We raced down the hallway of our dormitory floor and practically flew down the staircase toward the main hall. As we reached the bottom, a flash of ebony skin and brown braids caught the light, and a small noise escaped my throat—a mix of panic and relief.

"Leena!" I shouted. Her beautiful, honey-coloured eyes met mine, her face crumpling with emotion. As I leaped down the last steps, Leena took several strides of her own to close the distance between us, and we collided in a tight embrace. I could feel her noticeably shaking under my grip. Just then, a hard chest crashed against my back, and large arms wrapped around both of us, threatening to squeeze the air from my lungs as I found myself squashed between Jaxon and Leena.

"Tap out," I rasped, patting one of Jaxon's bear-like arms. "Tap out!"

As we broke apart, I took several deep breaths, resting my arm against the stone wall of the staircase to steady myself. People pushed past us, and Lex, who hadn't joined in the bear hug, ushered us forward so we weren't blocking the way for everyone else trying to get through. Although Lex had softened toward me after the attack, she remained her usual catty-self toward Leena. Still, I could have sworn I saw a glimmer of relief in her eyes as she took stock of Leena.

Leena was still in her nightdress and socks. Being on the other side of the building, she must have jumped straight out of bed when she heard the screams to rush over and check on us. A small kernel of guilt curdled within me for taking those extra minutes to sort myself out. If something had happened to Leena during those few precious moments, I would never have been able to forgive myself.

"Over here!" A deep voice I didn't recognise shouted from the main hall.

"That's weird," Leena said. "I didn't see anything when I ran through there a moment ago."

The four of us fell into step with the crowd starting to gather at the base of the stairs. As we finally edged our way through the archway that separated our dorm's staircase from the main hall, we spotted hundreds of people clustered together on the cobbled path outside the entry arch. Following the throng, I reached for

Leena's hand, and she entwined her fingers with mine in a vice-like grip. Whatever was happening, it was not good, and I began to understand what Jaxon had meant earlier about something not feeling right.

"Have you seen Nathaniel?" I asked Leena.

"No, I knocked on his door when I first heard the screaming, but I didn't wait for him to answer. I wanted to get to you. After everything that happened to you at Olos, when you were all alone..." Her voice broke at the end of the sentence, and I squeezed her hand reassuringly.

"I'm fine, Leena. It wasn't me. Besides, they would have to get through Lex first."

"Damn straight, little mouse. The only person who gets to torment you, is me." Lex said from behind us. I rolled my eyes at her barb, but a small warmth fluttered in my chest at her words. I knew that was her way of saying she had my back, and in that moment, I realised I would have hers too. Not that I'd be much help if anyone did come for her, but the sentiment remained.

As we made our way under the gilded dome of the main hall, the frenzied whispers and cries from the front of the fortress bounced around the space like a mournful song.

"What is going on?" Jaxon asked, glancing back at Leena and me.

As I skimmed the crowd, I saw a flash of auburn hair hurtling toward us with a larger silhouette in tow. Oliver and Nathaniel.

When they reached us, Oliver swept Leena into a tight embrace, burying his face in her hair as if drawing strength from the familiar scent of his closest childhood friend. His relief was palpable, a silent acknowledgment of the fear that was gripping us. Meanwhile, Nathaniel enveloped me in his arms, his warmth radiating through the fabric of my shirt. He pulled away to look me up and down, his hand cupping my cheek as he did so. His forehead was slick with sweat, and dark circles lined his eyes, making him look more exhausted than I had ever seen him. He had thrown on the same white shirt from earlier, but the buttons were done up haphazardly and didn't align properly. His chestnut hair was damp, as if he had just left the washroom, but his eyes had a frantic, haunted look. As I glanced toward Oliver, I saw the same look mirrored in his.

"What's happened, Nathaniel? Is someone hurt?" I asked, my voice thick with anxiety.

Nathaniel offered nothing more than a small nod, gently pulling my hand from Leena's to guide me toward the front of the gathering crowd, his other hand taking my rapier from me. As we descended the steps below the main archway onto the cobbled path, I became acutely aware of the way everyone was staring at us. Frowning, I glanced down at my own dishevelled appearance and then over to Nathaniel. We might not have looked our best, but we were certainly in better shape than some of the others present. I scanned the faces of the crowd once more, searching for answers.

No, they weren't looking at us—they were looking *above* us, and they looked petrified. I began to turn my head to see what had captured their attention.

"Don't do that," Nathaniel said, his voice soft yet sharp enough to cut through the rising tension.

"Why not?"

"You need to prepare yourself, Aela."

A knot of dread formed in my stomach as I took an audible gulp, tears welling in my eyes.

"Who?" I whispered, fear creeping into my voice.

"I'm so sorry, Aela. It's Mei."

CHAPTER TWENTY-ONE

The sight in front of me was something that would stick with me until my soul left this world—yet another vision to plague my nightmares. Mei, the small but fearless warrior, the quiet yet constant companion throughout my training over the past few weeks, was unrecognisable.

Her hands, bound together with rope, were raised above her as her lifeless body swung from the centre of the main archway of Solarus' War College, right above the spot where I had first met Leena. Any resemblance to the formidable woman I was coming to call a friend, was gone. Her once silken dark tresses were matted and scorched almost to her scalp. Her already pale skin now drained of any colour it once contained. Black veins spread from just above her chest, as if Shadows had entwined themselves around her heart. Her once white silk night dress was now soiled with blood and… other liquids. The most harrowing sight of all, however, was her face. As if she was frozen mid-scream, her mouth hung wide open, revealing a vacant space where her tongue should have been. Her beautiful dark eyes that once sparkled with knowledge well beyond her years were no longer present. Whether they had been removed intentionally or vultures had already started to believe that she was their next meal, I was unsure.

"By the Gods, what monster could have done this?" I heard Leena whisper to the right of me, her voice shaking with unshed tears. I understood now why people throughout the crowd had been crying. Bile started to rise up my throat and tremors began to rack my body.

"What's that on her stomach?" I heard Jaxon ask from behind me. I followed his line of questioning, squinting my eyes to see what he had noticed.

"It's a lightning bolt," Lex said slowly.

"Painted in her blood." Oliver tacked on grimly.

"*Who* would do such a thing?" Leena asked again, sobs now evident in her voice.

"We think it's the same people from Olos," Nathaniel answered her, "Aela said they painted the same symbol on one of the buildings there."

"You should be cautious with your words around the shadows, my young warriors. Their whispers slither through the air, reaching ears that hunger for secrets. I sense that someone not of this place may already be lurking, having gleaned all they desire. If you value your safety, steer clear of the main hallway tonight."

"No", I responded to Nathaniel on a whisper, remembering Azrael's words, "this was a warning."

The distant drum of hoofbeats approached, a pulsing cadence that felt like the beat of a song, the sobs from my fellow Cadets serving as the haunting lyrics.

"Bellum's on his way from the stables," I heard someone say, but my thoughts were already starting to tumble over one another. If Mei had been somewhere else last night, she wouldn't have been reading that book. She wouldn't have spoken to me about Kera and how she didn't believe in the dangers of saying her name. She might not have even been in the library at all. Maybe if I hadn't scolded her… was it my words that had drawn the Shadows' attention? My inner voice chanted at me, two words over and over, relentless in their accusations.

{My fault,
My fault,
My fault.}

I stared at the petite, brave woman, who had been so patient and kind towards me — something she rarely offered to just anyone.

She had been a steady pillar of strength during the times when I felt my weakest, always ready to share her culture, her history, and her teachings with me, asking for nothing in return. She was the strongest Cadet in our class, Bellum's shining example to the rest of us.

She was so far from her family in Shangnon; it would take them weeks, *months*, to learn of this… I didn't even know her story, how she had come to live in Olympia, and I would never know it. She was just… gone.

My heart pounded in my chest, each beat echoing the weight of my guilt. A suffocating sense of loss engulfed me, mingling with the fear of what had happened, and what could happen next.

{My fault,
My fault,
My fault.}

"Blondie… are you okay? You're… glowing."

I heard Jaxon's voice from behind me, but it felt distant, disappearing like a stone as it fell toward the bottom of a well.

The whole world around me seemed to blur, leaving only Mei in sharp focus. Her gaunt, colourless face, her singed hair, and her soiled nightdress made it seem as if her corpse had been hanging there for weeks instead of mere moments. A pressure built within me, and I raised my hands to my temples, a scream lodged in my throat. Pain. There was just so much *pain*.

It was relentless in its pursuit, suffocating me, clawing at my lungs as I struggled to breathe. Why wouldn't it stop? Ever since I had arrived here, it's felt like I was surrounded by a storm of suffering, the constant sting of failure and embarrassment, the man at Olos, the weeks of gruelling training—all culminating in this unbearable moment. Each breath felt like a battle; it was as if misery and violence clung to me like shadows, stalking my every step, waiting to pounce once my back was turned.

My knees hit the ground as I fell, but I barely registered the impact. A tide of anguish threatened to engulf me, pulling me toward the familiar darkness of my mind, just like it had in Olos. It called to me, offering the sweet solace of nothingness—where no anger, no sadness, no *pain* could reach me.

{My fault,

My fault,

My fault.}

The words chimed through my mind in time with my pulse.

"Aela, what's going on with you?" Oliver's soft voice came from my side. I felt his calloused palm touch my shoulder, but a hiss left his mouth. He jerked his hand away, as if burned.

"Gods... your skin, Aela," his voice sounded muffled as he turned his face away from me. "Guys, I think something's happening, her skin is practically on fire, it's like she's burning from the inside out, and her nose is bleeding."

"Aela, you need to snap out of it. You're having a panic attack."

Nathaniel's face came into view, blocking Mei from my sight. Crouched in front of me, he placed both hands on either side of my face, trying to pull me back from the swirling chaos inside. He grimaced in pain from the heat of my skin, but he didn't let go. The familiar spark of electricity that sometimes accompanied our touch flared to life and seemed to ignite my inferno further, stoking the flames to roar louder. Sweat dripped into my eyes, mingling with my tears and the blood from my nose. I attempted to blink the tears away, but they continued to fall, unrelenting.

"You're not helping her Cadet, step away, Everflame." Bellum's steady voice sounded from nearby.

"I won't leave her, not this time," Nathaniel responded.

"You heard him, Everflame, step back before you put the rest of us in danger." A low voice rumbled from behind me.

"Get away from us, *Blake*; like I already said, I am not leaving." Nathaniel spat, venom lacing his words, his gaze locking on Kieran.

"In case you hadn't noticed, you're a second-year cadet, so I outrank you. Your Commander has also given you an order. So I'll say it again… step, *the fuck*, back."

Nathaniel bared his teeth, but reluctantly released my face and rose to his feet, stepping away from me as he watched Kieran with a predatory gleam. The heat within me subsided slightly, but the roaring of my thoughts continued as Mei's body came back into view.

{My fault,

My fault,

My fault.}

Silver eyes suddenly filled the space Nathaniel had vacated moments before. They reminded me of pools of water basking in the moonlight, and something about the sight of them soothed me slightly.

"You need to ground yourself, first-year. Your magic is in touch with your emotions and naturally wants to protect you from whatever threat it senses coming for you. In this case, however, the attack is coming from within you, so it has nowhere to go. Here, dig your nails into the soil. Like this."

I looked down to where Kieran's hands were braced on the ground in front of him as he crouched before me. His fingertips dug into the soil, and he pushed them deep until his palm lay flush atop the surface. "Feel for the natural channel of magic in the earth, let it wash through you, then send your magic into it, like you're pouring a glass of water into a river."

I closed my eyes, trying to block out my surroundings, which only made the voices grow louder.

"*Trust him…*" an ethereal voice whispered, seemingly louder than the rest. It was the same one I had heard in Olos.

Lowering my hands from where they had still been pressed against my temples, I laid them flat on the ground, feeling the coolness of the earth beneath me. I repeated the motion that Kieran had demonstrated, curling the tips of my fingers until they broke through the soil's surface. The sandy earth felt soft and yielding under my touch, almost as if it welcomed my presence. As my fingers pushed through the top layer and delved deeper into the firmer soil beneath, I searched for the channel of magic that Kieran had described.

I had never attempted this before, but it felt instinctive, like a hidden part of me was awakening. Nanny Rosie would often tell me that the Gods created all beings, as well as the lands we walked upon; magic was not just a distant concept but an essence that surrounded us, woven into the very fabric of the earth. I took a breath, allowing that thought to ground me as I continued my search.

Moments stretched on for what felt like hours as I searched for some familiar sensation of magic within the soil. It didn't help that I didn't know what I was searching for, but the act of searching did temporarily distract me from my turbulent emotions. The distraction, however, didn't last as long as I had hoped, and my gratitude soon made way for frustration.

This was impossible, and I felt utterly ridiculous.

On the verge of giving up, I started to pull my fingers from where they were buried in the earth, my head pounding as the voices began to stir again.

Wait.

There.

A *spark*.

It wasn't as strong as what I felt when Nathaniel and I touched, but it reminded me of the connection I felt with the opalescent horse near Thellas. I pushed my fingers back into the soil, deeper than before, and focused on the sensation, pulling it toward me like I did when channelling my power. As I beckoned it, the energy surged toward my call.

Suddenly, I found myself standing at the edge of a shoreline. Rolling sand dunes rose behind me, and an endless blue ocean stretched before me, reaching as far and wide as the eye could see. The sun beat down on my face, and I squinted against its brightness. Looking down at myself, I saw that I was ankle-deep in the clear water, the cold waves skimming across my skin. I took a deep breath, savouring the fresh salt air that filled my lungs. Noticing a presence in my left hand, I looked to see that I was holding someone else's.

A very large hand, in fact. The hand was attached to a thick, muscled arm, and I traced the line of it up to broad shoulders, and then I took in the full figure of the man standing next to me. He was breathtaking. His long, black hair cascaded to his toned waist, nearly as long as my own, and was neatly tied back in a braid that accentuated his strong jaw and high brow. His dark eyebrows arched over silver eyes that shimmered in the afternoon sun. They reminded me of Kieran's, but there was something different about the warmth and softness in his gaze—something deeper, something like... *love*. Warmth flooded my chest at the emotions his look conveyed, and I got lost in his eyes for longer than I cared to admit.

"Who are you?" I asked, my voice melodic and ethereal as if someone else were speaking through me. The man offered a gentle smile, and if I thought he was breathtaking before, this expression made him appear purely magnificent.

"The earth holds memories that the soul has forgotten." The ethereal voice from before whispered, seemingly from all around me.

Air left my mouth in a whoosh as I was flung back to the present. The darkness of the night enveloped me once more, save for a low glow that I realised was emanating from my own skin.

"Good," I heard Kieran say softly from in front of me. "Now, I need you to channel your magic back into the earth; otherwise, this will have been for nothing. Your magic needs an outlet."

"Not today, our brightest ember. Use what we are offering. You'll know what to do…" The ethereal voice whispered once more.

Looking to Kieran, I shook my head.

His brow furrowed and a shadow of confusion seemed to pass over his face. Then, as if in understanding, he stood, offering an outstretched hand to help me up. I hesitated, remembering how the fire within me had roared louder when Nathaniel had touched me only moments before.

"I'm a Shade, Aela; I can't add to your magic. If anything, I will counter it." Kieran jerked his hand slightly, as if urging me to take it. Trusting him once again, I placed my palm in his, both of our hands coated with sand and earth. Electricity danced along my skin at the contact, surprising me. Instead of the anticipated heat, a calming sensation spread from where we touched, making the hair on my arms stand on end. The feeling reminded me of… belonging. Of *home*. One I had only ever experienced with Nathaniel and my dream horse.

As I stood to my feet, I raised my gaze to Kieran's, his eyes were wide, darting between our interlocking hands and back to my face. He must have been just as confused by the sensation as I was. As soon as he realised that I was capable of standing on my own without his support, he released our connection, taking a large step back from me. The moment he did, the flames within me began to burn hot again, rising with every heartbeat. Kieran must have seen the panic flash in my eyes.

"You'll be okay. This is expected; remember, you need to channel your magic to find that release. You know how to do that, don't you?" I offered him a shaky nod. "Good. Raise your hand and focus."

I did as he instructed, closing my eyes once more and focusing inward to find the small ember I often sought deep within me, but this time, I was greeted by a raging storm of fire. More power than I had ever felt writhed just beneath the surface, desperate for an order, desperate for release.

"Focus, Everflame. The flames do not control you. You are their General, command your army." Kieran's voice urged, closer now, sounding like a battle cry. I squeezed my eyes tighter.

I thought of Mei—of her darting in and out of Bellum's advances like a wraith during our training sessions. I remembered the small smile she would flash just before her wooden rapier connected with his side, and the applause she would offer me when I got a complex footwork sequence right or anticipated one of Bellum's thrusts. Tears stung my eyes at the memories; she had so much more life ahead of her. *So* much more to give.

Grief threatened to overwhelm me, but I pushed it aside, focusing on channelling my flames to my palm, not caring about the shape they formed, as long as I could release them.

"That's it; you've got it. You're doing great." Kieran encouraged, speaking to me as if I were a toddler trying to take my first steps.

Finally, I managed to take a deep breath, the panic gripping my chest receding a fraction. I slowly opened my eyes to look down at my hand. A small gasp escaped me at the sight that greeted me: a straight sword, much like Mei's description of the one she had used growing up, was clasped between my soil-covered fingers and thumb. The flames twisted and thrashed along the hilt like a living thing, but did not burn me. I stared in awe, realising for the first time in my life that they were simply just an extension of me, a part of me.

Tears flowed freely down my cheeks, but a small smile graced my face. This was the tribute Mei deserved. I took a step forward, and Kieran moved out of my way. I walked several more paces until I reached the base of the steps leading to the main hall, directly beneath the central arch. Looking up at Mei, I placed a closed fist to my heart with my left hand. Raising my right arm, I lifted the straight sword above my head, pointing its tip toward Mei's hanging body. Forcing myself to keep my eyes open and not shy away from the sight of her, I delved deeper within myself and asked my flames to give her the dignity she deserved.

They answered my plea.

Flames burst from the straight sword in a wide arc toward Mei, the force of the heat creating a wind that blew my hair away from my face. They reached her, and within seconds, she was fully ablaze.

I watched for several heartbeats until she was nothing more than ash on the wind.

Exhausted, I lowered the straight sword, which had grown cool in my hand, and let my shoulders drop with a long exhale. Realising I was no longer channelling my magic but still holding something, I looked down at my right hand, confused.

"*Impossible.*" I heard several people in the crowd whisper behind me.

In my hand, I no longer held a sword of flame, but one forged from metal - *iron*. I furrowed my brow in disbelief. I had never heard of magic actually *creating* weapons. Yes, those powerful enough could channel their energy to mimic the shapes of weapons—like Lex with her daggers or Leena with her arrows. The Crown's Mage could imbue steel weapons with magic, but those were man-made objects, not born of pure enchantment. Iron was also particularly rare, having mostly been depleted in the last war.

I heard soft, steady footsteps approaching and looked up, expecting to see Kieran or Nathaniel. Instead, I was met with the familiar salt-and-pepper hair that had become my daily alarm. Bellum's silver-lined eyes met mine, and a small smile accompanied his words.

"The earth's magic can be a mysterious thing," he said, glancing down at the sword.

I looked down at my hand wrapped around the straight sword's hilt, still covered in the dirt and sand from where I had dug my fingers into the ground. I remembered the vision of the stunning man at the edge of the ocean—how real it had felt and how loved I had felt in that moment. A small sob escaped me. How right Bellum was.

I looked back at him, but he was now focused on the spot where Mei's body had hung only moments before.

"We will find out who did this to her, Aela; we owe her that," he said quietly, just for me to hear.

I nodded, tears still streaming down my cheeks. I wanted nothing more than to curl into a ball and weep. I wanted to wale until my voice grew hoarse.

I watched as Bellum raised his left hand to his heart in a closed fist, much like I had done. He beat it to his chest in a steady rhythm, mimicking a heartbeat. I did the same, realising what he was doing.

In unison, we turned to the crowd still gathered behind us and raised our other fists above our heads, aiming them toward the Gods, my iron sword pointing toward the sky.

Like a rippling wave, one by one, our onlookers did the same. All that could be heard in the still night air was the collected, rhythmic beat of several hundred fists against chests.

A Warrior's salute.

The highest honour the Olympian Army could offer one of their fallen. The full-body sobs I had been holding in moments before broke free as Bellum recited the parting prayer.

"By the grace of the Gods,
We ask for their soul to return home.
Though their heart cannot beat forever,
We guide them with the drumbeats of our own.
As we reach towards the sky,
To show them the way,
We vow to remember our fallen,
Until we meet again one day."

CHAPTER TWENTY-TWO

Grief felt like being thrown overboard into a raging ocean at the heart of a storm. Wave after wave pummelled me, relentless and unforgiving, while the endless darkness below loomed like a hungry beast, patiently waiting to swallow me whole. Just when I thought I'd found a fleeting moment of respite—enough to catch my breath and convince myself the worst was over—the waves would surge back with greater fury, as if the storm itself were mocking my hope and testing my resilience.

Amidst the swirling tempest, I faced a daunting choice. I could succumb to the depths, allow the waves to drag me beneath the surface, to fill my lungs with saltwater and extinguish the last flickers of life within me, or I could muster the strength to fight. I could choose to swim toward my distant boat for the safety it represented.

The next week passed as if I were trapped beneath that wave of grief, caught between the limbo of drowning or swimming. I was so tired, so *exhausted*, I wasn't sure I had the strength to fight the sea of darkness that surrounded me.

Bellum did not call on me for our morning sessions. Whilst a part of me was grateful for the extra sleep, another part of me longed for the distraction as my nightmares had only worsened since Mei's death. Most of all though, I found myself wishing that I could turn back time. Back to a time when Nanny Rosie's stories were the most exciting part of my day. A time before I had ever set foot on Solarus' soil. A time before the attack and the cloaked man at Olos. A time before Azrael's cryptic warnings and his haunting milk-white eyes. A time before I had felt the weight of a parting prayer for a friend.

The grief that had consumed me after Bellum recited those words was unlike anything I had ever experienced. I had been fortunate enough to not really experience grief in my short eighteen years. I had no memories of my parents, and the Nannies at the orphanage had surrounded me with all the love I needed growing up. Although I was ultimately grateful for this, in the last week, I found myself resenting my lack of experience in coping with such heartache. Was this what the real world was like? As opposed to the sheltered bubble I had grown accustomed to?

Each morning, I bolted upright in a panic, fearing I had overslept and had kept Bellum and Mei waiting. I would picture her face on the other side of the roof terrace, a wry smile dancing on her lips, eager to demonstrate another manoeuvre from her seemingly endless arsenal. But then reality would crash down on me, and a part of me would wish I had never woken up.

Our classes continued as if nothing had happened, but an air of nervousness hung over the college. I tried several times to speak with Commander Bellum about any leads regarding Mei's death, but he either seemed reluctant to share any information with me or truly had no idea who had wanted to do this to my friend. People walked in larger groups than usual, and Bellum seemed to push the Cadets harder in Combat Studies. After my display on the front steps, he focused extra attention on me, urging me to delve deeper into my power.

The fire within me that had allowed me to set Mei's hanging corpse aflame and create an iron weapon was now dormant, and my meagre embers had returned. Strangely, I felt relieved by this, chalking it up to the fact that my surge of power must have stemmed from channelling the earth's magic. It was the only logical explanation I could muster.

Now that I was no longer spending evenings with Mei in the library, Leena had insisted that I resume our magic training sessions in her dorm. At first, all I wanted was to decline and retreat to my room, hiding beneath my covers and praying for sleep, which had been so elusive lately. However, by midweek, I found myself grateful for the interference and even more appreciative of her company. Leena was kind-hearted and remarkably perceptive; she knew just how far to push me without asking about my feelings. Instead, she hugged me a little longer than usual when we said goodbye at night, a silent promise that she was there for me whenever I was ready to talk.

Nathaniel attempted to join us on several occasions, much like before, but every time he came near, I flinched away, recalling how his touch had only heightened my turmoil just days earlier. From the look on his face, I could see that the intimate moments we had shared before Mei's death felt increasingly distant. To be honest, I had barely considered what those moments meant for our relationship; so much had happened since then, and I didn't have the energy to untangle the chaos of my emotions. No good decisions came from grief, at least that I knew.

"Are you and Jaxon *'off'* again?" I asked Lex over my shoulder as I tidied away my parchment and pencils from my bed that Friday night, preparing for another night of broken sleep. I had noticed that Lex had slept in her bed every night that week. Since I started at the War College, she had rarely spent two consecutive nights in our dorm, and I had grown accustomed to burying myself under the covers and covering my head with a pillow whenever she was next door with Jaxon. The walls were thin, and I could hear practically everything they got up to in there, leaving very little to the imagination.

Lex barely looked up from the book she was flicking through, lying on her stomach in nothing more than a bandeau and her undergarments. If I had her physique, I would probably walk around naked all the time too. She was the perfect blend of toned and curvaceous. No wonder Jaxon was smitten.

"No, but we decided we can't risk you being on your own, little mouse. If someone could take down someone as skilled as Mei, there would be no hope for you if that bastard decided he wanted round two."

I blinked, taken aback by her casual delivery. Directness was Lex's way, but I understood the underlying meaning.

"That's... oddly nice of you, Lex," I replied as I turned down my bed in readiness to clamber in. She was *actually* starting to like me. Sure, she would never be the nurturing type like Leena, but I would gladly ride into battle with her.

"It was Jaxon's idea. He seems to like you," she waved her hand dismissively in my direction as a small flush crept up her cheeks. I rolled my eyes but couldn't suppress a small smile. "Speaking of liking you..." she continued, "Kieran asked me about you today."

I turned fully toward her, a frown replacing my smile.

"Oh?" I asked, sitting down on the edge of my bed to hear more.

"Yeah. He said he felt your power just before you channelled your magic to create that sword." She pointed to the iron straight sword propped against the wall next to the doorframe, where it had been sitting for the better part of ten days. I had no idea what to do with it.

"What's so strange about that?" I asked, confused. I had always been able to feel Nathaniel's power. I was so accustomed to it that I barely noticed it anymore. Lex scowled, finally looking up from her book. She must have sensed my sincerity.

"You do know that you can only feel someone else's power, or their 'essence' as some call it, if they are of equal power level to you?"

My jaw dropped at her statement. I had never heard anything like this before.

"Who do you sense?!"

"I sense Jaxon," Lex said, trying to hide a smile at his name, "a few of the other second-years, and... Mei." Her eyes shifted away awkwardly, her throat bobbing. "Oliver and Leena can sense each other; that's why they were so close growing up. Jaxon always thought he was weaker than them until he joined Solarus and met me." A smug smile graced her face as she flipped a dark lock of hair over her shoulder.

"What about Kieran? Who does he sense?"

"Nathaniel," Lex replied, "but Kieran always said he didn't feel... quite right."

"What do you mean?" I asked, my hackles rising as I got prepared to defend Nathaniel.

"Kieran thinks Nathaniel has been holding back. He believes he has more power than he lets on."

My shoulders relaxed a little.

"Nathaniel has always been incredibly powerful, even since we were children. I have no doubt he has more to tap into." I almost let it slip that I sensed his power growing stronger, but I kept that to myself. People often said Nathaniel and I shared a special link, but I knew it had nothing to do with our 'essence'; he had more magic in his pinky finger than I did in my entire body. Explaining that to Lex would only raise more questions, ones that I didn't have the answers to.

"Perhaps," Lex shrugged, seemingly content with my answer, "but then there's the question of you..." She rested her chin on her hand, giving me an appraising look. "You claim you have next to no magic, yet Kieran sensed you just before you burned Mei's body. Kieran is one of the most powerful Shades the Continent has seen in decades. So, for him to sense you raises a lot of questions, little mouse."

I shrugged, trying not to wince at her mention of what I had done to my friend. I gnawed on my bottom lip in thought.

"You're right; I did feel strong that night. When I reached for my power, it was like… nothing I had ever felt before—like actual lava was running through my veins. But since then, it feels like there's even less inside of me than before. Bellum has been on my case all week about it, but whenever I try to pull my power to my palm, it just sputters out. He finally gave up today, saying we should resume physical training next week. The only explanation I can think of is that the earth's magic was still in my system. I didn't channel it back into the ground like Kieran told me to do, instead I was like…" I waved my hands in the air trying to find the right word, "a sponge." I settled on, letting out a weary exhale. This was the most I had spoken about that night since it happened, and a small weight felt like it had lifted from my chest.

Lex considered me for a moment.

"That makes a lot of sense, actually." She tapped her lip with a finger in thought. "My mum used to tell me stories about magic wielders who used the earth's powers; she called them 'witches.' I haven't been able to find any books about them, so I always figured she made them up. She said they had to make a sacrifice to ensure balance or some shit like that. It could be as small as a couple of tears or a few drops of blood. Apparently, some got so drunk on power that they started to get out of hand; she said some even sacrificed their own children. The Gods finally decided enough was enough and wiped out their bloodline completely."

I stared at her in horrified silence. Nanny Rosie had told me many stories growing up, but I had never heard of anything like that.

"That's awful," I said quietly.

"Like I said, she could have just made it up. She liked to scare Kieran and me when we were younger; she said it kept us in line." A fond smile hinted at her lips as she walked to the armoire and pulled out her nightdress.

A knock at the door interrupted our conversation. We exchanged glances, silently questioning whether one of us was expecting company. When we both shook our heads, Lex flexed her fingers, and a dagger of shadow appeared in her right hand, hidden behind her back. She walked to the door, unlatching it and pulling it open without caring that she was still half-naked.

"Cadets, I apologise for the late hour, but General Zaneer requests your presence in the War Room."

CHAPTER TWENTY-THREE

After throwing on the closest clothes we could find, Lex and I were out of breath by the time we reached the War Council chambers on the mezzanine level; it appeared we hadn't quite realised how long Bellum's legs were until we had to keep up with him. He seemed to have barely broken a sweat on the journey over.

Instead of his normal fighting leathers, Bellum was dressed in loose-fitting black slacks, knee-high riding boots, and a loose linen white shirt. The ensemble seemed to take ten years off him, making him appear more relaxed—as if this were the man he truly was, underneath the weight of his warrior persona. In another life, I imagined, he might have been content to live out his days as a stable hand, far removed from the rigid, formidable fighter he'd become in this one. He smelled strongly of horse—though not in a way that was unpleasant. In fact, it was oddly comforting. I made a mental note to visit Juniper soon.

As Lex, Bellum and I entered through the War Room's archway, I noticed that there were already several other Cadets seated around the familiar round table. I first saw Oliver, whose auburn hair was rather unkempt, and his tunic not quite fully laced. Clearly, he had been pulled from bed for this. He offered me a small wave upon entering, and Lex an almost imperceptible nod as she followed in behind me. There were two seats available on either side of him, so Lex and I swiftly made ourselves comfortable.

On the other side of the table from us was Bartholomew, the bird-like first year, who I remembered had been friends with Mei. We still hadn't spoken in the classes we had together, but I gave him a small nod of recognition, nonetheless. A pang of sadness pierced my heart at the memory of our shared friend, and I found myself almost having to blink back tears. To my surprise, Bartholomew offered me a genuine smile and a two-finger wave from where his hands rested atop the table. He looked much more put together than the rest of us, his black tunic immaculate and like it had been recently ironed. His eyes were bright and alert, his mousy brown hair combed back neatly from his youthful face, and I realised I may have just found the only other night owl in the entirety of the War College. Perhaps we could be friends after all.

Two other Cadets sat to his left. I couldn't sense any magic from them, but a formidable aura seemed to swirl around them, hinting at the potential for violence. One was female with short-cropped blue hair, and the other a male whose dark hair was in a buzz cut, no more than several millimetres on his head. They wore pristine fighting leathers (almost putting Bartholomew's tunic to shame) and both had two steel swords strapped to their backs. Third-years then.

"That's Theresa, or Tess, and her twin brother, Tatum. Individually, they aren't as strong as Kieran, but he said to me once that he has never seen two fighters work so in sync together before, both with their magic and with their weapons." Lex whispered over to me from the other side of Oliver. Oliver nodded in agreement as she spoke, and I took in the siblings more closely at her words. Now that Lex mentioned it, it was obvious they were twins. Their bronze skin and dark brown oval eyes were stunning, framed by dark eyelashes and eyebrows. Their full lips were pressed together tightly as they sat so incredibly still that it was both unnerving and rather impressive. Bartholomew didn't seem particularly fazed by their presence, appearing relaxed and almost overjoyed that he was here, but I couldn't help but think of him as a worm next to two hungry crows, blind to the danger in front of him.

I had barely noticed General Zaneer's presence as I had been taking in my fellow students, but there she was, her dark hair in her familiar plait, her medals on her Olympian uniform glimmering in the lamplight. She stood, bent over our table at the waist, her lean arms braced either side of a large scroll in front of her as if she had the weight of the world on her shoulders.

No, not a scroll, one of the maps from the wall.

Bellum stood dutifully behind her, to the right, his arms crossed behind his back and legs shoulder-width apart—his standard military stance whenever his General was present. His sharp eyes scanned the room for threats, eyebrows furrowed, which accentuated the scar that sliced through the one on the left. I might have inwardly laughed at his vigilance before; however, given everything that had transpired less than a week ago, I found a strange comfort in his alertness and keen attention to detail.

As I looked back at the twins, I noticed they were mirroring his vigilance, their gazes sweeping over each member of the room, the doorway, and even the shadowy corners, before returning to us. The tension I hadn't realised I was holding in my shoulders eased, and I sank deeper into my chair, reassured by the presence of the warriors around me.

Professor Sephere occupied the seat to the left of the General, proudly donning his familiar brown woollen cardigan with elbow patches that were starting to fade. With his glasses perched at the tip of his nose, he held a quill and a long piece of parchment, casting expectant glances toward the General. I presumed he was ready to take notes for the meeting, eager to capture every detail of what was sure to be an important discussion.

"Thank you for joining us Cadets, and I can only apologise for the late hour." Zaneer's sharp female voice cut through the silence from the head of the table.

"May we ask why we are here, General?" Oliver asked in his soft, steady voice. I had often thought he was shy, but the more I got to know him, the more I realised he was just composed. He would make a fine warrior one day.

Zaneer let out an audible exhale, running her eyes over the map in front of her. Rising from her hunched position, she took a step back and looked each of us in the eye.

"I was going to hold a War Council meeting after the Realm Announcement in the morning; however, it appears I will be pulled away with haste shortly after."

Hands now clasped behind her back, adopting a similar stance to Bellum, she nodded towards the map in front of her. "I received a missive by hawk last night that is quite concerning. I won't go into all the details, but in short, it appears that there have been more attacks, much like the one in Olos, spreading across our Realm. In the last month alone, there has been four more."

A heavy silence swept over the room, as if all of us were holding our breath. She continued; "While the bandits didn't strike as much damage to the villages as they did in Olos, this escalation is concerning. I didn't want to waste time awaiting a response from the Olympian Council back in Mytos, so Bellum and Sephere suggested that I call on the six of you, as you are the best strategists here in Solarus."

Commander Bellum leaned forward, his movements deliberate and commanding, to slide the map into the centre of the table. As I looked it over, I noticed that it was the same map that I had made a mental note of the last time I was in these chambers, except several more markers covered the parchment to indicate the increase in skirmishes.

"Do you think they are looking for something?" Bartholomew asked after several moments of us absorbing the plan in front of us.

"Apart from a few menial items, it appears that destruction was their main motivator," Bellum responded solemnly.

"Casualties?" Tatum asked, his voice low and filled with gravel.

"A few injuries, but no deaths. We were informed that the groups are often between six to twelve men on horseback, all in dark cloaks, and they sounded a horn on their approach and then circled the village's outskirts while people fled. They didn't invade until it was mainly empty." A memory of the cloaked man in Olos flashed to my mind, the image appearing so real in front of my eyes that it was like I had been transported back there. *He* had no issue harming someone, that was for sure.

"They wanted to invoke terror," I said softly, mulling over Bellum's words.

"We believe so, too," General Zaneer nodded at me. "But the question is, why?"

"Were there any lightning bolts painted at the scene?" Lex asked. There was a tense silence after her question as we waited to see if there were repercussions for her suggestion. Even though it was an innocent enough inquiry, and she hadn't mentioned the Lost God's name, the insinuation was enough.

"Yes," the General responded after several heartbeats, and the tension eased slightly.

"Do we think the assault on Mei was part of this?" Oliver asked, a sombre tone coating his question.

"We aren't sure." Sephere responded in his grating, nasally voice.

"Their methods were different," I offered. "These attacks are to create fear and chaos – they aren't killing people. It's almost as if the person who…" I took an audible gulp, "killed Mei knew about the Lightning Bolt signature and wanted us to believe her death was linked."

I pulled the map closer towards me to look at the pattern of attacks. Pointing towards a marker in Monacus, I continued, "We know that this skirmish was no more than a dispute between an inn owner and some disgruntled customers." I put my palm over it to block it from view. "If we take that one out of the equation…" I tilted my head to take in the shape, "I think these two might be distractions, or may even be completely unrelated…" I pointed at two markers that were near the wall, moving my palm so they were covered also. I frowned at the map, lost in thought.

"Well, Cadet, what do you see?" Bellum pushed me, sounding slightly impatient.

"I think… well, if we ignore these three attacks, it looks like they might have started from Orouras, which means that they might have come in from the docks… which means…"

I looked up at Bellum and Zaneer, the silence in the room palpable, broken only by the hurried scratching of the Professor's quill against parchment; at least he was finally doing something useful.

The General and her Commander exchanged a tense look, and I could sense the weight of unspoken thoughts passing between them. Zaneer's shoulders slumped almost imperceptibly, a flicker of fatigue crossing her features as she broke her gaze from Bellum and stepped forward. She reached for the map, her fingers brushing its surface as she rolled it up, a finality in her movements that made my heart race.

"That's what we feared, too," Zaneer said quietly, her tone strikingly soft and resolved compared to the formidable strength she usually commanded.

"What do they want in Solarus?" Tess asked, her voice higher and more melodic than I had expected from her, given her appearance.

"There's nothing here apart from dessert," Bartholomew said.

"And us..." Oliver's soft voice seemed to ring loudly in the space as the gravity of his words settled over us.

After a flurry of panicked questions from myself and my fellow Cadets—wondering if we were truly safe, whether the cloaked figures wielded magic, and if they carried weapons—the General excused us, expressing her gratitude for confirming her suspicions. I found the entire interaction unsettling; why would she convene a meeting so late if she had already reached her conclusions? A pit of dread began to form in my stomach, an ominous feeling that something vital was slipping through our fingers.

The Uprising—those who fervently believed Kera was still alive and the rightful ruler of the Continent—had never shown such aggression before. Their presence had always felt more like a whisper of myth than a tangible threat, causing many to dismiss them as mere folklore. It was rumoured they didn't have a base, but instead circled the Continent by boat, living their lives at sea and only coming ashore when absolutely necessary. The thought that these attacks could be their doing, and that they were growing bolder, sent a chill down my spine, deepening my anxiety about what lay ahead.

As we filed out of the room, I paused just before I exited, turning around to face the General.

"General Zaneer, may I make a suggestion if you are open to hearing it?" I said in a monotonal voice.

Two months ago, the very idea of being so bold as to make a suggestion to the Olympian Army's War General would have filled me with dread. But after everything that had happened, I found that I simply didn't care anymore. The weight of recent events had shifted something inside me, igniting a newfound resolve that drowned out my former fears.

"Of course, Aela," the General cleared her throat, "I mean, Cadet Everflame. That's what a War Council does."

"You have thousands of warriors at your disposal, just sitting in Mytos' barracks waiting for a war that may never come. If I were in a position of authority, I would suggest that a thousand, maybe as little as five hundred, could be utilised throughout the Realm. We have, what, five large towns and about forty villages?"

I wrung my hands together as I mentally counted, "You could position five or ten soldiers at each village, and a larger number—maybe twenty to fifty—at the towns. Not only could they provide a line of defence for the people there, but they could also teach the villagers how to fight. A lot of the villagers in Thellas don't have magic and have never received training in self-defence. I know that none of the Nannies carry weapons or would know how to defend themselves at the orphanage where I grew up, and whenever there are brawls at the nearby taverns, no one ever walks away particularly injured because no one knows how to throw a proper punch."

I stopped, realising that I had gone off on a bit of a tangent. I offered a small shrug to detract from my awkwardness. "Apologies if I've overstepped General; it's just something I have been thinking about for a while."

General Zaneer looked me up and down, her eyebrows raised as if she was taking me in for the first time.

"Thank you, Cadet Everflame, but it's late and you should get back to your dorm. It appears your friend is waiting for you."

I looked back towards the open exit and saw Lex leaning against the mezzanine's corridor wall, her posture radiating impatience. She tapped her foot periodically against the marble floor, wearing a small scowl that deepened the furrow in her brow. Her arms were crossed tightly over her chest. The tension in her stance was palpable, and I could tell she was ready to leave.

Turning back to the General, I offered a small nod in farewell, trying to mask the disappointment that tugged at me after her dismissal. As I made my way toward the exit, I heard the General's parting words, her voice closer than before, as if she had taken a step toward me.

"Aela, if you keep coming up with suggestions like that, I would be honoured to have you as part of my Council one day."

CHAPTER TWENTY-FOUR

The next morning, I could barely keep my eyes open throughout the Realm Announcement. General Zaneer's update had been vaguer than normal and hadn't hinted at the escalation of attacks throughout the Realm. She had informed us that our afternoon class with Professor Sephere was cancelled, as he would be joining her to record the findings of a '*trip*' they were taking that afternoon. An excited buzz had circulated among the students at the thought of a free afternoon; however, I couldn't ignore the nagging feeling in my gut. A feeling that this was only the beginning.

"Will you take a walk with me?" Nathaniel's low voice sounded from just behind me as we filed out of the dining hall. I tried to suppress my flinch. I knew I had been avoiding him since Mei's attack, but I just couldn't erase the memory of when he had touched me that night, of how he had felt like an accelerant to the flames that roiled within me.

"To where?" I asked over my shoulder, as I was jostled by Cadets on either side of me, while we attempted to make our way through the dining hall's archway.

"I think it would be good if we got some fresh air. If we… could talk."

It took Nathaniel and me over thirty minutes to walk the mile between the War College and the shoreline, the sandy terrain slowing our progress as we navigated the multiple dunes that rose and fell like the waves we sought. Each of my steps sank slightly into the warm sand, pulling at my legs, and by the time I finally reached the edge of the water, my dark tunic was damp with sweat. I paused for a moment, wiping my forehead to prevent the salty droplets from getting into my eyes. The action reminding me so much of when I had first arrived at Solarus, a time filled with both excitement and uncertainty.

The short journey had been awkward, to say the least. The conversation felt strained, and we had only managed to mutter a few words to each other: *"Watch your step!" "Gods, it's hot today," "Not much further now."*

Each exchange felt like a fragile attempt to bridge the growing distance between us, and the weight of my guilt gnawed at me with every step. I was painfully aware that I was pulling away from my closest friend, but I didn't know how to fix it or how to close this widening gap. However, as soon as I caught sight of the sparkling blue waves of the Marian Ocean reflecting the late morning sun, a sense of calm washed over me. The cadenced sound of the waves crashing against the shore filled my ears, soothing my frayed nerves, and the guilt simply fell away like sand slipping through my fingers.

I removed my boots and socks and set them down on the ground a few paces from the water's edge, making sure the socks were neatly tucked into my shoes so they wouldn't fill with sand. Rolling up my breeches, I stepped forward until my feet were submerged in the water. Closing my eyes, I relished the feeling of the cool water against my skin, as its final ripples danced over my toes. The sound of light splashing from beside me interrupted my thoughts, and a warm hand enveloped mine. The familiar spark of electricity zinged across my skin, and before I had time to pull away, to react, the comfortable feeling of home settled within me. I released a long, relieved breath.

This was *Nathaniel;* I was being stupid; he knew me better than anyone.

Opening my eyes, I turned towards my oldest friend. His eyes were soft as they looked at me, and when we made eye contact, a gentle smile graced his beautiful face. The way he was looking at me—with so much admiration and understanding—and the fact that we were standing together, hands interlocked at the edge of the ocean, my feet in the water, reminded me so much of the vision I had experienced the night of Mei's death.

"I'm sorry about Mei," he said quietly, the smile falling from his face as if he was reading my thoughts. "And I'm sorry that I couldn't help you in the moment that you needed me. I wish I could have been the one to calm you, to make you feel better."

He broke his gaze away from mine to stare across the water, his throat bobbing as he swallowed. "As much as I hate that it was Kieran who was there for you in those moments, I'm just glad nothing happened to you. Without you, the future I have planned for us is impossible."

My heart did a small somersault at his words.

"The future?" I asked shyly.

He closed his eyes as he dragged in a long breath before looking back at me. His green eyes almost appeared blue in the presence of the ocean.

"Whatever happens, whatever we face. I need you alive, Aela. I can't imagine my life without you. It's like… I would be broken in two." He cleared his throat. "I'm not sure I could survive without you." He stared so deeply into my eyes I almost looked away; open vulnerability evident on his face.

He had said similar words before, but something about the urgency and longing in his voice ignited a spark within me.

I closed the distance between us, raising my free hand to his cheek.

"I'm not going anywhere," I said softly.

"We are linked, Aela, you and me. Even before I met you all those years ago, I knew I would find you. It's like I had been searching for you, and nothing was going to stop me from reaching you. I couldn't live with myself if anything happened to you now. I would rather lock you away somewhere and throw away the key if that meant keeping you alive." Nathaniel responded, a small bit of humour leaking through the last of his words.

Without thinking, I leaned forward onto my tiptoes and crashed my mouth against his. A few moments passed as Nathaniel remained still, clearly shocked at my actions. However, once he realised what was happening, he released his hand from mine and cupped the base of my neck, his other arm snaking around my waist, pulling me deeper towards him. I felt him open his mouth and his tongue darted across my lips, encouraging me to open mine. I did as he wished, and our tongues entwined together in a hungry embrace.

Electricity danced across my skin from everywhere we touched, and I let out a moan at the sensation. Heat started to build within me as our kiss became more frantic; I couldn't seem to get enough of him. I balled a fist into his shirt as my other rested on his shoulder for balance. I needed him closer; I needed *all* of him.

As if reading my mind again, Nathaniel moved his hands to grip just below the back of my thighs and lifted me up. I automatically wrapped my legs around his waist, water splashing beneath us with the motion. I ran my fingers through his hair as we continued to kiss, my mind blank except for one word ringing through me, over and over.

{Mine. Mine. Mine.}

The heat inside of me continued to build and I started to feel the back of my neck prickle.

"Take it, take it all..." The familiar ethereal voice whispered in my ear.

Nathaniel pulled his lips away from mine and a desperate noise escaped me at the lack of contact, a noise I had certainly never made before.

"You're burning up again," Nathaniel said huskily, his voice low and thick with intensity. I opened my eyes and met his gaze, only to find that his usual moss-green eyes had transformed into a deep, dark abyss, the pupils nearly entirely dilated. The feral look he gave me sent a rush of adrenaline through my veins, making my heart race wildly in my chest. I felt my breath quicken, panting like a rabid animal caught in the grip of primal instinct. My skin flushed with warmth as the sun beat down on us and I felt the heat of his desire radiating from him, it was an energy that pulsed between us like a live wire. It was like the air crackled between us with unspoken tension, the world narrowing down to just the two of us wrapped around each other at the edge of the ocean.

"I don't care," I said in a sultry tone, trying to pull his face back to mine, my fingers digging into his scalp in an attempt to tug him forward. I didn't know what was wrong with me. It's as if I had been starved for years, and he was my lifeline. I needed to have him. Have him *all*.

"Well, I care. I'm not having a repeat of last week." Nathaniel said firmly. He adjusted his grip on me slightly, raising me higher against him. The friction of the movement created a pleasant sensation between my thighs, and I bit my lip, another moan building in my throat. Nathaniel waded deeper into the water until we were waist-deep, and I swore I heard the water sizzling against my skin.

"You have no idea how long I have waited for this," Nathaniel said, running a wet hand through my hair. The sensation of the cool water running through my long strands all the way to my scalp was intoxicating, and I shuddered. He leaned forward, "You are the reason for all the best parts of me, Aela."

Our lips collided once more, and Nathaniel consumed me with a renewed sense of ferocity, clearly, he had been holding back before. Now that we were submerged in the water, he released his hold on me and proceeded to run his hands along my skin. First, they moved down the back of my neck, his touch sending electrical shivers down my spine. He then trailed his fingers across my arms, down my back, and even lower to cup my rear. He squeezed both of my cheeks in his hands, and I involuntarily ground my hips against his body at the sensation. He released a low growl from the base of his throat.

"Remember when I said that if we crossed this line, I wouldn't be able to stop?" He whispered, kissing the most sensitive area of my neck just below my ear. The warm wetness of his lips against my delicate flesh sent even more heat through me, and I felt my magic rising as if in answer to his call, fuelling my lust. I ground against him once more and he inhaled raggedly, sucking air in between his teeth.

"I need you, Nathaniel." I moaned the words. A desperate plea.

One of Nathaniel's hands moved to the space between my thighs where our bodies met. He swiftly untied the knot from the drawstring and reached below the waistband of my breeches. With his thumb, he found the small bundle of sensitive nerves just above my core with surprising accuracy. He expertly moved his thumb in slow, gentle circles against it, and my whole body jerked forward at the sensation. With every circle, the pressure within me built. My breathing was now out of control, and my moans continued to grow louder. I tried to kiss Nathaniel to smother my sounds, but it was like I had lost the ability for all reasonable thought, my mind unable to communicate with my mouth. So instead, I tipped my head back, deciding to just let the ocean hear my cries of ecstasy. Nathaniel continued to kiss my neck, nipping and sucking at intervals.

{Mine. Mine. Mine.}

"It's yours to take." The ethereal voice whispered again.

"I need you to cross the line, Nathaniel, this isn't enough." I managed to choke out between moans. Opening my eyes, I looked at him and saw a wicked smile on his face.

"Take off your clothes." He growled, looking down at my drenched tunic and breeches. Unwrapping my legs from his waist, I pushed away from him, my feet touching the ocean floor. Where I was so much shorter than Nathaniel, the water was all the way up to my shoulders as opposed to the waves that gently rippled against his waist. I made quick work of removing my clothing, as did Nathaniel, our hurried movements frantic and unrestrained. Taking my clothes from me, he rolled them into a tight ball and tossed them toward the shore. They landed with a soft, damp thud against the sand, settling next to my shoes in a slightly crumpled heap. I winced slightly at the sight, already imagining the discomfort of the damp fabric and the gritty sand rubbing against me when I eventually had to put them back on; the thought of the rough texture against my skin making me screw my nose up in distaste.

Facing back to me, he pulled me into his arms once more, the cool water contrasting against the feeling of his hot skin. I relished the feeling as I ran my hands across his bared flesh, I wanted to touch every part of him, as if I couldn't get enough, as if it would never be enough. I trailed my fingers up his strong forearms to his muscular biceps and across his wide shoulders. Moving my hands lower, I ran the tips of my fingers through the delicate sprinkling of golden hair on his chest, along the rigid muscles of his torso, and then proceeded to move lower to follow the V of his stomach as if it was pointing the way. My view was obstructed by the movement of the water, but my palm grazed over a soft, hard length. I wrapped my fingers around it and looked up at Nathaniel's face. His eyes were closed, and his jaw was clenched so tightly that I saw a vein pulsing in his forehead.

"I… I don't know how to do this." I said quietly, trying to hide the embarrassment from my words.

"Just move your hand up and down, there's no way you can do it wrong, Aela. Any touch from you is a blessing."

I followed his instructions, moving my fisted palm up and down his length, squeezing slightly as I did so. His body spasmed and twitched at the action, and he started to rock back and forth to match my movements. He raised a hand to the base of my neck once more, his fingers tugging at the strands there, causing a small sensation of pleasurable pain. With his other, he cupped one of my exposed breasts and ran a thumb over the peak of my nipple. I let out a startled gasp as a feeling of electric pleasure coursed through me.

His thrusting picked up pace, so I matched the rhythm of his movements with my wrist. Nathaniel's lips crashed against mine, consuming me, and there was no control in the kiss. It was frenzied and sloppy, and our tongues danced together without rhyme or reason.

Without any warning, Nathaniel's hands reached for the back of my knees, lifting me against him once more. I wrapped my legs around his waist, the feeling of his hard length pressing indecently against me. Nathaniel broke away from our kiss as he looked down to align the tip of himself with my entrance.

"Are you sure?" he whispered in my ear. My heart softened at the question, but I could hear the desperate hope in his voice. Squeezing my eyes shut, I tried to slow my heartbeat. Although the water was helping, the heated tempest inside of me was still rising, and the feeling of nervousness was also starting to bubble up.

"Yes," I whispered in response, my voice shaking from my arousal and my nerves.

Nathaniel slowly pushed his hard tip inside of me and I let out a gasp. The pain that shot through me was sharp and instant, it felt like he was stretching me from the inside out. I let out a whimper as my body squirmed around him, a desperate attempt to try and alleviate the pain.

"I'm sorry. Just give it a moment and relax." He said softly.

I did as he said, trying to breathe through the bite of discomfort. Nathaniel pulled back out slightly, then pushed back in. He did this several more times, gradually deepening himself with every thrust. As he did so, the pain started to subside, mixing with a feeling of indescribable pleasure. I tilted my head back, letting the sensation roll through me, and I started to rock my hips in time with his.

A feeling of completeness settled over me. This was right. We were meant to be together. Like the two halves of us made a whole.

My magic surged as my pleasure increased, and I swore I could feel Nathaniel's doing the same. In my mind, I saw our essences entwining together, much like our bodies. Flames danced across my skin, and I heard a distant rumble of thunder. Nathaniel's grunts and moans filled my ears as he continued to thrust inside me, his pace growing more erratic than before. He was pumping hard now, and the sounds of water slapping between us created an almost erotic song. A crescendo continued to build inside of me and the muscles in my lower stomach tightened and quivered.

"Let go, Aela, let… *go*." Nathaniel rasped.

At Nathaniel's words it was like a dam broke within me and my magic burst free from me along with rippling, unending pleasure. My body felt weightless, as if it was falling through open sky. My head started to pound as visions flashed behind my eyelids.

A man with dark hair tied in a long braid rode atop a large black horse, a sword raised above his head in a fierce battle cry as he galloped toward danger. An enormous tree reached toward the clouds; its massive trunk adorned with vibrant vines. Winged animals of all different colours and species soared around its leafy branches. A beautiful blonde woman with blue eyes that could rival the Marian Ocean looked down at me, tears falling from her eyes as she kissed my forehead, knowing that this was goodbye.

As the visions began to fade, I slammed back into my body, jolted by the intensity of what Nathaniel and I had just shared. My limbs shook with lingering energy, yet I could swear I still felt the woman's tears coating my forehead, warm and heavy.

Opening my eyes, my head still tilted backward, I noticed Nathaniel resting his forehead against my shoulder, trying to catch his breath after finding his own release. I stared up at the sky, and it struck me that it wasn't tears I felt against my skin now. Large, dark clouds loomed above us, hovering like a thick blanket. A strong wind whipped through my hair, a wild, untamed force, as thunder rumbled ominously in the distance. Rain poured down on us in torrents, as if the Gods themselves were weeping. Whether this was a blessing or an omen, I did not know.

CHAPTER TWENTY-FIVE

*B*OOM. *BOOM. BOOM. BOOM.*

"Someone better be dead if that's how we're getting woken up!" Lex mumbled angrily from beneath the pillow, smothering her face the next morning.

A small surge of panic speared through me at her words, my mind flashing back to the night of Mei's death. {*Not again, please Gods, not again*} my mind seemed to beg.

Forcing myself from the warm comfort of the duvet, I stood on tired and shaky legs, reminiscent of a newborn foal learning to walk. I suppressed a wince at the soreness between my thighs from the previous day's activities. Nathaniel and I had walked back from the beach in companionable silence, and after changing into dry clothes, we joined the rest of our friends for dinner that evening. No one mentioned anything; however, I had noticed furtive glances exchanged between our group, clearly aware of the stolen looks and lingering touches shared between Nathaniel and me. Once we had finished eating, he walked me back to my door afterward, and when he leaned in to give me a gentle kiss in farewell, it held a tenderness that chipped away at the protective inner walls I had been building around my heart since Olos, since Mei. For the first time in as long as I could remember, I didn't have a nightmare.

Now, stumbling toward the door of our dormitory in my nightgown—having actually remembered to change out of my clothes for once—I wiped the sleep from my eyes as I released a wide yawn. Casting a look toward the window, I noticed the blue of dawn settling over the sky. In less than an hour, the sun would peek over the horizon, signalling the start of the day. *Early*. It was far too early.

Unlatching the door and swinging it inward, ready to bite the head off whoever was trying to disrupt mine and Lex's peace, my shout lodged in my throat. I blinked several times, believing I might be dreaming, but the person in front of me didn't disappear.

"Kieran?" I asked, my voice croaky and my brow furrowed in confusion.

I heard sheets rustle behind me, and light footsteps padded across the floor as Lex crossed the room to stand beside me.

"What are you doing here, cousin?" She asked in a soft voice that I had never heard her use before.

"It's Sunday. You both should join combat training today. I'll wait." He replied, his tone clipped and leaving no room for argument. He wore his impossibly tight fighting leathers, clinging to every inch of him and revealing the solid muscle beneath. His dark hair was still damp from a recent bath, slicked back from his face in a way that accentuated his sharp, chiselled features. The blue morning light danced across his skin, highlighting the contours of his jaw and cheekbones, while his silver eyes gleamed like polished metal, enhancing his fierce demeanour. How did he look so put together, so alert? What time did this man get up?!

Lex and I exchanged bemused looks. Lex frequently attended combat training sessions on Sundays, but I was yet to do so. Bellum had informed me in Combat Studies on Friday that our one-on-one training would resume on Monday, so I had hoped to use today to catch up on some much-needed rest before the inevitable torture began again tomorrow.

"You guys carry on," I said, pointing between Lex and Kieran. "I have other plans for today." I racked my brain for a suitable excuse but decided that was answer enough. It was none of their business how I spent my time; I could be saving the Realm for all they knew.

"Cancel them." Kieran bit back, his features unwavering as his emotionless silver pools scrutinised me from head to toe. "Get dressed. You have five minutes." He reached forward and shut the door, effectively closing himself off from us as he remained in the hallway.

I blinked at the now-closed door and turned to Lex, hoping she would offer some words of wisdom as to why it was essential we partake in today's activities. All she did was offer a small shrug before reaching for the trunk at the end of her bed to retrieve her fighting leathers. Letting out a weary sigh, I followed suit to retrieve my tunic and breeches.

• • •

One thing I quickly became certain of over the next few hours was that Kieran must be some sort of sadist. He made my sessions with Bellum look like a spa retreat. Several other Cadets were already waiting on the roof terrace when Lex, Kieran, and I arrived. Tatum, Tess, and Bartholomew were there, along with about ten others I recognised but didn't know by name. It was evident that Kieran believed himself in charge, evident in the way he seamlessly took control of the group. He barked out instructions with an authority that brooked no argument, and the rest of the Cadets fell into line without hesitation. There seemed to be an unspoken agreement among them, a mutual understanding that Kieran's word was law for the duration of training. Even those who might have questioned his methods remained silent, likely out of respect—or perhaps fear.

We ran ten laps around the terrace as a *'warm-up'* followed by as many sit-ups, push-ups, and burpees as we could do. It was clear that my week off had hindered my progress, but surprisingly, I wasn't a complete failure. My brief moment of celebration was short-lived, as Kieran soon returned with a short length of rope for each of us. He instructed us to hold either end and jump over it as many times as possible, as quickly as we could.

By this point, the sun had fully risen, and within just two minutes of attempting to jump over the 'skipping rope,' as Kieran had called it, I was drenched in sweat and gasping for air. I couldn't help but think that this might truly be the death of me. Not only did it demand fitness, but it also required coordination—something I hadn't quite mastered yet. Though I had made strides in my training with the wooden rapier, that skill didn't seem to translate to this at all. Every time I stumbled, catching the rope on my feet and nearly tripping, Kieran would unleash a stream of insults in my direction; *"You're useless, Everflame!", "Have you never used your feet before, Cadet?", "Start over and do it properly, you're embarrassing yourself!"*

After another painful ten minutes, I finally crumpled to the ground, waving my hand in the air like a metaphorical white flag pleading for surrender. Fortunately, Kieran seemed to be content with the amount of suffering I had endured, leaving me to wallow in my defeat and self-pity, while the others continued their relentless drills.

Now, after heaving myself up from the ground, I stood in front of the familiar row of targets, a ball of dread already rolling around in my stomach. I was still struggling to channel my power, and since Mei's death, it felt even farther away than before.

The terrace was significantly busier now, at least another eighty Cadets, with Leena, Jaxon, and Oliver also opting to join us today.

"You look like you've been through the ringer, Blondie. Did Nathaniel keep you up last night?" Jaxon asked with a devilish grin on his face, waggling his eyebrows at me in his signature taunting expression. I rolled my eyes, trying to disguise the blush rising in my cheeks.

"Kieran literally got us up at the crack of dawn and has been picking on Aela all morning." Lex chimed in, crossing over to us from where she had just finished an impressive demonstration of her fitness with the skipping rope. Jaxon bounded over to her before she could reach us like an excitable puppy and planted a loud, exaggerated kiss on her lips. Lex feigned disgust as she pulled her mouth from his, but a small, genuine smile tugged at the side of her mouth as she pretended to bat him away like a fly.

"Where's Nathaniel?" I asked Leena.

"Ahhh, that kiss reminding you of something?" Leena said quietly, bumping her shoulder against mine. I stroked my palm down my face, letting out a small moan of embarrassment as I felt my ears go red.

"Not you, too," I groaned, dragging out the last word. "Was it that obvious?"

"Well, firstly, you both had wet hair and smelled like the ocean. Secondly, I've never seen Nathaniel look so smug. Lastly," she held up three fingers in front of my face as if counting from a list, "you were so lost in each other's gazes that whenever we tried to speak to you, it was like talking to a brick wall. You didn't even notice when we got up to leave the table!"

I grimaced inwardly at her words, horrified at how blatantly Nathaniel and I had been wearing the change in our relationship.

"So... what happened? Was it good? Is he... *big*?" Leena asked conspiratorially in a quieter voice, her eyes twinkling with mischief.

I shooed her away with a wave of my hand, trying to take several steps back to remove myself from the conversation.

"Not here!" I whispered harshly, pointing at Jaxon. "He might look like a gorilla, but he has ears like a hawk, and you know he'd practically shout it across the roof terrace if he heard anything. People are already talking about me enough after losing my shit in front of everyone the other week."

Leena laughed at this.

"I heard someone saying that you ate the dirt as well yesterday. Some people are even calling you '*Dirt Girl.*'"

"Exactly! I'll come by your dorm later and provided Nathaniel doesn't press his ear to the door like a nosy child; I'll give you all the details."

Leena let out a delighted squeal, clapping her hands together in excitement. In that moment, she reminded me of one of the children at the orphanage celebrating their birthday. It amazed me how the simplest things seemed to bring her such unrestrained joy.

We watched the others for thirty minutes as they practiced their magic on the targets. For some reason, prickles of dread kept running their light fingers over my skin. Something felt… *off*, but I couldn't quite place it.

Lex was right about Tatum and Tess; they were formidable. Their shadows wove together like a spider's web, whipping through the air like thieves in the night. They hit each target with unfaltering accuracy, and had the targets not been magically warded to withstand magical blows, they would have been incinerated immediately. The twins barely broke a sweat during their exhibition of power and simply strode over to an empty spot on the terrace when they finished, drawing their swords from their scabbards to spar together. Tess's fluid movements reminded me so much of Mei's and I found myself absently rubbing my chest, as if trying to erase the stab of heartache I felt at the fact Mei wasn't standing alongside me.

"Everflame, you're up!" Kieran's voice cut across the space, interrupting my thoughts before they started into a guilty spiral.

Well, *shit*.

This had already been embarrassing enough in front of the other first-years over the past week, let alone in front of a larger crowd spanning all three classes. Taking a deep breath to steady my nerves, I stepped forward, feeling a tingling sensation at the back of my neck. When I turned around, I caught a glimpse of golden-chestnut hair and sparkling moss-green eyes. My anxiety eased slightly as Nathaniel's gaze met mine across the terrace, a gentle smile gracing his beautiful face. He offered me a small nod of encouragement, and with my shoulders squared, I turned back to the line drawn in the dirt in front of the row of targets. I clenched my fists tightly and focused inward, searching for those shimmering embers of power deep within me.

Nothing.

Not even a flicker.

I frowned and tensed my jaw in concentration as I burrowed deeper... deeper... *deeper.*

I searched so far inside me that it felt like I hit the bottom of a well, and there was nowhere else to go. I absently felt beads of sweat rolling down my forehead and the back of my neck as my hands began to shake.

"Everflame, what's taking so long?" Kieran barked. I jumped; having been so focused inward I hadn't heard him approach.

"There's... nothing there," I said quietly so only he could hear. He had closed the distance between us and now stood only several feet in front of me, arms crossed over his chest, biceps bulging. His silver eyes bore into me as if he were peeling back my skin and reading my soul like it was his favourite book. He really was attractive, and if his personality had been at all decent, I would have even said he was handsome.

"What do you mean... *nothing*?" Kieran asked, surprisingly soft with no judgment in his words.

"It's like I've reached a bottom of sorts. I can't seem to delve any deeper." I offered a small shrug to accompany my lacklustre explanation.

Kieran clenched his jaw.

"Have you used any magic today?"

"No. I think I may have used a bit unintentionally yesterday," I said, remembering the feeling of flames dancing along my skin in the ocean, "but I wasn't exhausted or drained afterward. It's felt depleted all week though, since... well, since Mei."

"How did you use it yesterday? What were you doing to bring it on? Can you do that now?"

"Ummm..." I searched for the right words as mortification flushed my cheeks.

"Sex?" Kieran said directly, without any embarrassment. I squeezed my eyes shut, hoping this conversation would just miraculously be over by the time I opened them again. Opening my eyes once more, I tried to search for the right words, *any* words, but before I could answer, Kieran whipped his attention to the edge of the roof terrace, towards the furthest wall.

"What's that noise?" I heard Leena ask from behind me.

"It sounds like a horn," Jaxon replied, his voice sounding confused. At his words, I strained my ears and heard it too—a distant, haunting blare of a horn, holding a single, continuous note that seemed to reverberate through the air. The sound was unsettling, sharp and persistent, as if it were carrying a message from some far-off, unseen place.

I spun around so quickly that I was surprised I didn't lose my footing. I instantly found Oliver's and

Lex's gazes among my friends, remembering what was discussed on Friday night with General Zaneer. Oliver had gone as white as a sheet and could only nod in confirmation, as if reading my mind. I looked over to where Tess and Tatum had been sparring only moments before, but they were already racing toward Kieran and me. Spinning back to Kieran, I said as quietly as my terrified voice would allow.

"I think we're about to be under attack."

CHAPTER TWENTY-SIX

The roof terrace erupted into chaos as news spread that we were about to be under attack. It was like watching a literal tidal wave sweep through the Cadets.

"This is what they want," I whispered to myself, but Kieran heard me anyway.

"Get to Lex; she'll protect you. Don't leave her side. Take this." Kieran reached behind his back and extended one of his two steel swords toward me.

"I can't take that. It might drain me."

"You have no magic. It won't do anything," Kieran said tersely, already focusing on the increasing mayhem behind me. I hesitated for a second too long, so he impatiently grabbed my wrist and forced the sword's hilt into my palm, essentially taking the decision away from me. Electricity sparked at my skin's contact with the hilt, and a surge of energy rushed through me. My eyes widened slightly as I looked up at Kieran.

"You good?" he asked, already turning away as he reached for his other sword, his steps carrying him toward the far side of the terrace.

"Good!" I shouted back, already making my way toward Lex.

Once by her side, I took in her expression. A mask of calm had settled over her face, leaving no doubt that she was related to Kieran.

"We stay back-to-back, okay, little mouse? Just like Leena and Oliver over there, do you see them?" She pointed to a space behind me, and I followed the direction of her finger. Oliver and Leena stood back-to-back, shoulders straight, legs shoulder-width apart and slightly bent in an attack position. Shadows were already forming around Oliver's wrists, and Leena's eyes were squeezed shut in concentration, most likely tunnelling into her own power. They weren't the strongest on the field, but both fought with such enviable self-control and precision that I would be surprised if anyone got close to them. Out of the corner of my eye, I saw Jaxon and Nathaniel. They were not back-to-back but stood within close proximity of each other. I could sense Nathaniel's power rising from where I stood, maybe fifteen feet away from him. He was diving into his magic fast and hard. Jaxon's expression, brows furrowed and jaw tense, told me he was likely doing the same.

"Shouldn't you be with Jaxon?" I asked Lex as I turned to press my back to hers.

"He can take care of himself." She said, but I heard an edge of concern in her voice.

"I'm sorry you're stuck with me," I said sheepishly, trying to swallow the shame clawing its way up my throat.

"Never apologise for anything, little mouse. You are enough just as you are; don't let anyone tell you otherwise."

I found myself blinking back tears as her surprisingly sweet words settled over me, adrenaline clearly heightening both of our emotions. I kept darting glances at Nathaniel, convincing myself he would be fine. This group didn't kill. They just wanted to scare us.

The roof terrace was hauntingly quiet. Nearly a hundred of us stood stock still, watching the walls that surrounded us, waiting.

The minutes dragged on as the roaring sound of my pulse filled my ears. I tried to steady my breathing, but the thumping in my ears continued to grow louder.

No, that wasn't my pulse.

Hoofbeats.

I strained to determine how many there were, but it was impossible.

At once, the drumming of the hoofbeats stopped, and silence prevailed once more. I darted my eyes around the top of the walls, my breath lodged in my throat.

"*Breathe, little ember.*" An ethereal voice whispered. I jumped at the sound, but metal scraping against stone sounded from behind me, and I whipped my focus away from the voice, bumping the back of my head against Lex's with the movement.

Another clang rang out to my right, then my left, and finally in front of me. The grating noise echoed through the air, and the fragile hold I'd tried to keep on my steady breathing faltered.

"What is that noise?" I whispered to Lex.

She cleared her throat.

"Hooks over the tops of the walls." Her voice trembled slightly, indicating that she did, in fact, feel some fear for our situation. I felt her adjust behind me as she straightened her shoulders. I did the same, trying to push down my own fear as I grasped the hilt of Kieran's sword tighter. I had to hold it with both hands; I wasn't used to the weight of it.

A gloved hand coming over the wall caught my attention to the right, towards where Tatum and Tess were gathered. Quicker than I thought possible, the hand heaved up a cloaked figure—all in black, dressed just like my attacker in Olos. A spiked mace was clasped in the figure's other hand, and I squinted to try and make out the brownish colour that covered the metal of the spikes.

Blood.

The hairs on my arms stood on end at the harrowing revelation.

Realising I had spent several precious seconds staring at the cloaked figure's weapon, I cast my eyes upon the rest of the field once more, searching for Leena and Oliver. A small gasp escaped me. Nearly thirty cloaked figures now surrounded us, all carrying various weapons: swords, maces, crossbows, and even a few pointed spears.

"I can sense at least three of them," Lex whispered to me.

Shit.

So, they did have magic. I looked to my left and made eye contact with Kieran. He looked just behind me to Lex and held up two fingers.

"Kieran can sense two with the same power level as him," she confirmed.

Double shit.

My heart sank, and all I wanted in that moment was to fall to my knees and weep. I was a sitting duck. If Kieran could sense two of them, it meant they were powerful.

A pregnant pause hung in the air, stretching between the two groups, each side waiting to see who would make the first move. Then, without warning, as if a switch had been flipped, it was as though the underworld itself had descended upon us.

Havoc reigned around me like a swirling storm. The sharp clash of metal on metal rang through the air as weapons collided, arrows screamed past, and the battle between fire and shadows unfolded — darkness crashing violently against light.

Lex and I subtly moved to the centre of the fight, meaning the cloaked figures had to make their way through the rest of our comrades before reaching us. I felt a little selfish for doing this, but Lex had pointed out that I would "*be dead in a heartbeat*" if we didn't move. So, shuffle we did.

Oliver and Leena had already taken down one of the cloaked men. Leena's fire arrows had forced the man backwards until he was pressed against one of the terrace's walls, and Oliver had used the advantage to send a slim spear of shadows hurtling toward the man's shoulder. On impact, the man released a blood-curdling scream that swiftly cut off as he slumped to the ground, unconscious.

Jaxon had been doing what he did best—essentially burping shadows at the opposition. I had laughed at the sight, knowing a part of me was becoming hysterical; the adrenaline and fear eating away at my sensibility. Unfortunately, as powerful as Jaxon was, it was very hard to change the direction of that much magic, so a few of the cloaked figures had been able to dance out of reach before his shadow-flames engulfed them entirely. Fortunately, however, Tatum and Tess were there to pick up the slack.

They really were a work of art. When Tatum went high, Tess swung low, cutting some of the men into thirds. The image was truly gruesome. When Tatum sliced away a man's head while Tess removed the legs from the body simultaneously, I nearly vomited.

Bartholomew was holding his own near Nathaniel, a wise choice to stay close to him, I thought. Nathaniel, however, had yet to use any of his magic, instead remaining in a defensive position and forcing anyone who came near him back with a pointed spear he must have swiped from one of the fallen cloaked figures.

"Why aren't you using your magic?" I shouted at him as he passed by the centre of the circle, several feet from Lex and me.

"We're all too close together. I might kill one of our own." He shouted back. I barely managed to hear him over the chorus of mayhem that surrounded us, but I offered him a curt nod in understanding.

Scanning the circle around me, about eight of the cloaked figures were either unconscious or dead. However, the other twenty circled us like hungry hyenas, pressing us in closer together. Even though we outnumbered them, it was clear the men were extremely well-trained and had been fighting together for quite some time. Their movements seemed strategic; professional.

"We need to create an opening so we can get behind them. We're all too close together, they will just pick us off one by one." I said to Lex over my shoulder. I felt her nod in agreement.

"KIERAN!" She shouted at the top of her voice, and I couldn't help but wince at the sound as my eardrums nearly perforated due to her being so close.

I looked behind me and saw Lex making a whipping motion with her arm. Following the direction of her gaze, I locked onto Kieran, who lightly dipped his chin in acknowledgement to his cousin. His face was speckled with blood, and his silver eyes glowed with a manic expression.

I watched in what felt like slow motion as Kieran took a deep breath. Shadows started to curl around his free arm, reminding me of a swarm of locusts. They swirled and extended from his open palm, taking a semi-opaque shape about twenty feet long, fanning out at the end like a clawed hand.

"What is that?" I whispered to Lex, mesmerised.

"It's his five-tail whip."

She grunted as I felt her shoulders move against mine; a distant squelch followed by a heavy thud sounded from a few feet behind me. She must have thrown one of her shadow-daggers.

"Got one!" She exclaimed in triumph.

I was still watching Kieran, too focused on him to congratulate Lex on her achievement. His eyes scanned the nearest surroundings and landed on a cloaked figure edging his way to some of the trembling first-years who had huddled together like vulnerable ducklings. I watched as his jaw tensed, in rage or concentration, I wasn't sure. He pulled his arm back and took several long breaths as he steadied his focus, his chest rising and falling with the movement. In a singular, fluid motion, he slashed his arm forward and directed the whip as if it was an extension of himself, at a speed I didn't think humanly possible.

The whip's talons reached for the cloaked man, but instead of encircling him like a large hand as I was expecting, they sliced through the man like he was made of butter. The sound of flesh tearing and the wet sounds of organs falling to the floor was something I didn't think I would ever be able to forget. The blood from the man's now lifeless body sprayed the petrified first-years. One of the females let out a scream of pure terror whilst the burliest-looking male of the group wiped the blood from his eyes and swiftly proceeded to vomit. Bile rose in my throat at the sight of another human being throwing up, but I refused to succumb to it, clenching my teeth together so hard I could hear a grinding sound in my skull.

"Aela, look out!" I heard Oliver cry.

"Duck!" Leena shouted, but it was too late.

Searing pain burst through my chest, just below where my necklace sat. I looked down to see an arrow protruding from the centre of my chest. Blood started to bloom, and an iron taste filled my mouth. Heat started to rise within me, and my heart started to race. I knew this feeling.

"It is not your time yet, little ember. We will save you. You know what to do." The ethereal voice that I had heard several times now whispered into my mind.

"Lex, you need to step back from me," I said softly, a cool calm settling over me as I dropped Kieran's sword to the ground.

"Aela, you're hurt; how can I help? What can I do? Do I pull it out?" Leena was in front of me now, her eyes wide with panic as she reached for me.

"You need… to step back… Get back, get away from me." I said, my words coming out gargled as my mouth filled with blood.

"What?" Leena said, a sob already hanging on her words as her lower lip started to tremble.

A cool hand pressed against my forehead.

"She's burning up, Leena; we need to step back," Lex said in a monotone voice, ever the warrior.

"We can't leave her!" Leena cried, desperation lacing every syllable.

"If we don't step back, she will kill the both of us and then she won't want to live, so step the fuck back, Du Preez," Lex said in a biting tone, sounding a lot like her cousin as she tugged Leena back towards Oliver and Jaxon, who had also edged closer during the commotion.

The tempest within me prowled at the edges of my mind like a caged tiger, but I somehow managed to hold it back until Lex and Leena were about twenty feet away. The stinging in my chest was no longer there, or at least I just no longer noticed it. Instead, everywhere was pain. Everywhere hurt. My blood felt like it was burning me from the inside out.

"What's happened?" I heard a frantic voice shout from just behind me. *Nathaniel.*

"Blondie has been hit," Jaxon shouted back.

"What? Where is she? Move, let me get to her." Nathaniel shouted, but his advance towards me was cut off as several cloaked figures stepped in his way.

I sank to my knees, digging my fingers into the ground, just as Kieran had shown me. I closed my eyes and searched for the familiar spark of the earth. As if it recognised me this time, it hurtled toward me without me having to call.

A man with dark hair, tied in a long braid, stood by the edge of the ocean, his eyes filled with nothing but love as they met mine. In the next breath, I saw him again—this time, atop a large black horse, sword raised high in a battle cry as he galloped toward danger. An enormous tree stretched its limbs toward the clouds, while winged creatures of every colour and species darted around its branches. A beautiful blonde woman, her blue eyes as deep and endless as the Marian Ocean, gazed down at me, tears falling as she kissed my forehead one last time. The sky cracked open with lightning, and a woman's mournful wail echoed through the air, joined by the heart-wrenching whinny of a horse. Above the mountaintops, a red beast soared, its roar so loud it seemed to shake the very earth beneath my feet.

The power of a thousand stars filled me, and I let out a battle cry of my own. Light bloomed from behind my eyelids, and power filled my limbs—a power I had never felt. Releasing my hands from the earth, I pulled myself to my feet. Flames danced along my skin, coating the ground in a circle around me. I delved deep into the swell of magic now raging within me. Channelling its essence, I thought of Mei's straight sword and the shield that Bellum had said I would need. Fire raced down my arms to my open palms as the shapes began to take form, a heavy weight settling in both of my hands. Iron.

Yes. This was power. This was what it felt like to be a God. This... was immortality. I bit my lip at the feeling of exquisite pleasure the power sent through me, and I could feel the wound in my chest knitting together.

"LEENA!' Jaxon's horrified scream cut through my feelings of bliss. Turning my head towards where my friends were last, I took in the sight before me, and the power drained from me like a tap turning off water, my shield and sword clattering to the floor.

Leena was clutching a hand to her throat; her beautiful honey-coloured eyes met mine across the space, so full of fear and panic. Blood started to seep between her fingers as she fell to her knees. Oliver and Jaxon reached for her in an attempt to keep her up, but she was too heavy. She let go of her neck and I saw the metal of an arrow protruding through it. It had gone straight through her neck, straight through to the front of her.

{No, no, no, no.}

This couldn't be happening. Not Leena. She was the best of us. This wasn't the end, it couldn't be.

I looked toward Nathaniel, who was still separated from the group. He was trying to make his way toward me, but four of the cloaked men surrounded him. He wielded the spear with impressive precision, still too nervous to use his magic so close to our group.

I made to step toward Leena, hating that I wasn't next to her. I needed to get to her. Maybe if she could channel the magic from the earth like I had, she could fix herself too. As I took a couple of steps forward, rough hands grabbed my shoulders and pulled me back against a hard chest.

One arm snaked around my waist and held me there, the strength of it unwavering as a metal knife was held to my throat.

"Let go of me!" I shouted, squirming and kicking and flailing my arms in a bid to escape, my eyes never leaving Leena's. I felt the tip of the knife break my skin as I flailed, a hot trickle of blood running down my neck. Jaxon's large hands were wrapped around Leena's neck now, trying to stop the bleeding, as he frantically barked instructions at the other Cadets gathering nearby. Oliver knelt beside Leena, as if the rest of the battle had fallen away. One of his hands clasped her bloodied fingers while the other stroked away a single tear that was tracking its way down Leena's beautiful cheek. He whispered in her ear, and whatever he said seemed to ease the panic from her face, but her eyes never left mine.

I noticed that Kieran had made his way over to his cousin, and they were both fighting off several cloaked men who were trying to take advantage of my friends' distraction. Lex's daggers were flying at a break-neck pace, one after the other; if her strength was waning, she didn't show it. Kieran was wielding his sword in one hand whilst he controlled a shorter version of his five-tail whip in the other. Two of the cloaked figures fell to the ground, one of Lex's daggers going straight through a man's skull, whilst Kieran managed to remove the other man's legs with his whip. He left the man, or at least what was left of him, to sob hysterically on the ground. The man used his arms to pull his torso across the grass in a bid to escape Kieran, the movement leaving a trail of blood behind him from the open wounds just above his knees, turning the green blades of grass to a dark shade of brown. It would be a slow, painful death. Kieran was not offering this man any mercy. A dark, vindictive part of me hoped that this was the man who had fired the arrow at my friend.

I scanned the floor around me desperately as I still fought against the man's hold. Where was the sword Kieran had given me, or the straight-sword I had dropped when the arrow pierced my chest? Surely, they were nearby - could I somehow retrieve one of them with my feet and kick it up toward my hands? A hard yank from the arm around my waist squeezed the air from my lungs as the flat of the knife pushed against my windpipe, and my vision wavered at the lack of oxygen.

"You're coming with me, I'm afraid. If I let you go, I'd be better off dead." A low voice, carrying the stench of decay, whispered in my ear, reminding me so much of the man in Olos. I kicked and flailed harder, but the man's grip didn't loosen.

"No! Let me go. LEENA! You cannot die, you hear me? You cannot die on me."

Tears began to fall from my eyes as I looked back at my friend. Leena's honey-coloured eyes met mine again, tears also streaming down her cheeks. There was an unsettling calm in her expression—something almost peaceful, as if she had accepted the weight of what was happening. She raised a closed fist to her chest, and the sight filled me with dread, prompting a scream to erupt from my throat.

"No, Leena, it's not your time. We were meant to do this together! I can't do this without you." I tried to shout over to her as the man began to pull me even further away, but sobs were forcing their way up my throat, making it hard to speak. I tried to dig my heels into the ground, but it did nothing; his grip only tightened around my waist, a vice that threatened to crush my ribcage. Panic surged within me as I fought against his hold, desperation driving my struggle.

"I love you, until we meet again, my friend." Leena mouthed to me over the growing distance between us.

A loud wailing filled the air, and it took me a moment to realise the sound was coming from my own throat. Leena slumped backward, and Jaxon caught her before she could hit the ground, still kneeling beside her. He rocked her in his arms, lowering his forehead to hers, and loud sobs broke from him. The sound of his raw grief shredded what was left of my soul. Oliver bowed his head gracefully, but I could see his shoulders shaking with silent sobs.

I squeezed my eyes shut, mentally reciting the parting prayer for those we love that Nanny Rosie had taught us when we were young, in case anything ever happened to her. The words flowed through me like a desperate lifeline, even as the world around me crumbled.

"By the grace of the Gods,

We ask for their soul to return home.

Though their heart no longer beats,

Do not let them wander alone.

As they travel the endless sky,

We pray you show them the way,

Whilst we vow to remember them,

Until we meet again one day."

Opening my eyes, I tried to find Nathaniel. The roof terrace was covered in blood, making the grass appear brown, and bodies littered the floor. So much for this group not killing people.

Around ten of the cloaked attackers still stood, but it was becoming hard to decipher who was who amongst the Cadets in dark leathers or black tunics. Tatum and Tess had one cornered against a wall, while another third-year I didn't recognise guarded their backs, two blue flames roaring from each of his palms. To their left, Bartholomew fought a man at least twice his size, desperately trying to protect the first-years huddled behind him with his flames—or what remained of them. The girl who had screamed earlier lay motionless on the ground, while the burly male crouched over her, seemingly ready to fight anyone who dared approach and take her from him. It reminded me of a male lion defending its cub, refusing to accept that death had already come to claim her.

Continuing to scan the scene, I noticed Kieran and Lex were no longer near my group of friends. Oliver, who had somehow managed to compose himself, fought the cloaked man with the spiked mace, trying to protect his brother. Jaxon still cradled Leena, grief evident on his face as he stared vacantly into the distance. My eyes searched through the chaos as best as they could while the man continued to drag me away, my heels digging into the ground, leaving lines in the grass. *Where* was Nathaniel? Reaching my hands up behind me, I dug my nails into the man's face, dragging them downwards; I could feel his warm blood welling beneath my nails as I did so.

"*Bitch!*" He hissed in my ear.

A damp cloth covered my face, and a sweet smell suddenly filled my nose. I tried to shake my head to get it off me, but the man pressed it so firmly against me that all I managed to do was twitch. My limbs started to feel heavy, and it took all of my energy just to keep my eyes open. My flailing dissipated, and all I could do was watch as Oliver, Jaxon, and Leena grew farther and farther away.

"Why are you here? This was never the plan. Who sent you, was it my father?" A low voice said from nearby, sounding confused.

Who was that? I recognised it, but my mind was becoming foggy.

I tried to scan the surroundings one last time before the world inevitably went completely black. Where was Nathaniel? Where were Kieran and Lex? How many of the cloaked men were left?

A figure caught my attention at the Fire Spire's archway; the pale, stained robes stood out like a beacon among the sea of dark clothing.

Azrael. What was he doing here?

My vision darkened and narrowed as I struggled to concentrate, the sweet-smelling cloth still covering my mouth and nose. I tried to scour my hazy mind for what Nathaniel had told me about Leena's beliefs regarding Azrael.

"Leena likes to taunt Jaxon, who is petrified of him by the way, by saying that Azrael used to help Ouran by transporting the souls of the dead."

My heart fluttered with a small sense of panic as realisation dawned. I looked at the fallen cloaked warriors, then towards Leena, who lay painfully still. I focused on her chest, willing to see the rise and fall of her lungs, but nothing happened. Jaxon had stepped away from her to join his brother, leaving her a crumpled heap on the ground.

I glanced back at Azrael, who was now no more than a pale speck in the distance, as I was dragged away to the furthest wall.

"Please don't take her from me, Az. Not her." I spoke in a croaky whisper through the cloth that covered my mouth. I knew he couldn't hear me; I could barely hear myself.

Just as my vision darkened for the final time, I swore I saw Azrael raise a bony fist to his heart and nod in understanding.

PART THREE

*When the time comes,
He must save the war bringer.
For if he does not,
I fear,
Two halves will remain torn,
Beasts will continue to slumber,
And the land of truth will stay forgotten.*

CHAPTER TWENTY-SEVEN

Sienna jolted upright from the warmth of her fur-covered bed, her red locks tumbling over her face with the movement. She had dreamt of a small blonde-haired woman tied up near the bow of a ship, her clothes torn, and a threadbare woollen blanket draped over her waist. Cloaked, silent figures surrounded her, all rowing in tandem with military precision. The petite girl looked dirty, save for the evidence of tears that had tracked down her cheeks. Her hair was matted, one side singed, clearly burnt at some point, making it several inches shorter than the other.

Decades had passed since Sienna had seen anything from so high above, the steel necklace around her neck suppressing her other form. The roaring of her beast, silent for almost as long, filled her mind in time with her racing pulse. Now awake, she tried to tell herself it was just a dream, but a pulling sensation in her chest persisted. With every breath, the tugging intensified, urging her to stand, to *act*.

Sienna furrowed her brow in confusion; she hadn't felt this feeling since her time in her homeland. A pang of sadness speared through her heart as she recalled the beauty of her birthplace. The endless forests and rivers, the clear open skies where she had spent so much time, the warm air of the enchanted lands as it caressed her skin. Memories of her friends and family, with whom she had served with for a millennium, flooded her mind. She missed her brother, Sebastian, whose sharp features had faded from her recollection with each passing day. His laugh, once a familiar melody, now felt like a muffled lullaby whenever she tried to grasp it.

Home.

As sleep cleared from her mind, her senses sharpened, and she shoved the sadness deep within herself. She pulled the covers from her naked body and stood on steady feet, reaching for the silk robe she had carelessly draped across the armchair beside her bed before the King's visit the previous night. Her once-toned physique had become weak and bony, her ribs jutting out like a fragile cage, and her once-luminescent skin now appeared sunken and grey, as if life had drained from her. She wrapped the robe around herself, the fabric whispering against her skin, and loosely fastened it around her too-thin waist before edging closer to the window opposite her bed.

The King had given her luxurious quarters—only the best for his prized possession, and what a prize she was. His men had caught her in a steel net five decades ago while she was on a scouting mission for her people. Since then, she had resided in this grey, soulless castle, biding her time until one of her own came for her—a sign that she was to return home and that the Uprising would soon be upon the Continent. She had tried several times to escape in the first decade, but with only one way in and out of the castle, she hadn't gotten very far. Each failed attempt had only reinforced her captivity, binding her further to this life she had never chosen for herself.

Kneeling on her plush window seat, forehead pressed against the cool glass of the windowpane, she placed a delicate, manicured hand to her racing chest, as if trying to feel the invisible string tugging at her. Sienna focused her yellow-gold eyes over the dark horizon of the barren landscape of Idernan. Although the cover of night obscured her view, she let the pull in her chest guide her gaze. It snapped to the southeast, towards the distant shoreline of the Thalattas Sea. In that moment, she felt a clarity wash over her: what she had seen was not merely a dream.

Squinting toward the ocean, she focused intently, willing the ship to emerge from the inky blackness.

But all she could see was an endless void, a seemingly unending darkness that swallowed any trace of light. The ocean lay at least a two-day ride from the castle, and even with her enhanced vision, there was no way to pierce the dark shroud. A frustrated rasp escaped her lips, fogging the glass closest to her as she exhaled.

If only she could take her other form, she could be at the coast within an hour. Instead, she was trapped in this useless mortal body, reduced to being the King's entertainment—a pretty face for when he wished to showcase her before his minions, a pawn in a game she had never agreed to play.

Raising her hands to her hair, she pulled at her scalp—a habit she always resorted to when annoyed. Sienna leaned back from the seat and turned on her heels, pacing between the window and the end of her bed. Her steps were silent on the plush, colourful rug beneath her feet, a '*gift*' from his Royal Highness last year for being such an accommodating prisoner.

The Gods wouldn't have given her this vision for no reason. It had been a long time since she had been granted such a gift, and she was determined not to waste it. Whoever the girl was, she was important, and if the tugging in her chest was any indication, she belonged here as much as Sienna did. The roaring in her mind quieted, replaced by a singular mantra that echoed within her:

{*Protect, protect, protect.*}

It was time.

CHAPTER TWENTY-EIGHT

I opened my eyes to a clear blue sky, the soothing sound of waves lapping gently against something solid beneath me. A cold breeze brushed over my face, carrying the unmistakable scent of salt and seaweed. My mind was thick with fog, but I could make out the faint murmur of voices drifting toward me on the wind. The words were too muffled to understand, and I couldn't focus long enough to make sense of them. My body felt heavy, stiff, as though I had been lying there for ages. I tried to sit up, but my limbs refused to cooperate, and I could only manage to prop myself up on my elbows, lifting my head a few inches off the ground.

Why was I so weak?

As I shifted, something tugged at my wrists. I looked down, and my breath caught. Two steel bracelets were locked around my wrists, fastened tightly against my skin, connected by an interlocking chain. Shackles.

Panic flared briefly before I pushed it down, forcing my sluggish mind to process my surroundings. Slowly, details came into focus. I was on a boat—no, a ship—somewhere out in the open water. The vessel was about thirty to forty feet long, with around twenty men rowing in unison. Their dark cloaks billowed in the wind, hoods drawn low over their faces, obscuring their identities. My heart skipped a beat, and my mind flashed back to another time: a cloaked man with wretched breath, rough hands grabbing at me, and another dragging me away from my best friend as she took her last breaths.

I blinked the memories away before grief could swallow me whole. Focus. I needed to focus. I looked around as a horrible thought tugged at me; was this group... the Uprising?

Several men stood nearby beneath a large sail, the fabric billowing in the ocean breeze. Sunlight glinted off it, casting ever-shifting shadows across the deck. I realised I was lying at the front of the ship, just beneath a platform where a solitary figure stood behind a weathered wooden wheel, steering the ship through the rolling waves.

One of the men noticed my gaze. The muffled conversations nearby ceased, and I could feel their eyes on me. He broke away from the group, his dark cloak swirling in the wind with each measured step. As he drew closer, I noticed his size—he had a broad, muscular frame, reminding me strangely of Jaxon. For a fleeting moment, I almost smiled, my mind briefly mixing him up with my gorilla-like friend. But then a small, urgent voice inside me whispered: {*You are not safe here. This is not your friend.*}

He knelt down in front of me, his shadow falling over my face. I could only make out the bottom half of his features—rough stubble, several days' worth, and small scars were evident along his jaw. His eyes remained hidden beneath his hood.

"Welcome back to the world of the living, Princess," he said, his voice low and gruff. "Naz will be pleased to hear that the blow I delivered to the back of your head didn't kill you off."

"Naz?" I croaked, my voice raw and hoarse, like I had swallowed sandpaper. My mouth felt like it had been coated with wool, faintly tasting of old vomit. How long had I been unconscious? Why couldn't I remember being hit? And who was this *Naz*?

"He's the reason you're here," the man replied, his hood tilting slightly as though sizing me up. "Our leader seems to have taken a real liking to ya." His tone was casual, as if we were discussing nothing more serious than the weather. "Bit scrawny for me, but I'm not one to question our master's taste."

Before I could react, he reached out with a gloved hand and traced his fingers along my chin. I flinched and instinctively tried to pull away, but my body felt sluggish, unresponsive.

"Who is Naz? What do you want from me? Where are my friends?" I tried to inject authority into my voice, but the words came out feeble and desperate. I was too weak to demand anything.

The man clicked his tongue in disapproval and reached into his cloak, pulling out a familiar-looking rag. My heart dropped.

"One thing I don't like," he muttered, "is a woman who asks too many questions. If you ask me, women should only open their mouths for one thing."

His voice was low, almost seductive, as he leaned in closer, his hand now cupping the back of my head. Relief briefly washed over me at the thought of not having to hold my head up any longer. I found myself almost instinctively leaning back into his grip, too tired to resist, the weight of my head sinking into his palm. I was so exhausted.

"Take a deep breath," he whispered into my ear, his words smooth and coaxing.

The cloth was cool against my face, and as the sweet scent filled my nostrils, my thoughts began to slow. I fought to hold my breath, knowing what was coming. But it was no use. The world around me dimmed, and between one heartbeat and the next, everything faded to black.

CHAPTER TWENTY-NINE

My senses gradually began to return, the first awareness cutting through the haze being the dull ache that enveloped my entire body. I lay on a firm, damp surface, a chill seeping into my bones. As I adjusted slightly to ease a sharp throb in my right hip, I became aware that I was curled up on a cold stone floor. My body shivered involuntarily, and my skin felt parched as if coated in a layer of grime that made me feel utterly filthy.

I focused on the sounds around me, but my surroundings appeared to be silent, save for a repetitive *drip, drip, drip*. Dank air filled my nose, the scent of mildew almost overwhelming me. I coughed at the smell as I took in a deep breath, my ribs feeling tight as if they might be bruised. I tried to swallow, but it felt like someone had raked knives down my throat. My head pounded as I tried to peel my eyes open. They were slightly crusted at the corners, so I raised my hands to clear them, realising much too late that my fingers felt gritty. Adjusting to wipe at my eyes with the heels of my palms, my attempt to keep any more dirt from getting into them, I felt a tugging at my wrists; something was fastened around them. Slowly cracking my eyelids open, I peered down at my wrists, trying to understand what the sensation was. Two steel bracelets encircled my wrists with an interlocking chain dangling between them, linking the two together. Fragmented memories started to flash behind my eyelids.

Arms around my waist. A ship. Leena's eyes. Azrael.

I took a shaky breath. My mind felt addled, each thought sluggish and tangled, but I could sense panic simmering just beneath the surface. With a determined effort, I forced myself into a sitting position, grunting softly at the strain it took.

As I settled, I glanced down at my appearance. I was still clad in my standard black tunic and slacks, but they were now soiled and torn, evidence of a struggle I couldn't fully recall. My gaze drifted to my ankles, where I noticed a set of heavy shackles binding me to the floor. Panic surged again; I was no longer wearing any shoes. My feet were caked with a mixture of dirt and dried blood, the sight grim and unsettling. My toenails were chipped, some missing altogether, revealing several infections already starting to form. It occurred to me that I must have been dragged at some point for my feet to be so torn up. A crease formed between my brows as my dazed mind tried to piece together what had happened.

I slowly looked away from my dishevelled state, forcing myself to take in my surroundings. Dark stone walls loomed around me, their surfaces cold and damp, creating a claustrophobic atmosphere that seemed to close in on me. The floor beneath me was equally grim—a patchwork of dirt and filth that whispered of neglect and despair. A small bucket was to the left of me, presumably where I was meant to relieve myself. The foul stench wafting from it made me wrinkle my nose; clearly, I would not be the first to use it.

I forced myself to look away from the harsh reality of my makeshift toilet and shifted my attention ahead. There, directly in front of me, loomed a set of vertical steel bars, cold and unyielding. As the truth settled in, my heart began to race, leaping and stuttering in my chest.

I was in a cell.

Suddenly, memories crashed into me, flooding my mind like a tsunami, relentless and overwhelming. The attack on Solarus. Kieran's five-tailed whip as it cut through the air. The earth's magic, roaring and surging through my veins. Leena's lifeless eyes, vacant and unblinking as she lay motionless in Jaxon's arms. A man dragging me away, his grip unyielding. Jaxon's blood-curdling screams as he called Leena's name, begging her to wake. A cloth pressed against my mouth, stifling my breath. Azrael raising a hand to his chest as he watched me, a silent, haunting gesture. The ship rocking beneath me, the salty breeze stinging my face. Cloaked figures surrounding me, rowing in unison to a song only they could hear. Another cloth, the sweet smell suffocating my senses.

A sob surged up from my throat once the memories faded, unbidden and raw. No, not Leena—my kind, selfless Leena. Grief bubbled up within me, threatening to overflow, and a small sound escaped my parched lips. She couldn't be gone; she simply *couldn't* be. That warm, beautiful soul couldn't have been torn away from this world in such a horrific way. She deserved so much more.

She had died trying to protect me, too focused on whether I would survive rather than fighting off our attackers. If only I had been stronger, more alert—she would still be alive.

Tears pooled in my eyes, and I quickly blinked them away, fighting against the tide of emotions that threatened to swallow me whole. I couldn't give in to despair; I needed to understand where I was and how I could escape. I had to get back to Solarus and see what remained of my friends. Jaxon, Oliver, Lex, and even Kieran. Most of all, I needed to know that Nathaniel was okay—I had lost sight of him in the chaos, and that uncertainty gnawed at me, a reminder of everything I still had to fight for. I couldn't lose him too. Not after Leena, after Mei.

The sound of heavy footsteps jolted me from the haunting images in my mind. I turned my stiff neck toward the echoes reverberating off the cold stone walls. As the footsteps drew nearer, the racing in my heart increased, pounding in my chest like a drum. Every instinct screamed at me to stand and prepare to fight, that whoever approached was undoubtedly a threat. But my muscles felt heavy, as if they were being weighed down by lead. All I wanted was to close my eyes and slip back into oblivion. Why did I have to wake up? My reality was worse than any nightmare.

The air around me seemed to darken as an outline of a man emerged just beyond the bars of my cell. Shadows cloaked his face, but I could tell he was at least six feet tall, clad in leather breeches and a dark emerald tunic adorned with intricate gold stitching and buttons. His figure was lean, yet his posture was straight and rigid, exuding an unsettling stillness that suggested he possessed the predatory grace of a hunter ready to pounce at any moment.

"Well, you look like you've seen better days," he said in an amused tone. His voice was low, but something in the back of my mind flared in recognition. "It's nice to finally put a face to the name, Aela Everflame. My son has told me so much about you."

I frowned in confusion, and alarm bells began to ring in my mind. Was this the man the cloaked figure on the ship had referred to, their leader?

"Who are you?" I croaked back weakly. I cleared my throat slightly. "Where am I? What do you want with me?"

The mysterious man chuckled.

"An inquisitive little thing, aren't you?" The shadows peeled back from his face slightly to reveal a strong jaw and a mouth that slanted upwards in a cruel smile. "You've been here for a couple of days, but it took you several weeks to get here. My men had to keep sedating you throughout the journey; I was told you were blubbering like a fool for most of it."

He cocked his head slightly, and I saw his fingers twitch. Shadows began to peel from the edges of my cell and surged toward me. They reached for me, and I pushed myself back into the wall to try to escape them, but it was no use.

Whispers filled my mind—too many voices to count, and the pounding in my head increased ten-fold. Men's voices, women's voices, children's voices; it was all of them but none of them at the same time. Black spots swirled in my vision, and the pressure on my mind was so intense it felt like I was deep underwater. The shadows started to run themselves over my body, feeling like a pair of hands caressing my skin. My mind screamed at me to push them away, but the whispers only grew louder in protest, and my body involuntarily arched into their touch. The caress felt intimate, and my body craved the sensation.

Images of a man and woman flashed in my mind, a look of ecstasy on both of their faces. They were unclothed, and I saw glimpses of their naked flesh rubbing against each other. The woman opened her mouth to let out a cry of pleasure, and I heard her moan so clearly in my head that it was as if she was in the cell with me. Their bodies continued to move together, increasing in momentum until they appeared frenzied. I saw sweat glistening on the man's chest, but when I tried to focus on both of their faces, their features slipped away as if I was looking through mist. Who *were* they? I squeezed my thighs together as dampness started to pool between my legs; memories of mine and Nathaniel's shared moment in the ocean starting to mix with the images of the couple in my mind. The feeling of Nathaniel deep inside me, the friction of his length as he pumped harder, the perfect blend of pain and pleasure whilst the salt water of the ocean cooled the rising flames within me as I edged closer to my climax. I bit my lip at the memory and could feel sweat gathering on my forehead as the temperature of my blood rose.

I looked down to realise that my thighs were no longer clamped shut, my knees were spread, and I had been rubbing myself through my breeches with one of my shackled hands. How long had I been like this? It felt like only seconds had passed. My breath billowed in front of me in the frigid air as I panted rapidly, I was so *close*. I tipped my head back as my impending climax started to rise within me, like the sun over a mountain, and the back of my skull whacked against the stone wall behind me.

As if the movement had knocked some sense into me, embarrassment started to pierce through my lust-filled mind, an awareness that this wasn't the time or place for this to be happening. I looked over to the man looming outside my cell, as if only just remembering he was there, and noticed that his mouth had curled further into a now menacingly seductive grin.

Well, I guess there was my answer as to whether he had been watching me.

He reached down with his left hand to re-arrange himself through his breeches, clearly aroused, and the movement reminded me so much of the cloaked man that attacked me in Olos. The memory that single movement evoked was like a bucket of iced water had been tipped over my head, and the lust cleared from my mind entirely, along with the voices. My mind was silent once more; the repetitive *drip, drip, drip* was the only thing to be heard throughout the space, save for my ragged breathing. Shame seized me, forcing away any lingering feelings of desire. I suddenly felt so angry, so violated; how *dare* he? What gave this man the right to take control of my mind like that? But as quickly as those feelings rose, a wave of overwhelming exhaustion crashed over me, washing them away entirely. I heard the man release a dark, raspy chuckle.

"Impressive; not many people have the strength to push away my magic." He started to pace slightly in front of my cage; his hands now clasped loosely behind his back, his erection still straining against the leather at his crotch. He was shameless.

"Who are you?" I asked again, more firmly than before. I'm not entirely sure what had just happened, but it wasn't something I had consented to. The man's pacing paused, and he turned his body, facing me once more.

"My friends call me Lucius, but most know me by a different name."

I let out an exasperated sound at his lack of response from my dry throat. Whoever this person was—Lucius—I didn't have the energy for his riddles. I wasn't particularly thrilled about the clear violation I had just endured and the fact I was clearly a fucking prisoner.

"Why am I here?" I repeated through gritted teeth, my temper rising again through my drained energy reserves.

"Let's just say… my son's future depends on you being here. You know him, actually, but just not by the name he was born with. In fact, it was his men that captured you from Solarus, under my orders, of course. I don't think he was particularly thrilled to be caught off-guard. A bit of a control freak, that child of mine." Lucius let out an amused snort.

I tried to recall what the man on the boat had called their leader.

"Naz?" I asked on a whisper.

Lucius smiled whilst looking down at the nails of his right hand, as if this conversation was now becoming nothing more than a nuisance.

"I've been keeping my eye on you for a while now you know, been getting yourself into all sorts of trouble recently, haven't you?"

"What?" I responded in confusion.

He moved to crouch down on the other side of the bars, so our gazes were parallel; however, the shadows still clung to his face, obscuring his features.

"Oh child, you really haven't pieced together anything, have you?" He said in a tone of false kindness.

Before I could ask anything further, Lucius rose to his feet in one fluid motion, returning the way he came. Just before he exited from view, he called back, "Sienna will be down to see you shortly. We must make you presentable for the ball this evening; it is the Night of Shadows, after all."

CHAPTER THIRTY

I awoke several hours later to the sound of light footsteps echoing in the corridor. My heart clenched in my chest at first, but I quickly realised these footsteps were far lighter than Lucius's heavy tread. The dimness had faded a little, a small ray of sunlight filtering through a narrow window at the end of the row of cages. The light illuminated a female figure that came into view just outside my cell bars.

The woman was several inches taller than me, her thin yet womanly figure accentuated by a ruby red velvet dress and an elegant fur cape draped over her shoulders. The weak light in the space highlighted metal around her neck.

A steel collar.

Was she a prisoner too?

Even beneath the opulence of her attire, I could discern her curves. As my gaze travelled up to her face, I was captivated by the shade of her eyes—they looked yellow, almost gold, glowing faintly in the dimness, reminiscent of the last embers of a dying fire. Her hair cascaded down to her waist in waves that shimmered like melted red diamonds, mirroring the colour of her dress. She wasn't traditionally beautiful like Leena, but her sharp, unusual features took my breath away, evoking images of the formidable warriors of the Gods I had read about.

The striking redhead inhaled deeply, tilting her nose slightly, and after a moment, I realised what she was doing.

"Are you… smelling me?" I asked, my lip turning up slightly.

"I apologise," she said, her cheeks flushing slightly. "Force of habit." Her accent was peculiar—one I had never encountered before. It was quaint, almost regal.

"My name is Sienna," she continued, producing a key from a hidden pocket within her dress. In quick succession, she unlocked my cell door, swung it open, and stepped toward me. As she approached, her own scent wafted towards me. At first, it was lilac soap, making me yearn for a long soak in a tub. But as she drew closer, I detected undertones of pine and what could only be described as warm summer air. The scent felt strangely familiar, but I couldn't quite place it.

Bending down, Sienna deftly unfastened the chain connecting my steel anklets with another key, then gently clasped her fingers around my wrists, pulling me to my feet. It was the first time I had managed to stand, and surprisingly, her touch sent a small surge of energy through me, much like the feeling I had experienced when I touched the opalescent horse near Thellas, and when I had gripped Kieran's hand. It seemed this sensation I thought was unique to Nathaniel and me wasn't so rare after all.

"You have magic," I stated, more as a fact than a question. She answered anyway as she unlocked the chain between my bracelets, placing it on the floor.

"I used to, but that was a long time ago." A hint of sadness coloured her voice, but given that I had just met her, I didn't pry further. The small burst of energy I felt from her began to wane as I concentrated on remaining upright; I didn't have the mental capacity to ask more questions, even if I wanted to.

Sienna led me down the prison's corridor, which was lined with around twenty cells, each one just as filthy as my own, but all vacant. Once at the end, we made our way up a dark, winding staircase, and I had to pause several times to catch my breath, leaning against the damp stone walls to keep myself upright. Sienna didn't rush me or say a word, her grip on my wrist remaining firm. Given my shaky state, I clearly wasn't a flight risk, so I wondered why she felt her hold on me was necessary, but I was begrudgingly grateful for the extra support it offered.

As we exited the staircase, I took in my surroundings. Unlike the light, high ceilings of the college in Solarus, this building had low, dark hallways. They were illuminated by small flame-lit sconces every few feet, presumably to light the way but also to keep the passageways warm. The initial shock of my situation was beginning to wear off, and the cold was really seeping into my bones now. We were no longer in Olympia; that much was clear.

Eventually, she led me to a large wooden door and produced another key from her pocket. How many keys did this woman carry?! This one was much larger than the ones she'd used for my cell and shackles, engraved with intricate designs that matched the carvings around the doorframe. The symbols on the key likely corresponded to the door's patterns, rather than the numbered system we used in Olympia. I made a mental note of this detail for later.

Sienna unlocked the door and shifted her grip from my wrist to my lower back, gently urging me forward. I stepped into a small but cosy room, the warmth of it a stark contrast to the cold stone corridors. A four-poster bed, draped in privacy curtains, revealed a plush bedspread covered in furs and an array of cushions. Without thinking, I took two steps toward it, my body aching for the comfort of a proper bed after what felt like months on cold stone floors and damp wooden decks. If Lucius had been truthful, I hadn't slept in a real bed for weeks.

Sienna's hand remained on my back as she gently guided me toward an ornate wooden console table, positioned in front of a wall-mounted mirror, with a comfortable-looking green armchair tucked beneath it. I moved slowly, grimacing at the thought of my dirty feet ruining the beautiful rug that covered most of the floor. Lowering myself into the armchair, I let out a relieved sigh as my back finally pressed into something soft and supportive.

For a moment, Sienna stepped away from me, rummaging through an armoire to my left, so I turned my gaze to the window beside me. While the window itself was unremarkable, save for a cushioned seat beneath it, the view outside was what captured my attention. The sun was sinking below the horizon, casting a warm glow that signalled the arrival of evening. As the last rays of light spilled across the landscape, they reflected off a vast expanse of... *nothing*.

I was accustomed to the diverse terrains of Olympia—the sandy dunes of Solarus, the verdant farmlands of Thellas. There had always been something to focus on, whether it was a bustling town, rolling hills in the distance, or a winding riverbed. But now, as I gazed out, all I saw was a barren stretch of flat dirt that extended for miles—barely any trees, no hills, no signs of life or civilisation. Just an endless, desolate plain.

Sienna's return pulled my attention from the bleak view outside, bringing with it the harsh reality that escaping would require more supplies than I could imagine, and that there would also be no place to hide. My eyes met hers in the mirror, but before I could speak, I froze at the face that stared back at me. Disgust washed over me as I scrunched my nose. The face in the mirror did the same. It took several heartbeats for me to realise that the dishevelled heap staring back was, in fact, *me*.

I looked like a complete mess. My face was smeared with grime, save for the stark lines of dried tears tracing from my eyes to my jaw. My once-shiny blonde hair resembled a tangled bird's nest, one side shockingly shorter than the other. Had I been caught in the crossfire during the attack on Solarus, or had the flames I wielded done this? There was a hole in my tunic at my chest, the fabric stained with dried blood, pink skin and a faint scar peeking through it. That must have been where the arrow struck. Leena's vacant eyes flashed in my mind, but I quickly blinked the image away.

Defeated, I sank deeper into the chair. I wasn't vain; I rarely spent time on my appearance. Yet the realisation that I didn't even recognise the person staring back at me shattered something deep within me. After everything that had happened over the past couple of months, I didn't think there was more of me that could break; clearly, I was wrong.

Sienna moved swiftly to brush out the tangles in my hair, spraying a mist from a bottle to help the bristles glide smoothly. My scalp protested with each tug as she yanked and pulled, her determination evident in the way she worked. After what felt like an eternity, which was actually only about ten minutes later, she finally managed to work the brush through my hair without a single knot interrupting its descent. She must have given herself quite the workout. A glimmer of metal caught my eye, and I flinched at the sight, unsure of what to expect. She gathered my hair to the centre of my back and began snipping away without a word. The metal was scissors, not a dagger. I rolled my eyes at my own paranoia.

Once she finished cutting, Sienna pushed my hair back forward. My once waist-length locks now rested between my collarbone and the centre of my chest. She stood in front of me, blocking my view of the mirror, and began to add layers from the bottom of my chin.

As she stepped back to admire her handiwork after a few minutes, I caught a glimpse of her small smile in the mirror's reflection. Praise where praise was due; she had transformed my burnt monstrosity into a surprisingly decent and intentional-looking cut.

Putting down the scissors, Sienna reached passed me and pulled out a small tin box from the top drawer of her dresser. She opened it to reveal a white powder.

"You should probably sniff this," she said quietly, handing the tin to me. I eyed it cautiously.

"What is it?" I asked.

"It's what we call moon-powder. It's made from the bark of the trees in the Shangnon mountains. It will give you energy."

I looked up at her, suspicion evident in my expression, I had never heard of such a thing. Sienna rolled her eyes at me before taking one of her nails and scooping up some of the powder. She lifted it to her nose and inhaled sharply. Her yellow eyes flared slightly, but quickly settled.

"I promise, all it will do is boost your energy. If you weren't wearing those steel bracelets, it would enhance your magical abilities and might leave you feeling a bit drunk. But since the steel is suppressing whatever power you have, that won't happen. Instead, it'll just help you get through the evening."

Trusting her, I gave her a small nod, and she dipped her finger in the powder once more, offering it to me to take an inhale of my own.

...

After nearly an hour of scrubbing away the dirt in Sienna's copper bathtub, I felt a little more human. The water had only reached halfway up my thighs and was lukewarm, but it was a relief to wash away several weeks' worth of grime. When I stepped out, the water was nearly black and had stung my injured feet.

A few servants had brought in several gowns for me to try on, whispering quietly with Sienna at the doorway before passing them through. Now, standing in front of a narrow full-length mirror next to Sienna's bed, I examined myself. I had chosen a simpler gown, not quite accustomed to the opulence of the offered materials. The light blue velvet faded to indigo at the floor, with sheer sleeves reminiscent of spun cobwebs and a fitted corset with a sweetheart neckline. Sienna had also found a pair of boots at the bottom of her closet—they were several sizes too big for me, but we layered socks so they didn't feel overly loose. Given the state of my feet and the pain in my toes, I was actually grateful for the extra room.

"Let me add some finishing touches," Sienna said from behind me. I turned to face her as she gestured for me to take a seat in front of the console table once more. Smoothing imaginary wrinkles from my dress, I made my way over to the armchair, feeling more like a clumsy child than a graceful lady worthy of such attire. Thankfully, the moon-powder had started to take effect, and I was feeling a little more like myself. Settling in front of Sienna, I watched her as she pulled cosmetics from a small bag that was tucked under her arm.

She skilfully applied kohl to my eyes, emphasizing their shape, before brushing a berry-coloured formula onto my lips and cheeks, which added a fresh flush to my complexion. Then, with a purposeful stride, she moved to the armoire. Setting down her cosmetics bag, she pulled open the top drawer. Inside, she retrieved a necklace, two elegant clips, and a delicate mask.

With deft hands, Sienna changed my hair's parting from the centre to the side, tucking one side neatly away from my face with the golden clips, while allowing the rest of my hair to cascade over my opposite shoulder.

She fastened the necklace around my neck, which rested just above the glass stone Nathaniel had given me. This new piece was a rich gold, featuring a large, dark sapphire at its centre that beautifully echoed the bottom of my dress. Then, with a practiced touch, she placed the mask over my face, securing it with a dainty ribbon that wrapped around the back of my head.

The mask was nothing short of breathtaking. Its bright blue hue mirrored the colour of my eyes, while intricate gold paint defined the contours around them, as well as the edges of the mask. Golden feathers adorned the top of it, swirling around a half-sun just above the centre of it, giving the impression that the sun was rising from me, ablaze with light and life.

Once finished, she stepped back to take in my appearance.

"What do you think?" she asked, gesturing toward the small mirror above the console.

Finally focusing on myself, I gasped softly. My hair had air-dried into natural waves, and the jewellery and gold of the mask accentuated it beautifully, making it look like liquid gold cascading over my shoulder. The mask covered half my face, stopping just above my nose, and as I had hoped, the blue half harmonised perfectly with my dress and the hues of my eyes. I marvelled at the flush on my lips and cheeks, relieved that Sienna had managed to create such vibrant colour without the usual slapping of my face I often resorted to. The haircut, makeup, and dress combined made me look several years older than my eighteen, and for the first time in my life, I felt like a woman... I felt *beautiful*.

"You must be a witch," I whispered.

Sienna laughed lightly, the sound melodic and lovely.

"Oh, come now, child, you know there's no such thing," she said, waving a hand dismissively as she turned away to retrieve another mask from the armoire. "I've just had many years of practice enhancing natural beauty, with a few tweaks here and there."

I frowned at her words. She spoke to me as if I was much younger than her; though she looked only a few years older than me, I would place her in her early twenties at most. Sienna fastened the lace mask she had chosen for herself, her fingers expertly weaving through her fiery hair as she adjusted it into place. The mask was a stunning black, decorated with intricate red embroidered vines that curled and twined like the tendrils of a creeping plant, perfectly complementing her dress. It was evident that this mask had been crafted specifically for her, its delicate patterns accentuating the sharp angles of her face and the vivid hue of her hair, creating an ensemble that was both striking and harmonious.

Looking back at myself, I wondered if the mask I wore was also custom-made, given how well it complemented my features.

Sienna removed the fur pelt from her shoulders, revealing the swell of her bosom above the square neckline of her dress, and turned toward the door. I moved to follow but stopped in my tracks. Her dress was completely backless, exposing the canvas of her milky skin, unblemished except for two long, jagged scars that ran parallel between her shoulder blades and spine.

"What are they?" I asked, grimacing at my own intrusion. Though we had spent several hours together, our conversation had been limited, and I felt like my question might have been over-stepping.

"A reminder," she replied softly over her shoulder, avoiding my gaze. "Now hurry, we don't want to be late."

CHAPTER THIRTY-ONE

As Sienna and I stood in the archway of opulent double doors, my mouth remained slack as I took in the space around me. I stared at a large throne room, at least four times the size of the ornate entry hall of the college at Solarus. Although the rest of the fortress was dull and nondescript, the complete opposite could be said about the sight before me. As if only just realising the obvious, it dawned on me then that we were in King Aadhar's castle in Idernan, Anka.

Marble steps led down from the doors where we stood to a glass-like floor, where people drank, danced, and seemingly enjoyed one another's company. Towards the back wall sat a curved marble dais with a golden throne perched atop. Its design was intricate, made up of curving gold vines and golden carved leaves with inset gems, giving the appearance that it had grown out of the very marble itself.

Surrounding the dais were several men clad in exquisite emerald green and gold tunics, each garment a testament to the highest quality craftsmanship. I realised they must have been the King's inner circle, commonly referred to as the 'Elite.' As I took in their appearance, a familiar memory struck me: Lucius must have been one of them, given that he had worn something strikingly similar during his visit to me. However, from my vantage point, I was too far away to discern which one he might be. It also didn't help that each of them wore an assortment of masks, much like everyone else here, all varying in size, shape, and material; some faces throughout the crowd sported animal masks, and I could make out a few lions, foxes, and deer from where I stood above the gathered mass.

The 'Night of Shadows,' the reason for the ball, marked an evening of celebration for the longest night of the year. In Olympia, it wasn't particularly acknowledged, as the land had historically been inhabited solely by the Flames and lesser elementals, who revelled in light and warmth. However, I had heard whispered tales over the years—stories of how Shades, who were often cloaked in mystery, would host extravagant parties to honour the darkness. It was a night when the usual constraints faded away, and revellers engaged in all manner of debauchery—each celebration a tribute to the shadows that enveloped them, embracing the thrill of what lay hidden in the dark.

Sienna squeezed my hand gently, and as I looked toward her, she motioned for me to follow her to a table against the right wall, where goblets of wine and platters of food were laid out. My stomach growled as we edged closer, pushing our way through scantily clad women and men.

I was unsure what I had expected, but I was not prepared for the lack of clothing and the abundance of skin on display. The fireplaces inlaid into the walls every twenty feet or so gave the massive space somewhat of a cosy, warm feel. Given Anka's typically frigid climate, I guessed this was probably the only place where people could spend any length of time nearly naked. Sienna and I looked positively modest in comparison, our full-length dresses covering everything that needed to be covered.

As I filled a small plate with an assortment of foods, I noticed there was a lot more meat than I was used to. This didn't surprise me, given the weather conditions throughout the Realm, it was very difficult to grow any kind of fruit or vegetables in Anka.

"You'll need some wine if you're going to get through this evening," Sienna whispered.

"Why?" I responded, not really paying her much attention as I focused on whether I wanted more beef or pork to accompany my chicken.

"Because the King likes to put on a show when he has an audience, and they're not normally for the faint-hearted."

As the hours passed, Sienna and I stood close to the table, pushing ourselves almost flush against the wall, a desperate attempt to blend into the shadows as we opted to watch the revellers around us.

Dusk bled into night, and the sound within the throne room reached a fever pitch as drunken laughter, upbeat music, and dancing filled the space. Men and women beckoned others towards small doors that led off the throne room. Sienna explained that they were private antechambers containing daybeds with a plethora of pillows and cushions for those who couldn't quite wait until the night concluded to seek the affection of another.

Guards were strategically positioned throughout the room like silent sentinels surveying the rambunctious crowd. Their backs were straight, exuding an air of unwavering authority, while their hands rested firmly on the pommels of their swords, elegantly sheathed at their waists. Two guards stood on either side of Leena and me, clad in slightly cheaper-looking versions of the Elite's uniform. Their simpler emerald and gold tunics caught the ambient light as they scanned the merrymakers with sharp, discerning eyes, poised to spring into action at the slightest hint of trouble. There was no way we would be able to slink out of the throne room unnoticed.

In contrast, the Elite stationed near the dais seemed slightly more relaxed, mingling with the merriment. They danced with those who offered their hands, drank heartily from the ornate goblets, and engaged in animated conversations with anyone bold enough to approach. Yet, even in their revelry, their eyes remained vigilant, constantly scanning the crowd for potential threats. One of the Elite darted glances back toward me so frequently that I couldn't ignore his scrutiny. I recognised his physique and the stillness of his presence, but I couldn't quite place my finger on who he was.

"Who is that?" I asked Sienna, around a final mouthful of meat, subtly pointing to the lean-figured Elite, an intricate black, white, and red fox mask covering his face and hair. The whiskers curled upwards, appearing extremely lifelike. His sharp eyes were the only visible feature as he scanned the room, giving life to the predatory and cunning mask he wore.

A small frown appeared on Sienna's face as she examined him, trying to work out who was beneath.

"I think it's Blake, the King's brother. It's hard to tell beneath his mask, though."

"Brother?!" I spluttered back through a mouthful of wine. "I didn't realise he had family."

Sienna shrugged. "I don't know his first name; both he and the King are very secretive about that; many people in Anka are. Blake likes to go by his wife's maiden name to distance himself from the weight that the name *Aadhar* carries."

My mind started to race with the information, finally putting the pieces together.

"Does he have a son?" I asked quietly.

"Yeah, but he was sent away when he was young. I think he goes to Solarus' War College now, maybe you know him?"

My thoughts stumbled over each other, each one louder than the last, desperate to be listened to. My conversation in my cell earlier that day replayed in my mind:

"My friends call me Lucius, but most know me by a different name."

"Let's just say... my son's future depends on you being here. You know him, actually, but just not by the name he was born with. In fact, it was his men that captured you from Solarus, under my orders, of course. I don't think he was particularly thrilled to be caught off-guard. A bit of a control-freak, that child of mine."

This man went by his wife's maiden name, *Blake*. I only knew two other people with that last name, and one of them was female.

Kieran Blake. Kieran *fucking* Blake. Kieran Blake was Naz. Kieran Blake had been the reason for my capture after the attack. Kieran Blake was the reason I was now a lamb amongst wolves. Kieran Blake was the reason my best friend was dead.

My wine and food turned sour in my throat.

"Are you okay?" Sienna asked from my side. I pulled my focus away from Blake, or should I say *Lucius,* to look at Sienna, but she was looking down at my hand, which held the goblet of wine I had been sipping from. I followed her gaze to realise that I was holding the chalice with a white-knuckle grip, small droplets of liquid spilling out onto my skin as I trembled fiercely.

I took a long, deep breath, attempting to steady my shaking, much like I had done during the attack at Solarus. Taking several more breaths, the tremors subsided, but my iron grip remained steadfast. Taking onboard Sienna's advice from earlier, I raised the cup to my lips and downed the entirety of the wine. I grimaced after my final swallow; the wine wasn't as fresh as what I was used to back in Olympia—in fact, it tasted slightly of vinegar. Gods, the things I would do for a tankard of ale from the local Thellas tavern right now.

I looked over at Sienna's goblet, which she held gracefully in her left hand, and noticed that her cup was also relatively full. Without much ceremony, I took it from her and drained its contents as well. With both empty goblets now clutched in my hands, I finally turned back to face her. Her eyebrows were raised, the question that I had yet to answer still plastered across her face. She didn't seem too bothered that I had just robbed her of her drink, not that I would have cared much if she did.

"It seems that I have just managed to piece together who arranged my capture, but I just can't seem to work out why."

CHAPTER THIRTY-TWO

A hush fell over the throne room as the double doors at the top of the stairs swung open. I followed the room's gaze to see who was entering, finally managing to peel my eyes away from 'Blake', but I couldn't loosen my grip on the goblets in my hands. Rage simmered just below the surface, and I knew that if it hadn't been for the steel bracelets around my wrists, my magic would have been roiling inside me as well.

Several nearly naked men and women descended the staircase towards the onlookers. I noticed that they, too, wore steel in a bid to suppress their magic, but the metal was fastened tightly around their necks, resembling the collar of a hound, much like the one Sienna wore. They were unnaturally thin, and the pallor of their complexions reminded me of how I had looked before Sienna applied cosmetics to my face—grey and joyless. Each of the gaunt, hauntingly graceful figures wore masks that covered half of their faces, crafted from dark feathers that shimmered in the light of the lamps and fires, the sight both eerie and hypnotic.

"Who are they?" I whispered to Sienna, nodding in the direction of the spectacle.

"It's the King's harem," she whispered back, her voice barely above a breath. "He calls them his *crows*."

I looked back at Sienna and noticed how her posture had stiffened, as if she were trying to shrink further back into the wall to go unnoticed.

"Do you not agree with it?" I asked cautiously, running my eyes over her to gauge her reaction.

"I used to be one of them before my position was… '*upgraded,*'" she raised her delicate fingers in air quotes around the word. I wanted to press her for more information, but something about the way she spoke sounded so hollow and empty that I refrained from asking anything further, redirecting my focus back to the group descending the staircase.

False smiles were plastered across their mouths, the only part of their faces I could see, as the crowd parted for them to make their way toward the throne. Once they reached the dais, the five of them perched themselves on the steps, leaning back and spreading their legs in a suggestive posture. They appeared relaxed, but given how unsettled Sienna seemed next to me, a part of me wondered whether their ease was merely for show.

The crowd, who had been drinking in the entrance of the crows like a starving pack of lions, looked back toward the top of the staircase as a tall figure filled the frame. A petite woman rested on his arm, her long dark waves flowing past her slender hips. She wore a narrow bandeau around her chest, and two delicate chains held up a strip of fabric between her thighs, similar to the rest of the crows. Unlike the others, however, she did not wear a mask. She wore an expression of quiet serenity, but her sharp eyes scanned the room with a keen awareness, reminiscent of how the Elite had observed the gathered crowd just moments before.

When her gaze collided with mine, I swore we held eye contact for several seconds longer than necessary. She was undeniably beautiful, but I would have guessed she was at least a few years younger than me. The apples of her cheeks were full, still bearing the signs of youth, while her lack of womanly curves was evident in the scant amount of clothing she adorned, which only emphasised her delicate frame.

"How old is she?" I asked Sienna.

"The fact that she is unmasked means she is underage, so technically she is off-limits, but the King has been known to grow impatient at times." Sienna raised a hand to her hair and started to tug on the strands near her scalp—a nervous tic, perhaps.

Underage. That meant the woman, the girl, was younger than sixteen. I silently prayed to whatever Gods were listening that she wasn't younger than fifteen.

I forced myself to pull away from the dark-haired beauty to focus on the man she was latched onto. He was tall and lean, and I thought to myself that Bellum probably looked like this in his prime, about twenty years ago. He had the build of a warrior. His leather breeches clung to his muscular thighs, evoking memories of Kieran the first time I saw him, and I couldn't begin to imagine how he had managed to pull them on—had he been sewn into them? He stood shirtless, revealing a sculpted, pale torso. A swirling tattoo of black fire curled up the left side of his ribcage, appearing to shift with every breath he took, its pattern reminding me of Jaxon's shadows when he released them on an exhale.

A feathered mask covered the entirety of his face, intricately designed with flecks of gold woven throughout the black, silken feathers—a more opulent version of those worn by the crows. A long, dark feathered cape adorned his shoulders, trailing behind him like a black cloud as he descended the staircase toward his throne. The most breathtaking thing about him, however, was the golden crown perched atop his head. Like the throne, it featured a complex design interwoven with rubies and emeralds, resembling vines that had been intricately crafted and then enveloped in shimmering gold, forever imprisoned beneath the metal. A soft glow emanated from the ornamental headpiece, and I swore I could feel the hum of magic radiating from it even twenty feet away.

My eyes remained glued to King Aadhar as he crossed the glass-like floor, people bowing their heads and offering small curtsies as he passed. It was hard to tell if he took any notice of their gestures from beneath his elaborate mask, which obscured his expression entirely.

Upon reaching the throne, he turned and adjusted the long train of his cape, allowing it to flow gracefully behind him as he settled into his seat. The material rippled from the arms of the throne down the steps of the dais, undulating like a serpent in motion. The underage beauty moved to kneel at his ankles in obedient submission, and the King proceeded to rest a hand on her head, treating her as if she was no more than a pet.

Blake then moved to stand by his side, much like how Bellum guarded General Zaneer's back, obviously Blake was The King's right-hand. With a casual wave of his wrist, the King issued a command, and dark shadows began to pour from the throne, rolling down the steps like mist over a still lake. The shadows gathered just in front of the crows perched on the dais steps, creeping forward slowly, as if drawn to them.

The crows appeared to wait patiently, their expressions unreadable.

At the moment of contact, the five crows began to writhe as if on cue, and loud moans escaped their lips, reminding me of how I must have looked in the dungeon only hours before—lost, tormented, consumed by lust and utterly helpless.

The men gripped their now erect bulges that were barely covered under the thin piece of material. Moving their fists up and down at a hurried pace, they proceeded to thrust and buck their hips against their hands, soft grunts coming from their mouths as they did so. One woman grasped her breast as she threw her head back, loud cries bursting from her throat. The other two, closest to the King's throne, simply moved the thin material between their legs to the side and plunged their fingers deep inside themselves, the sounds of their wetness reaching me from where I stood over thirty feet away.

The entire spectacle was positively indecent, and I was torn between looking away in embarrassment, or continuing to stare with fascination, horror and much to my mortification… *arousal*.

The harem seemed to grow bored of their self-pleasure after a few minutes, and quickly turned their attention to one another. The two women at the top of the dais reached towards the man closest to them and started to move their bodies against his, hands roaming over his skin like he was the most exquisite thing they had ever touched. Their thin pieces of material got disregarded, and the threesome gyrated together in ecstasy. Mouths and hands disappeared between each other's legs, and their groans grew even louder. My focus shifted to the remainder of the crows, the man and woman at the base of the steps. The man had the woman bent over the bottom step as he thrusted into her from behind, a hand fisted in her hair to keep him steady, reminding me of Lex and Jaxon against the tree just outside of Olos. The slaps of their bodies coming together reverberated off the stone walls of the room and I found myself having to clench my thighs together. What was *wrong* with me?

I finally pulled my gaze away from the group and scanned the room. A thin veil of shadows now blanketed the space closest to the dais, the crowd growing increasingly more excited at the scene unfolding in front of them. Murmurs quickly changed to whimpers and shrieks of pleasure. More and more people began making their way to the antechambers off the main room, eager to escape into private spaces, while others unabashedly indulged right in front of the crowd, displaying a boldness that left little to the imagination.

Women's barely-there dresses were being hiked up to their hips as they allowed men's hands to push between their thighs, the men's wrists moving up and down, in and out. Some men were even beginning to kneel in front of other men to remove their slacks, hungry looks in their eyes as if they were about to indulge themselves on their last meal. Several pairs of women were eagerly removing each other's clothing, the air thick with a sense of abandon. It became evident that it didn't matter what gender you were here—there was a palpable freedom, and no hint of discrimination could be felt.

A clattering of dishes falling to the floor beside me made me jump. A woman had been lifted onto the edge of the table; her clothing now bunched around her middle. Her legs were entwined around the waist of a broad, naked male who was pumping his hips into her in wild, jerky movements, entirely unrestrained. Her face was buried in his neck as she sucked and nipped the skin there.

Averting my gaze, I cleared my throat as I tried to focus on a brick high up on the wall on the opposite side of the throne room, my go-to distraction technique. What a lovely brick—a very, *very* interesting brick.

"What is going on?" I asked Sienna quietly, shifting my focus to the next brick on the wall. I wondered how long it would take me to count them all—perhaps all night? I silently prayed that would be the case.

"It's the shadows," she responded just as quietly. "Powerful Shadow Whisperers can influence people's emotions—lust, rage, sadness, you name it."

I already knew this, but witnessing it unfold before me was an entirely different experience.

Remembering what had happened earlier in the dungeon and how Lucius' shadows had affected me, I glanced back toward the throne. 'Blake' still stood next to the King, and it occurred to me why he must be there—the shadows must be *his*, not the King's.

As if sensing my attention, Blake turned toward me, and our eyes locked. My posture stiffened involuntarily. Reaching into the pocket of his emerald tunic, Blake pulled out a sheet of parchment and handed it to the King. King Aadhar opened it and read over it for several minutes before looking back up to ask Blake a question. Blake raised his gaze back to mine and extended one of his lean, muscular arms, pointing in my direction. My stomach plummeted at the gesture. What could they possibly want with me?

Looking back at the King, I saw that his masked face was now turned toward Sienna and me. He raised a large hand and beckoned us over with a casual wave. I glanced at Sienna, who did the same, her mouth tight in an expression of concern and curiosity.

"Do we go?" I asked her, praying she would say it was fine to leave.

"We have to." She whispered in a defeated tone, placing her hand against the small of my back, much like she had earlier, and gently urged me toward the dais.

Trying to keep my attention on the King as I ascended the steps of the platform was no easy task. I found myself having to look down several times to see where I was stepping, and it was difficult not to glance at the crows, who continued their intimate displays without a care in the world.

One of the women had grasped a small hand around my left ankle and had yanked on me with impressive strength, encouraging me to join in on their *fun*. Sienna, who was also much stronger than she looked, had managed to pull me free and proceeded to kick the woman's hand away. I had winced at the crunch of bone that Sienna's boot caused when it made contact with the woman's fingers, but the crow didn't seem to notice and had just continued to ride the male beneath her.

"Aela Everflame," the King said, his voice so reminiscent of Lucius's that a chill ran down my spine. "Or shall I call you '*War Bringer*'?"

Blake's shoulders stiffened almost imperceptibly at the King's words.

"I beg your pardon, Your Majesty?" I replied, trying to project the strongest, most confident tone I could muster. Lex would have been proud.

"One of your Queen's minions has been in touch, demanding your return," Aadhar stated, stroking the feathers at the base of his mask as he assessed me from head to toe. "Tell me, Miss Everflame, why would the

Queen be so concerned about ensuring you are returned to Olympia in one piece?"

I frowned at him. "I don't know Queen Elena, Your Majesty. I can't imagine she even knows who I am."

"See for yourself, my dear."

The King handed me the piece of parchment that Blake had given him only moments before. The red of the Olympian Armies seal still evident at the top.

"For the Consideration of His Royal Majesty, King Aadhar,

It has come to our Queen's attention that you have captured a first-year Cadet by the name of Aela Everflame. We seek to understand your interest in this Cadet; however, we must express our unequivocal disapproval of any violence against one of the Queen's own.

You may be interested to know that the recent barbaric attack on Solarus' soil left behind an injured but living man. While we initially believed that the Uprising were responsible for the violence throughout our Realm, the results of our subsequent interrogations have proven to be incredibly enlightening.

Should you return our Cadet within one month of receiving this letter—unharmed—to the Guardians of the Passage, or to the Docks of Orouras, we may consider leniency regarding your heinous actions across our half of the Continent.

If you choose to disregard this request, we will view this as an act of war, and Anka shall face the full might of Her Majesty's army.

Let this letter be considered an act of mercy from Queen Elena.

*Yours sincerely,
General Zaneer."*

CHAPTER THIRTY-THREE

Sienna and I had been excused from the ball after The King had hounded me with questions regarding my relationship with Queen Elena. I could see the flicker of frustration in his eyes as he quickly became uninterested in my useless replies, mainly because I had never even met her, let alone knew her personally.

Once dismissed, Sienna had reluctantly taken my arm, guiding me away from the opulence of the ballroom, its gilded decor and laughter echoing behind us. The atmosphere shifted from vibrant and alive to cold and oppressive as we navigated the stone corridors back toward the dungeon. The hallways felt frigid, each gust of air creeping in from the stone walls like an unwelcomed ghost, the memory of the warm fireplaces in the throne room now feeling long forgotten. Two guards trailed us closely, their presence feeling like a looming shadow behind us as their heavy tread filled the silence of the passageways. My steps were beginning to feel heavy as we descended the staircase back towards my cell, the moon-powder clearly starting to wear off. I was so tired. All I wanted was a bed — a soft pillow to rest my head on, or even just a warm blanket to wrap around myself. I had no idea how I was going to survive in this cold, especially now in the sheer material of my dress.

Once we reached my cell, Sienna hesitated, her eyes scanning the dim corridor to ensure we were alone. With a resigned sigh, she opened my cell's bars, re-fastened the chains to my bracelets, then secured my ankles to the steel shackles anchored to the cold stone floor, which only allowed me to move about five feet or so. Each clink of metal echoed in the small space, a sound that was starting to become all too familiar. Her hands trembled slightly as she secured the locks, and I could sense her reluctance. It was a silent acknowledgment of my plight, one that filled me with a mix of gratitude and despair.

"I wish things were different." She murmured, her voice barely above a whisper. I offered her a small, bittersweet smile, knowing full well that there was little hope for change.

•••

As the days blurred into weeks, I truly started to lose faith that I would ever be free again. The guards, thankfully, had grown bored of my fragility and had ceased taunting me through the bars of my cage after a few days. One guard, Lennox, whom the others called Len, had even started sneaking me extra portions of bread. Granted, it was stale, but it made all the difference when I was only getting one meal a day. After weeks at sea and weeks in the cell, my already lean body now resembled a bag of bones. My ribs had started to protrude from my chest, and any minor womanly curves I had once possessed were now non-existent. I had no doubt I could probably pass for a child if I really wanted to.

The tears I had quietly let fall in the middle of the night for Mei, Leena, and the crushing weight of my situation had long since dried up, leaving only the faintest sting in their wake. The grief that once felt so sharp had faded into a dull ache. I no longer allowed myself to mourn, although their faces still plagued my nightmares. Thoughts of Nathaniel, Nanny Rosie, or the children at the orphanage barely skimmed the surface of my mind, like distant memories fading with every passing day. In truth, I didn't think of much at all anymore. I had become a ghost of myself, existing only in the present, where the cold, the hunger and the endless hours blurred together into a single, unending moment.

On my second day in the cell, I found a small rock and had started using it to draw lines on the stone wall next to me every time the day turned to night, when I got my meal. There were twenty-six lines on the wall now. I had been here almost a month, which meant that the King would rather risk a war than return me home.

Sienna had visited me a few times, normally when the guards had changed shifts, as though she feared being seen. She would appear as if emerging from the shadows themselves, the sounds of her light footsteps rarely filling the space. She was a woman of few words, but each time she appeared, there was a quiet defiance in the small acts of rebellion she offered. Whenever she could, she managed to sneak me scraps of food—dried bread, a small chunk of cheese, and occasionally a meagre piece of cured meat. But the most significant act of kindness came last week when she smuggled in a thicker blanket. The woollen one I had been given on the boat was rough and thin, offering little protection against the ever-deepening chill that seemed to grow more severe with every passing day.

For a moment, wrapped in the warmth of that clean, fur-lined quilt, I had felt a little more like a human-being, rather than a caged animal. It had been almost enough to make me feel something, something akin to gratitude—*almost*. But of course, my brief comfort didn't last. The next morning, when the guards spotted me curled up beneath the quilt, they didn't hesitate. It was snatched from my grasp, and even my original, tattered blanket was taken as punishment. I was left shivering in the same dress from the masquerade ball—a dress that had been designed for beauty, not for warmth. It had now been six nights since my blankets were taken from me, and I hadn't gotten much sleep since. Between my constant shivering, malnutrition, and the steel that drained my energy, I realised I was probably going to die here.

I had come to this grim realisation several hours ago. The thought had crept in quietly, as though it were an inevitability rather than a sudden shock. I waited for the familiar surge of panic, that frantic rush of adrenaline—the fight or flight response that would push me to scream, to thrash, to do anything to escape. But it never came. Instead, I was left with an overwhelming emptiness, a detachment that clung to me like a wet blanket. Some might call this acceptance, or even bravery, but I knew the truth. It was just a sign that I had given up—that I had stopped fighting, stopped hoping, stopped feeling anything at all; just a thick, suffocating numbness.

The grim reality was that I was now starting to welcome the idea of death. I was just so cold, so tired, so *done*. I had stopped asking why I was being kept here, because no answer ever came. There seemed to be no reason for my captivity—no clear purpose for why someone would go to the trouble of trapping me and keeping me alive. What did I have to offer? A flicker of magic and a knack for memorising historical texts? Reciting Olympia's last ten rulers hardly seemed like a good enough reason for Blake, or should I say, *Lucius*, to keep me locked away. How was he convincing the King to keep me here and risk a war... did the King even know I was still here?

Just as I watched the last ray of light disappear from the window at the end of the cell corridor, I heard boots shuffling from the other end towards the winding staircase that led to the above level. Expecting to hear Len's footsteps, which I had come to recognise, I was surprised to hear several sets of them instead. Len came into view in front of my cell bars and offered me a small but hesitant smile. Weird; he had never done that before. Two more guards stood behind him, their eyes unable to meet mine, instead focusing on a spot on the wall just above my head.

Cowards.

The guards all wore a less ornate version of the Elite's uniform: a green tunic with a gold embroidered patch just above their right breast, the opposite spot to where the Olympian Army wore their crest. The Ankan crest was made up of two swords crossed over a full moon, with crow's wings outstretched on either side, honouring one of Nykus' forms. All I could think of whenever I saw the wings was the young girl who had knelt at the King's feet, knowing she would be the next to join his harem of crows. I wondered what misery she had faced in the last month since I had seen her last.

All three guards also wore dark fur-lined cloaks that covered their swords and daggers, presumably because temperatures had dropped so low over the last few days. *Lucky them.*

In the early days of my captivity, when I still had a morsel of strength, I had reached for one of Len's daggers when he came to deliver my evening meal. I don't know what drove me—perhaps a need for protection, or perhaps the dark thought of ending my misery on my own terms. Len let me graze the handle before stepping back. I had scurried to the back of my cell like a terrified cockroach, bracing for a beating that never came.

One small mercy was that no guard had entered my cell without reason. I could have easily faced worse: attacks, torture, rape, but none of that had happened. It made me question the truth behind the stories of the King we were told about as children—tales of his insatiable thirst for violence and pain. The only real assaults I had endured were Lucius' whispering shadows on my first day and the guards tearing my blankets away.

"You've been summoned," Len said in a low voice. I frowned in confusion, realising that it was the first time I had heard Len speak. His voice was deep but non-descript. I had no doubt I would forget it as quickly as I heard it.

"By whom?" I croaked back, my throat dry. I hadn't had any water today, and it showed.

"You've been invited to dine in the King's quarters tonight."

...

After detaching my ankles from their shackles, Len and his comrades led me up several flights of stairs to the floor above Sienna's bed chambers and the Throne Room. I felt sick to my stomach from the movement, my muscles weak from being curled up against the wall for so long, and my energy still being drained from my steel bracelets. I had to stop several times to catch my breath during the journey, and I knew that Len was tempted to carry me when I had to stop for the eighth time.

The hallway on the second level resembled the one below, though there were fewer doorways. Presumably, the King only shared this level with those he trusted most, and I found myself wondering if Lucius Blake had a room up here.

Len stopped in front of a small door and pulled a key from his cloak pocket. The door bore only a few markings, and the key was unremarkable.

"This is the King's entryway?" I asked, slightly disappointed. Len scoffed at my question.

"No, this is a bath chamber. You will know when you reach the King's quarters; they're hard to miss. But I don't think your company will appreciate a dinner companion who smells like piss and shit."

He wasn't wrong; I probably did stink. I had definitely gone nose-blind over the past few weeks, but the fact that I hadn't washed in almost a month, had been relieving myself into a bucket, and that several rags tossed in through the bars every morning were all I had to clean myself up with, hadn't really crossed my mind on the walk up here. Trying to keep the nausea at bay had been my only focus.

Len unlocked the door and swung it inward, revealing a small antechamber with a copper tub, several steaming buckets of water already beside it. A toilet, and a sink with a mirror above, also inhabited the space. Len led me in by my wrist, unlocking the interlocking chain between my bracelets as he did, holding me much more gently than I expected. He proceeded to fill the tub with the buckets of water, and I was relieved that I didn't have to be the one trying to lift them. I began to remove my dress from my skeletal frame. Len looked over his shoulder and stopped mid-pour.

"What are you doing?" he asked, shocked.

"Undressing," I responded blandly, shrugging off the dirty velvet dress, my miserable undergarments, and my oversized boots. I perched my naked self atop the toilet seat and pulled off my socks very slowly. To my relief, the nail beds that had previously shown signs of infection several weeks ago had almost completely healed. I curled my lip at how ugly my toes looked without nails, but beggars couldn't be choosers, *literally*. Clearly, the bath I took in Sienna's room and the fact that I hadn't removed the shoes and socks had given them time to heal on their own.

Len finished pouring the last bucket of water and quickly turned his back to me. I scoffed at his reaction. I was fairly sure he had seen me shit in a bucket, but this was where he drew the line on modesty?

As I lowered myself into the tub on shaky arms, I couldn't help but let out a moan. Len had added some lilac liquid soap to the water, and the scent filled my nose in the most delicious way, the smell reminding me of Sienna. I dunked my head beneath the surface and held my breath for several moments, enjoying the warmth that surrounded me from head to toe. It was so *good* to feel warm again, to not be shivering.

As I surfaced for air, I saw that Len had cracked open the door and was taking a small parcel from someone on the other side. He turned back to me, eyes looking everywhere and anywhere apart from at me, and set the parcel down on the toilet seat with a few measured steps. Unwrapping it, he pulled out a towel, a black tunic, black breeches, a navy-blue cloak, and a small tin. *Moon-powder.* He quickly removed some socks, undergarments, and a bandeau for my chest, flinging them onto the rest of the pile like they were going to burn him. Swiftly, still averting his gaze from me, he turned his back and made his way to the door.

"A hairbrush and cosmetics are in the cabinet under the sink, as well as a toothbrush and mint paste. The soap by the sink smells of orange, and Sienna told me to tell you that it's a good way to perfume your skin on your wrists and neck once you're dry. It might feel a little sticky at first, but you'll get used to it."

"You know Sienna?" I asked quietly.

"Yes," Len responded. "She's somewhat of a friend. I told her you were cold and let her bring you a blanket. I should have known better." I could hear the shame coating his words, and the hard stone that had formed around my heart softened slightly.

"It's not your fault, Len. You've done all you can to make my imprisonment..." I searched for the right word, "...survivable," I settled on. Len let out a sigh, and his shoulders drooped slightly.

"We don't know why you're here," he said over his shoulder, "all we know is that we are to keep our distance from you and that we cannot hurt you. Most prisoners are executed or tortured to death after a few days."

Well, there went my theory about the King being a big ol' softy under all those rumours.

"Why are you telling me this, Len?"

"Because the King needs you for something… Aela," he said my name awkwardly, as if it were unnatural for him to treat a prisoner like a human. "Which means you have leverage. Try and use it."

CHAPTER THIRTY-FOUR

Well, Len was right about knowing when you reached The King's quarters. The doorway that Len had led me through only moments before was almost as ornate as the one that led to the Throne Room—tall, arched, and made of dark, polished wood, intricately carved with swirling patterns and symbols I couldn't decipher. Two guards, clad in crease-free emerald tunics, stood at attention on either side of the doors, their expressions stoic with assessing eyes that never left me as I passed.

Len politely excused himself, and I now found myself awkwardly standing in a grand foyer that led to a spacious living area. To my left, a large dining table made of a rich wood was set with eight velvet red chairs, each one tucked neatly beneath the table's edge, as though waiting for guests who might never arrive. To the right, a sizable, plush cream-coloured settee was framed by two leather armchairs set at an angle, pointing toward a fireplace with a roaring fire. On instinct, I edged closer, trying to soak up its warmth; my fingers tingling as the heat of the flames seeped into my bones. There was a small table to the left of one of the armchairs, with a decanter of amber liquid set atop it, and a glass next to it that appeared to be partially drained.

I barely had time to take it all in before a voice, low and dark, rumbled from behind me. It wrapped around me like a velvet ribbon, smooth and dangerous, reminding me of satin sheets and stolen kisses.

"So, we meet again, Aela Everflame."

The words felt like a caress, but they made the hairs on the back of my neck stand on end. I spun around instinctively, irritated at my own lapse in judgment for turning my back to one of the doors. There, framed in a doorway to what I presumed were the inner chambers, stood a lean, imposing figure. The predatory stillness of his presence made gooseflesh break out across my skin.

He wore simple leather breeches and a white shirt—casual, yet elegant in its simplicity. The top few buttons of his shirt were undone, revealing a dusting of dark hair that trailed down into the collar. There was something deceptively ordinary about his attire, but it didn't fool me. Everything about him screamed power, from the sharpness of his features to the way he held himself. I tried not to stare, but he was breathtakingly beautiful, as if the Gods had taken extra time to craft such a masterpiece.

I would have placed him in the latter part of his third decade, though the power of the crown not only granted the ruler immortality but also slowed the aging of their inner circle as well. This man could have been a thousand years old for all I knew. His chestnut brown hair fell to his shoulders in loose waves, and his dark green eyes sparkled as if they were the only light in the room. There was something unnervingly familiar about him, though I couldn't say what. I was certain I had never met him before, despite his claims. His cheekbones were sharp, his jawline a sculpted work of art, with several days' worth of stubble darkening the skin along his chin.

I caught myself staring a little too long before tearing my eyes away and blinking nervously, surprised at how his presence seemed to hold my attention there a moment longer than was comfortable.

"I don't believe we've met," I finally said, breaking the silence. My voice came out rougher than I intended, and I cleared my throat to hide the brief uncertainty that crept into me.

"You wound me, my dear. Did I not make a memorable first impression when you first arrived?"

The words made my stomach tighten, and I felt a flash of something stir deep inside me—a mixture of recognition and something far more unsettling. My mind spun, sifting through the fog of memories from the past month, trying to place where I might have seen him before. And then, as if a light flicked on in the dark, realisation struck.

"Lucius," I whispered, the name slipping out before I could stop it. I meant it more to myself than anything else. A small part of me had expected to meet the King himself tonight, not… *him*.

A wide grin spread across his face then, half-mocking, half-pleased with himself. He opened his arms in an exaggerated gesture, giving me a mock bow, as though relishing the moment.

"The one and only," he responded with a flourish, as if he had just performed some great and marvellous trick.

Straightening, he took a few steps toward me, his presence pulling the space between us taut. With an easy gesture, he motioned toward the grand dining table behind us.

"Please," he said, his tone suddenly all charm, "it would be an honour if you were to dine with me this evening."

. . .

Ten minutes later, after having awkwardly settled myself onto one of the red velvet dining chairs while several servants brought in countless trays of sizzling food, I could hardly contain my drool as I took in the roasted meats and vegetables set before me. The only time I had eaten anything like this in the past few weeks, months, was at the Night of Shadows ball, and the revelations of that night had made the food taste like ash on my tongue.

Once the servants left, I proceeded to stack food onto my plate like it was my last meal—which, it very well might have been—and dug in with as much grace as a feral beast, not waiting for Lucius to start. Lucius, thankfully, didn't interrupt me and let me devour half of the contents of my plate before speaking.

"You do realise if you don't slow down, that's going to come right back up?" he said in a taunting tone that distantly reminded me of someone. I decided to ignore him and carried on with even more vigour just to spite him. I leaned forward to take several large gulps of water from the glass set next to me.

"I could've poisoned your food, you know. Did that even occur to you?"

I shrugged. "I'm going to die here anyway; might as well find some enjoyment where I can."

I looked up from my plate to meet his shining green eyes and noticed that he was frowning at me.

"Why do you say that?" he asked.

I raised one arm and showed him one of the bracelets surrounding my wrist.

"Firstly, this *lovely* piece of jewellery is practically draining the life from me. Secondly," I raised my fingers as I counted, "I've had no blankets for the last week, with just the flimsy dress I wore to the ball providing the only protection from the freezing temperatures of the dungeons. And thirdly, I've lost so much weight from the measly scraps that get passed through the bars each evening that I'm surprised I've lasted this long."

I swallowed the contents in my mouth, not caring that I'd been talking with my mouth full, and that several chunks of food had landed on the table as I spoke.

Lucius was seemingly silenced by my proclamation. Content with this, I resumed gorging myself on a chicken leg, picking it up with my fingers and tearing the meat from the bone like a bear.

"I didn't realise you were suffering so much; I can only apologise for your treatment so far," he said after several moments.

I let out a huff. His apology was worthless, no better than pissing in the wind.

Setting down the chicken bone, I wiped the juices on my trouser leg.

"So, why am I here, Lucius? Why did you and Naz go through all this effort to capture me and keep me here? You know there could be a war over this, right? You read Queen Elena's letter, she gave you a month, but I'm still here."

Lucius's left eye twitched at my direct questioning, but I swore I saw a glimmer of approval cross his face.

"Why don't we retire to the more comfortable seats by the fire, and I'll answer your questions?"

I stood from the table eagerly, relieved that I didn't sway on the spot. The calories from my meal, the water I'd guzzled between mouthfuls, and the moon-powder I had inhaled, were clearly doing their jobs at replenishing some of my energy.

With both of us now seated in the plush leather armchairs, the fire warming my legs, I relaxed into the backrest. Lucius handed me a fresh glass and poured me some of the amber liquid from the decanter, filling his own swiftly after. I took a swig and almost coughed it back up. It tasted like molten lava and burned a trail all the way to my stomach.

"Before I answer any of your questions, tell me about this man that you love… Nathaniel, is it?"

I almost choked on my drink again at his question. How did he know about Nathaniel? He clearly saw the look of confusion on my face and let out a dark chuckle.

"I've got spies everywhere, Ms. Everflame. I wouldn't be doing my job properly if I didn't know everything there was to know about those who reside within this castle." He took a large gulp of his drink, and I was envious of how effortlessly he swallowed it. "Have you fucked him?" he asked over his glass, his green eyes burning into mine.

My mouth hung open at his brazen question, and I felt my cheeks heat. Another laugh left his mouth before he continued.

"Ah, I forget how prudish you Olympians are," he waved a hand as if to dismiss the shock on my face. "I was only interested in who you were imagining in the dungeon when we first met, that's all."

My mouth snapped shut, and I shot a glare in his direction. I would've loved nothing more than to wrap my bony fingers around his perfectly sculpted throat and throttle him, but the answers to my questions were too important.

"Tell me why I'm here," I said through gritted teeth, the amber liquid making me feel bold.

"Not until you answer my question."

"Yes."

"Yes, *what*?"

"Yes, I have… *slept* with him." I clenched my jaw so hard I was surprised my teeth didn't crack from the force.

Lucius's smug smile teased at my anger, but I clamped it down, reaching for the numbness within me that I'd grown so accustomed to since Olos. Gods, had that really been two months ago? Lucius leaned back in his armchair and rotated his wrist in a circular motion, swirling the liquid in his tumbler.

"I've only ever loved one woman in my long life. You remind me so much of her. You have the same hair, the same colour eyes, but there's also a feistiness within you, a *spark,* that reminds me of her most of all." A small smile tugged at his lips, much gentler than anything I had ever seen from him before. His expression changed in an instant, and the menacing smile from the dungeon spread across his face once more. "I wonder whether you would enjoy fucking me more than your Nathaniel, though."

Before I had time to process what he had said, the room darkened between one heartbeat and the next, and his shadows reached toward me, just like they did when we first met. I recoiled away from them, now knowing what their touch could do, but I had nowhere to go. As soon as they touched my skin, whispers entered my mind, growing louder with every breath, drowning out all of my own thoughts.

My nipples peaked and molten heat began to gather between my legs as the voices consumed me. My whole body came alive, my dormant energy flaring to life once more. His shadows completely enveloped me, and I struggled to suck in enough air into my lungs. Images flashed in my mind once more, but I could make out the faces of the couple this time. I released a gasp as I recognised Lucius, and then myself. My hair was tousled and spread out behind me on a pillow as I laid on my back, surrounded by luxurious furs, on a large four-poster bed at least twice the size of Sienna's. My cheeks were flushed pink, and I was panting in anticipation, gazing up at Lucius like he was the moon in the sky. My body was more curvaceous than how I was now and sweat glistened off my full, round breasts. I looked healthy, beautiful, *alive*.

A naked Lucius was propped above me, his biceps rippling as he supported his weight. He adjusted himself slightly so his weight was supported on his left side. Raising his right hand, he trailed a delicate line from my collarbone to my left breast with deft fingers. Distantly, I could feel his shadow hands following the same path whilst I remained seated in the armchair.

Cupping my breast with his hand, he lowered his mouth to swirl a warm tongue over my nipple and a raspy moan left my lips both in the vision and in the present. He lifted his head from my breast and stared up at my face hungrily as his hand released its grasp. I whimpered slightly, desperate for his touch and a small, crooked smile graced his beautiful face. He used two fingers to trail a line down my body, his touch feather light as it travelled across my ribs, the flat plane of my stomach, then lower. Finally, after an agonising moment, it drifted towards the aching space between my legs. In the present, a keening noise escaped my mouth, and I parted my legs to allow the shadows more access. I could feel my hips starting to rock back and forth in the armchair as the invisible fingers of his shadows dipped below the loose waistband of my trousers, and rubbed circles around the sensitive bundle of nerves just above my core. In my vision, I watched as Lucius plunged his two fingers inside of me; my wetness clearly evident as he moved them in and out of me. His shadow fingers expertly moved my undergarments to the side, and pushed themselves deep inside of me, stroking the exact spot that craved their touch. They felt as if they were growing and expanding with every thrust and buck that I offered them. My breath came out in short gasps and my head slammed back against the armchair's backrest behind me so hard that I saw stars behind my eyelids. I had never felt lust like this; it was all encompassing.

I bit my lower lip as I felt my climax rising. Raising one of my wrists, my hand squeezed one of my breasts to add some pain to the experience, a sensation I didn't realise I craved until this very moment. His shadows encapsulated my hand to squeeze myself harder, and I felt myself on the very verge of losing control. A small ember of power fluttered inside of me, and I knew that if it weren't for my steel bracelets suppressing my magic, my flames would be racing along my skin, igniting the armchair and everything else in the nearby vicinity. The shadows that were wrapped around my hand expanded and reached towards my neck. I expected to feel the pressure of them wrapping around my throat, I weirdly wanted them to, but instead, I felt an absence of weight on my chest. I reluctantly peeled open my eyes, the vision of myself and Lucius disappearing, to see that my stone necklace was levitating amongst a bed of shadows, hovering over where it normally sat just above the swell of my breasts.

"My sweet, naïve girl," Lucius purred, "you really have no idea what this stone is do you?" He tsked at me like I was an ignorant child. "It's a shame that poor girl from Shangnon got so close to you, such a powerful Shade; a clever one too. She was the only one who had truly started putting things together after all these years. Nazakeel had no choice in the matter really, he had to get rid of her. That being said, the theatrics of it all weren't exactly to my taste, that boy sure does love to get a reaction." He chuckled fondly, as if he wasn't talking about his son murdering someone.

My body froze. He was talking about Mei. It was Nazakeel, Kieran, that killed Mei – because of me? But why?

BOOM.

A loud sound from just outside appeared to shake the very earth itself; the ancient walls of the castle seemed to tremble and groan under the weight of the force.

I opened my eyes wide, my impending climax and thoughts about Mei completely forgotten. Lucius' shadows dissipated, and he bolted out of his armchair towards the window that sat just behind the dining table, his arousal still evident just below his waistband.

My body lay limp in the armchair, but strangely enough, shame didn't sear through me like it had during Lucius' first visit. I wasn't sure what that said about me—whether it was because I had grown numb or something else entirely—but I chose not to focus on it. Instead, I watched Lucius' back as he stood motionless at the window, his posture rigid, his attention fixed on something beyond the glass. Several long moments passed in silence, with no explanation for the noise that had shattered the stillness.

"What is it?" I croaked; my voice hoarse. I cleared it, trying to shake the rasp that clung to my words. "What was that sound?"

"An explosion."

CHAPTER THIRTY-FIVE

Another loud bang sounded as Len burst through the extravagant double door mere moments later.

"Apologies for the intrusion, but your brother believes we are under attack and said that you are needed… at once… sir," Len stammered at Lucius, a hand raised to his head in salute, slightly out of breath from wherever he had clearly run from.

Lucius turned from the window to face Len, an exasperated look on his face.

"No shit, Lennox, I'm not deaf. Pray tell, where does Bastian believe he can order me to go, Captain?" Lucius said, his tone dripping with sarcasm.

Captain. Interesting. *Bastian.* Even more interesting. That must be the King's first name.

"He said you're needed in the armoury, sir... I mean, y.. your Majesty, your Highness...sir." The Captain stammered, offering another salute with a shaky hand. I had never seen Len so flustered and dare I say, intimidated.

"That's all the way on the other side of the castle." Lucius stroked a palm down his face, a sign of weariness. He let out a sigh as he reached for an overcoat draped over the back of one of the red dining chairs. "Lennox, please take Miss Everflame back to the dungeons. Going forward, make sure she has a blanket."

My heart sank at his words. Although I was grateful to hear I'd at least be slightly warmer going forward, a small part of me had hoped this meal was a peace offering—that maybe Lucius wanted to get to know me as a person, not just his prisoner. That perhaps he would have spoken to his brother about my living conditions. Even though a part of me knew I wouldn't be set free, I'd secretly hoped I'd at least be given my own room. Nothing as lavish as Sienna's, of course, but I'd never wanted a bed and a working toilet so desperately before.

Numbly, I rose to my feet and took several paces toward Len, putting my hands behind my back so he could easily restrain me. He latched the familiar chain to both of my steel bracelets and led me toward the doors.

"It was a pleasure getting to know you, Aela, and I trust that whatever the shadows showed you will come to pass," Lucius called after me as Len led me away from the King's quarters. A shiver of dread tingled down my neck as I remembered the vision of us both in his bed. I kept walking, ensuring my inner walls of numbness remained strong.

As Captain Len and I walked the many corridors from the King's quarters back to the dungeons, Len continuously glanced over his shoulder every few steps.

"What are you *doing*?" I asked, after what felt like the tenth time of him doing so. Every time I had met Len, he had been composed, showing little emotion, but now he seemed almost frantic. "Why are you so nervous? Is it because the castle is under attack?"

"We are not under attack," Len said in a clipped tone, pushing my shoulder with his free hand to hurry me along.

"How do you know?" I asked, trying to turn my head to see his face once more, but he pushed me forward again, rougher this time, and I stumbled.

Catching me by the wrist so I didn't faceplant into the ground, he whispered, "Because the explosion is a distraction."

I frowned at his words as I continued to walk. What could a distraction be needed for, and how did he know about it? We finally reached the stairs leading down to the dungeon, and a wave of nausea hit me so suddenly that I staggered, my meal threatening to rise. The stench of damp stone and mildew already clung to the air, and just the thought of returning to that cold, suffocating place twisted my stomach into tight knots. How much longer could I endure this? How much longer before I broke? Before the darkness, the filth, the constant feeling of being caged like an animal, snuffed out the final bit of fight left within me, and devoured me fully? I felt the weight of it pressing down on me, suffocating every last spark of hope. Pressure gathered behind my eyes, but I couldn't cry.

{Please, Gods, if you're up there, please don't make me go back down there. I'll do anything. Just don't make me go.}

Len pushed my shoulder again to urge me forward, and I took a step toward the staircase. "Not that way." He whispered quietly. "Just keep walking. End of the hall."

"Huh?" I responded, confused. He didn't answer but continued to paw at my shoulder, directing me further down the corridor. On hesitant feet, I crept past the staircase toward the end of the hallway, where a knight's full armour—reminding me of a mummified soldier—was displayed in a corner that led to an adjoining corridor. I recognised the route from when Sienna had led me to her chambers the night of the ball.

Len tugged lightly on the chain shackles of my wrist as we reached the knight, a small twinge of pain shooting up both of my arms.

"Are we stopping?" I whispered.

"Quiet!"

Len reached forward and rotated one of the knight's fingers, and a faint click sounded as it turned ninety degrees. A few seconds passed, but nothing happened. I looked back at the Captain, a scowl already forming on my face.

"If you've dragged me up here just for me to watch you play with a metal fing…"

A loud screeching sound cut off my snide remark. Snapping my eyes back to the knight, I opened my mouth in shock as I saw the suit and the wall behind it rotating inward at an angle.

"I wish it wasn't this fucking loud," Len muttered, looking around us again. Distant voices began to sound from one of the staircases at the end of the hall as the screeching finally came to a stop.

"A secret doorway," I whispered in amazement. The gap was no more than two feet wide, meaning one would have to slide through sideways. A cold, damp breeze washed over my face from the small space.

"Hurry, it only holds for about twenty seconds before it closes," Len urged, pushing me forward, the movement feeling urgent.

As I shimmied my way through the small gap, I winced at the sound of my steel bracelets and chain scraping against the stone wall. Len followed closely behind me, grunting softly as his large frame barely fit through the narrow opening.

I let out a relieved gasp as I stumbled through the slither of the doorway into a large, dark corridor. I rasped out a cough and shook my head, trying to clear the cobwebs from my nose and lips. A large body crashed into mine as Len fell through the gap, clearly squeezed so tightly that he essentially popped out the other side. We both tumbled to the ground in a tangle of limbs, and I let out a hiss as my shoulder blade slammed into the floor, a sharp jolt of pain radiating through my left side.

"Shit, sorry Aela," Len whispered as he tried to move his body weight off mine.

"You'd benefit from a prison diet, you know. How much do you weigh?" I grunted as Len's body trapped the air in my lungs while he still lay atop me.

The screeching sound from the secret doorway started again as Len scrambled to his feet. The voices in the hall could now be heard over the noise, and my eyes widened in panic.

"Will they find us?"

Len reached forward once standing, put a hand under each of my armpits, and lifted me to my feet with ease. I felt like a limp ragdoll.

"Only a few of us know about the hidden passages, and I've made sure the guards working tonight are the ones that don't know they're here."

A small ball of flame formed in the Captain's hand, lighting up the space around us. I openly gawked at him as the heat pressed against my skin.

"You're a Flame," I said, shocked.

Len nodded.

"The King likes to collect us. I was captured from near the wall many years ago. I was given a choice, live my life as one of the crows, or as part of his personal guard." Len motioned for me to turn around while he reached into his pocket for the key to my chain shackles.

"Why didn't you try to escape? You know the Queen would protect you. She'd probably make you a member of the Olympian Army if you could prove you could fight." I asked him over my shoulder as he unlocked the chains from my bracelets and threw them to the floor.

"The King constantly reminds us that he always has eyes on our loved ones. I don't have much, but I would live my life in service to a monster if it meant keeping my baby sister safe."

"Where does she think you are?" I asked softly as I turned back to look at him, absently rubbing the skin around my bracelets.

"Dead," he said gruffly. "Now hurry up, your friends don't have long."

My stomach did a somersault at his words.

"My friends?"

"Yeah, they're with Sienna. A man and a mean-looking small woman."

For the first time in a month, a surge of hope crashed through me, wild and overwhelming.

Nathaniel had come.

The man I'd secretly prayed for in these long, agonising weeks. And Lex—Lex was here too. The thought alone took my breath away. She'd surprised me yet again, proving to be far more loyal than I'd ever given her credit for. It was a bittersweet sting in my chest, knowing how much I'd underestimated her. I struggled to blink away the hot, sudden flood of tears that burned behind my eyes, turns out I could cry. My lower lip trembled, despite my best effort to stop it.

Len pulled a small, unlit torch from a wall sconce, and a flickering flame sprung to life at the end of it with a quick twist of his wrist. He handed it to me with a brief nod, his silent command urging me forward. The weight of the torch was heavier than I'd expected, dragging at my arm. I rolled my injured shoulder, wincing at the sharp flare of pain that shot through it. It was still sore, but the relief of knowing it wasn't dislocated made it more bearable.

With the torch in my hand, and my heart pounding with a fierce mix of anticipation and fear, I turned on my heel and walked forward, more determined than I'd ever been. For the first time in a long while, I didn't feel alone.

CHAPTER THIRTY-SIX

We walked for what felt like hours. The darkness of the corridors seemed to close in on me, the passageways feeling never-ending. Adrenaline coursed through my veins, making me twitchy, every sound making me flinch. From the small drops of water that cascaded down the damp walls to the scurrying of rodents that had taken refuge in this forgotten place, clearly deeming it safer here than the castle's main corridors. I didn't blame them, honestly.

"How much longer?" I whispered to Len, wiping sweat from my brow as the flames from my torch continued to heat my face.

"Just a little farther. We should see the light at the end very soon."

As if on cue, a faint glow appeared at the end of the next corridor we turned down. It was only about a hundred feet away. I quickened my pace, my heart starting to pound in my chest.

{Almost there. Freedom. Nathaniel. Lex.}

The words blotted out all other thoughts, driving me forward. My steps quickened, as if ready to break into a run, but a large hand gripped my tender shoulder, halting me. A small yelp escaped me at the sharp tug of pain.

"Not yet. We need to wait for our signal."

"What signal?" I asked, frustration creeping into my voice. I shook my shoulder, trying to dislodge his hand, but he didn't release me.

"You'll know it when you hear it."

We stood in silence for what felt like an eternity, when realistically, it was probably no more than twenty minutes. My foot began to tap impatiently, and my lower lip caught between my teeth as I nibbled on it anxiously. I kept glancing at Len, but he was as still and unreadable as ever, staring ahead with grim focus.

"Are you sure we haven't missed it?" I said finally, my voice tinged with annoyance as I threw my hands up in exasperation like a petulant child. Len ducked back slightly, the flames from my makeshift torch dancing a little too close to his face.

"Believe me, Aela, there's no way we could miss it."

The minutes dragged on and I felt my anxiety reaching new heights. What were we waiting for? Why was it taking so long? Had something gone wrong?

Len finally broke the silence, halting my spiralling thoughts.

"I was there you know, I was the one who found you."

I frowned at his words. "At the attack in Solarus?"

Len shook his head. "No, in Thellas."

I stared at him, even more confused. "You were at the attack in Olos? I don't understand."

Len let out a weary sigh. "*Lennox* is my last name, a lot of people in Anka do not share their first name in respect to the King and his brother. But my first name, my real name… is Jesper."

"Jesper…" I said slowly, trying to rack my brain. I looked at his face. He was pale, with bronzed curly hair and brown eyes. He was attractive, but not someone who you would pay much attention to. Scanning his face, my eyes snagged on a mark just above his right temple. It was faint, so faint I hadn't noticed it before. I sucked in a deep breath.

"You were at the orphanage, in Thellas…"

Len pursed his lips and dipped his chin in confirmation.

"My aunt lives in Halydon and came for me when I was seven, after she learned my grandmother had given me up, so you won't really remember me, but I was the one who heard you crying the night you first arrived. You must have only been two years old, maybe three, when we left."

"We?" I asked.

"My aunt also took in Aggie, Agatha, one of the other orphans. We aren't related, but we shared a room for over three years and she became a sister to me. She's who I am protecting now, the reason I stay here."

Tears welled in my eyes.

"Is that why you've been sneaking me bread, letting Sienna visit me… why you're helping me now?"

"It's what Nanny Rosie would have wanted," Len looked away from me, a distant look of sadness crossing his face. "That's how I got caught. My aunt gave Aggie and me a great life in Halydon, but there was always a part of me that longed to return to Thellas. To see Rosie again, she was like a mother to me, y'know. I just wanted to see her, just one more time."

"But you didn't have a license or a Permit of Passage?"

"No," Len said gruffly. "I didn't have enough money. It was stupid really, reckless. But I was young, not much older than you are now, and I will have to live with my decision for the rest of my life." He turned back to me, his eyes sharp, a resolve hardening his expression. "I let down Aggie, but I won't do it with you. I saved you all those years ago, and I will save you again now."

BOOM.

Just as Len had finished speaking, another loud explosion rocked the very foundations beneath us. The sound was deafening, and I braced myself against the wall with my good arm, squeezing my eyes shut as debris and dust rained down. For a moment, the world seemed to shake apart.

"RUN!" Len shouted, grabbing my free hand and yanking me forward, his grip firm and urgent as he pulled me toward the light.

As Len and I burst through the end of the hallway, past the small sconce that had been guiding our way to the exit, I almost keeled over from exhaustion as a cool breeze hit my face. I had to clamp down on the vomit that lingered at the back of my throat, not used to this amount of physical activity since my capture—especially on a full stomach.

We emerged into a small clearing surrounded by sparse, thorny bushes. A cloaked figure stood nearby, nervously bobbing on anxious feet. The movement reminded me of myself just before Leena had walked us to Sephere's first lesson. Sorrow swelled in my chest at the memory of how kind my friend had been to me when we first met. Clearly, my inner walls, which had long kept my emotions contained, were starting to crumble.

"Drago!" Len shout-whispered from where we were camouflaged amongst the foliage. *Drago*. That was Oliver and Jaxon's last name.

The cloaked figure whipped around, and a small part of me expected to see Jaxon's or Oliver's faces under the hood from Len's use of their last name. The hood was pulled low, but there was no hiding the blazing red locks that peeked from beneath it.

Sienna.

She lifted one of her delicate hands and waved us over in a hurried motion.

Len and I moved swiftly toward her on quick, soundless feet. Once we were together, she reached up and closed a small fist around the end of my torch.

"What are you do—" My words cut off as the fire extinguished beneath her touch. I couldn't help but gape at her. "How did that not burn you?" I stared, flicking my gaze between the torch and Sienna, disbelief written across my face.

She offered no explanation apart from a small shrug.

"Where are the others?" Len interrupted my staring contest with the wooden stick.

"Near the river. Blake has sourced us a boat."

"Blake?" I guffawed. Why would Lucius be helping us when he'd just told Len to take me to the dungeons?

"He's the one who orchestrated the whole thing. He's been planning it with Len since the Night of Shadows," Sienna said over her shoulder as she turned to walk away. Like a little lamb trying to follow its mother, I started after Sienna, Len close behind me.

"Why would he do that? Didn't he want me locked up?"

"He said that Nykus came to him in a vision when his son was born. He never knew who the God was referring to, but when the Queen sent that letter and The King referred to you as the *war-bringer* at the ball, Blake knew he had to get you out—and that his son was a part of the prophecy," Len said, his voice steady as he walked behind me.

I got lost in thought as I stared at Sienna's back, trying to piece everything together, but nothing seemed to fit. Why would Lucius be breaking me out when he was the reason I was locked up, and what did Nazakeel, Kieran, have to do with anything?

A flicker of movement caught my eye, and I looked away from the back of Sienna's cloak. Three cloaked figures stood before a moonlit river in front of a small rowing boat—one significantly shorter than the other two.

I discarded my wooden stick without a second thought and broke into a sprint, all feelings of exhaustion and nausea forgotten.

{Almost there. Freedom. Nathaniel. Lex.}

The words blocked out all other thoughts.

I collided with Lex first, unsure which of the men was Nathaniel, and wrapped my arms around her. A small sob broke free from my throat. Well, the walls around my heart had well and truly crumbled now. Without hesitation, Lex wrapped her arms around me and squeezed me tightly.

"Shit, little mouse, where's the rest of you?" Lex moved her hands up and down my middle, clearly able to feel my bones through the thin fabric of my tunic and navy-coloured cloak. She pulled back, untied her thicker cloak from under her chin, and placed it around my shoulders. I let out a soul-deep sigh. It was fur-lined and still held Lex's body warmth. With the adrenaline, I hadn't quite grasped how cold I was; the cloak I'd been given was definitely for indoor wear only.

I took in Lex before me. She looked even more formidable than I remembered. Her fighting leathers peeked through under the layers of warm furs, and multiple daggers were strapped to a belt hanging low on her waist. Her long, almost black hair was plaited back off her face, reminding me of the dark-haired man who haunted my visions. Her face was set in a determined expression, but silver tears lined her dark eyes as she took me in. We held each other's gazes for a while until someone cleared their throat nearby.

"Miss Everflame, I don't believe we have formally met."

The familiar voice sent a chill down my spine, like someone walking over my grave. A tall, lean cloaked figure stepped forward toward Lex and me, and I instantly knew who it was. Removing his hood, I braced myself to insult Lucius for his antics, wishing people wouldn't play such ridiculous games.

"What do you mean we haven't m… wait, w…w… what?" I stammered, trying to process what I was seeing. The man was as handsome as Lucius, though his eyes appeared more grey than green in the dim light, and his hair was a darker brown as opposed to the golden chestnut I was expecting to see. His facial features were also slightly softer than Lucius', making him seem more approachable. But there was no mistaking that this man was a fighter. He stood even straighter than Lucius, and his gloved hand remained clasped around the pommel of the sword slung around his waist.

"You're not Lucius," I whispered.

"No, Miss Everflame, I am Bastian, his brother, though many know me as Blake, my late wife's maiden name. It's a pleasure to meet you properly. We didn't get a chance to speak at the Night of Shadows. I can only apologise for my brother's treatment of you up to this point."

I blinked at his words, and things finally started to click into place.

"I thought it was Lucius who went by the name Blake," I said with a trembling voice, my mind flashing back to the fox-masked Elite guard to the right of the King at the ball—the one I'd thought was Lucius. "Who is Lucius?" I asked in a quiet voice, but I didn't need Bastian to answer. I already knew.

King Lucius Aadhar.

How could I have been so stupid when I always prided myself on being smart? Of course, I had been in the King's quarters with the King, not his brother. It was The King whom I had shared dinner with. It was The King whom I had… pleasured myself in front of…. Twice. The realisation stripped back the final layer of numbness that I had been desperately clinging on to for composure.

Bastian saw the look on my face and chose to remain silent.

"Nathaniel?" I said softly, turning to the last remaining figure, hope in my voice. I needed my best friend. I needed the man I loved.

"He won't be coming within an inch of you," a low voice rumbled from under the hood of the cloak. I instantly recognised it. Rage surged within me, and I wished I still had my wooden stick to beat him over the head with it.

"*You.*" I hissed as I lunged toward him.

It was him.

Kieran Blake.

Kieran lurched back a step as Bastian and Lex stepped in front of him.

"What are you doing?!" I cried at Bastian and Lex. Len grabbed the back of my cloak and pulled me back as I frantically clawed at the air, trying to reach Kieran. "*He's* the reason I'm here! MOVE!" I squawked, sounding like a hysterical owl.

"Like fuck I am," Kieran responded, pulling the hood from his face. His hair was longer than before, and dark circles lined his silver eyes. He looked exhausted, but his high cheekbones and strong jaw left no doubt in my mind that he was related to The King.

"You are *Nazakeel*, you killed Mei, you're the reason Leena is dead!" I spat the words, saliva spraying from my lips as a sob nearly escaped my throat at the mention of Leena's name.

The trio exchanged glances, and it was Sienna who broke the silence, her melodic voice a stark contrast to my own.

"No, Aela, Kieran is Bastian's son, not the King's."

I glanced between Kieran and Bastian, my mind racing to make sense of the conflicting truths I had clung to for so long. I had been so certain that it was Kieran, that he was Naz. I had blamed him for Mei, the attack on Solarus, *Leena*. But now, standing there with Bastian, that certainty began to crack. Bastian and Kieran looked so alike. Their dark hair, the colour of their eyes, their strong jaws, even the way they stood.

The pieces of my puzzle didn't fit together anymore. If Kieran was Nazakeel, and the reason for my capture, then it wouldn't make sense that he would be breaking me out now.

The realisation hit me hard, leaving my shoulders heavy with the weight of it. I could feel the tension between us, Kieran's silent challenge, Bastian's almost imperceptible pity. I swallowed, trying to steady myself, but my mind kept tumbling through the same impossible conclusion.

"So, if you're not Nazakeel, and you're Blake's, I mean, Bastian's son, then what are you… Nazakeel's cousin?" I said in a defeated, quiet voice.

"Sort of," Kieran responded, raising one of his broad shoulders in a half-shrug.

"Kieran is also Nazakeel's brother," Bastian said.

I snapped my head up. "What?!" I asked.

Bastian Blake let out a tired exhale, and although his warrior's stance didn't change, sorrow and grief crossed his face.

"My brother used his shadows on my wife, Kieran's mother. She tried to resist the temptation, but she was a lover, not a fighter, my Lilly. Kieran was only a few months old at the time. Nine months after my brother took my beloved to bed, Nazakeel was born. My Lilly loved that boy with her whole heart, even after the events that led to his conception."

Blake shook his head, a small, sad smile tugging at his lips. "I swore to Lucius that I would raise him as my own, but my brother—well, you've met him. He is a proud but paranoid man. He sent Nazakeel away not long after his fifth birthday. Lilly held onto the hope that he would come back for as long as she could, but her heart was so broken she couldn't go on."

Bastian's voice cracked. "After she died, I wasn't the father I wanted to be. I was cold, angry, *mean*. She was the balm to my temper, and I feared what would happen to Kieran without the softness of his mother; of what he would become. When Lilly's sister, Alexis' mother, reached out and said she would take Kieran in, I knew I had to send him away to Olympia. It's what Lilly would have wanted—for Kieran to be surrounded by her family, to know love."

Bastian cleared his throat, and I could only stare at him, feeling the weight of the tragic story settle in my chest. Bastian Blake had lost everything because of his brother: his love, his son, even himself. How could he still serve him? Kieran had also lost his mother, a brother, and a father. I looked between the three of them, the sorrow of their tale washing over me.

"So... who is Nazakeel?" I asked hesitantly. "Lucius said I knew him, and why did he kill Mei?"

The three exchanged a long look once more, and I felt Sienna step closer to me. My stomach tightened, and dread coated the back of my throat.

"Who do you know that came to Olympia when they were five, Everflame?" Kieran asked, his voice softer than I'd ever heard from him.

A name instantly flashed in my mind, but I shook my head.

"No," I whispered, my heart sinking. Looking between them all, I settled my gaze on Lex. "Please, tell me this is a joke. This isn't possible. He wouldn't... he couldn't."

CHAPTER THIRTY-SEVEN

"I'm so sorry, little mouse," Lex said, her voice heavy with regret. "Kieran recognised Naz's essence last year but didn't know where from. He sent word to Bastian about his suspicions not long after the attack in Olos. Kieran only told me who Nathaniel really was when we were on our way here. I didn't even know he had a brother, neither did Kieran, up until a few months ago. If I had known, I would have done everything I could to keep you two apart."

"No," I said again, my vision going blurry. I dropped to my knees, my breath catching in my throat. "You're lying. Not him, anyone but him," I pleaded.

I lost the battle to keep my emotions in check. Tears streamed down my face as I struggled for breath between sobs. My whole life began to unravel in front of me. My best friend, the person I grew up with, the man I loved, the man I had trusted with all my secrets, with my *body*. He was a Prince. He was the Prince of Shadows.

I had been so stupid. I knew Lucius' face seemed so familiar to me; of course, it did. I should have recognised the chestnut brown hair and green eyes; even the way they spoke, the way they joked, the mock bowing, *everything* was so similar. I had convinced myself beyond all reasonable doubt that it was Kieran who was responsible for my capture, that I had ignored all the signs that had been literally staring me in the face.

I took a shaky breath, trying to compose myself. I still needed answers; none of it made any sense.

"But Nathaniel... I mean, *Prince Nazakeel*, he's a Fire Wielder. This isn't possible. Shades can't have children with fire abilities, can they? Surely this can't be true?"

Bastian gave me a sympathetic look as he stepped closer to me. With some effort, I pushed myself back to my feet, trying to steady myself for the answer.

"I'm afraid it is true, child," Bastian placed a gloved hand on my shoulder and gave it a light squeeze. He left it there, clearly sensing the exhaustion and shock threatening to overpower me. The dam holding my emotions back had finally burst, and for once, I was grateful for the steel around my wrists.

"The King kept his son's birth a secret. He knew his enemies would try to use Nazakeel against him. Only Lilly and I knew about the boy. Lucius felt your essence in Thellas on a journey back from Monacus when you were just a young child. The King knew your gentle Queen would let any desperate child into that Realm of yours, so he came up with a plan."

Bastian's face hardened, and he tensed his jaw, the expression and tone of his voice reminding me so much of Kieran.

"His plan meant that not only could he hide his son from his enemies, but he could also keep a watch on you; manipulate you, control you. No one suspects a child of being a spy. Nazakeel's powers manifested not long after his second birthday, and from a young age, he could whisper to the shadows, much like his father. All it took was a bit of guidance from the boy to get his shadows to convince one of the orphanage workers that they saw him use flames to create the stone from sand, rather than pull it from his pocket."

He laughed softly, shaking his head in disbelief at the nanny's stupidity.

"That friend of yours from Shangnon, the one Nazakeel strung up in the college, well, she must have realised what the stone was as soon as she saw it. One hasn't been used in centuries, but you know how those Shangonese are, they love passing down their ancestors' knowledge through generations. Anyway, that's not a glass stone, my dear. It's what we call a 'Syphoning Stone.' If the bearer can convince another to wear it freely, they can use the other's magic as if it were their own. It's a good job you haven't removed it, as there's a chance the surge of power could have killed you if you've been wearing it this long."

My mind swam. My essence? Surge of power? Why would The King want to control me when I had so little to offer? Bastian had clearly got something wrong.

I stared at Bastian as my mind processed the rest of his words. Nathaniel's betrayal ran so much deeper than I thought. Our whole lives together had been a lie. Nathaniel was not only responsible for the death of Leena, but he had also killed Mei in the most gruesome fashion imaginable. He had tortured her and put her on display for all to see. I knew Mei had an interest in my necklace, but I had never realised why. I thought she had died that night because she had spoken about Kera, not because of the stone around my neck.

Aadhar had been right. I hadn't put any of the pieces together—or at least, I hadn't put them together correctly. It was like I had been putting together a puzzle blindfolded.

My mind automatically started denying Bastian's claims. Surely, Nathaniel wasn't capable of murder, of *torture*. I felt like I knew him as well as I knew myself. Bastian was clearly mistaken about my power, so maybe he was wrong about Nathaniel, too.

I focused back on Bastian's final comment about my necklace. Looking down at my chest, I wrapped my shaking fingers around the stone, wanting nothing more than to yank it from the leather tie and throw it into the river. I raised my eyes back to him as my mind replayed what Nathaniel had said to me on the beach before we were… intimate.

"I'm just glad nothing happened to you. Without you, the future I have planned for us is impossible."

"Whatever happens, whatever we face. I need you alive, Aela. I can't imagine my life without you. It's like… I would be broken in two."

"We are linked, Aela, you and I. Even before I met you, all those years ago, I knew I would find you. It's like I had been searching for you and nothing was going to stop me from reaching you. I couldn't live with myself if anything happened to you now. I would rather lock you away somewhere and throw away the key if that meant keeping you alive."

"A Syphoning Stone? What do you mean?" I asked, pushing the memories of that day to the back of my mind. Nathaniel was right, I would regret giving my body to him if all this were true.

"You need to go to Alethia. Ask for Lord Killith. He will know what to do."

A memory of Mei holding a book to her chest in Solarus' library came to the front of my mind.

"Alethia?" I asked, trying to remember the title of the book Mei was reading all those months ago.

Bastian nodded.

"Yes, Kieran, Lex and Sienna will accompany you." He paused to look deeply into my eyes, ensuring I was listening. "You need to find Perseus. He will most likely be at the base of the Shangonese mountains. He'll be waiting for you. Kieran tells me you may have already met him. He will show you the way."

"But, the stone… what does it do? Why was I even captured in the first place?" I asked.

Bastian sighed and released my shoulder, stepping back toward the castle. I stumbled slightly, the loss of his support throwing me off balance.

"The King learned of the events in Olos; how you had nearly died at the hands of one of those bandits. Those weren't Naz's men, but a group they had been keeping an eye on, believing they might have been part of the Uprising. The King was always paranoid that you would be discovered once you left for Solarus, but became even more panicked when he heard you had been attacked and nearly died. Naz's men killed those bandits and proceeded to attack more villages under their disguise. It was the perfect ruse and allowed them time to evoke enough terror throughout Olympia that no one would be surprised when the War College was targeted."

I blinked up at Bastian, still struggling to make sense of things, but grateful someone had finally given me a straight answer.

"But… why does the King want me alive? What does he want with me? What does Nathaniel, I mean, Nazakeel want from me?"

"The King wants Nazakeel to command the Olympian Army. He wants to rule both Continents."

"And what's that got to do with me?"

"Because, those flames that Nazakeel wields that you were always so envious of, well… they do not belong to him, child. Nazakeel is using that stone to syphon them from you. That power is yours, Aela Everflame, and I believe you are more powerful than you and I could ever imagine."

The light-headedness I had been battling suddenly intensified, spiralling into a dizzying wave that pulled me under. I stumbled, and my legs buckled beneath me, sending me crashing to my knees. Darkness crept in at the edges of my vision, thick and suffocating, until it swallowed everything. In the brief moment before I lost consciousness, one thought pierced through the haze: *{Who really am I?}*

EPILOGUE

Sienna stared at the grey castle as it grew increasingly smaller in the distance, almost blending in with the night sky. A frigid breeze cut through the air, tugging at her long red hair, whipping the strands across her face. Raising her hand to clear it from her eyes, she lowered her fingers to the steel collar still encircling her neck.

Bastian had given her a key just before he had separated from her to meet his son and niece, just before Aela and Len had emerged from the secret passageway's exit. The key was a small, delicate thing, no larger than a needle. It had seemed so insignificant at first, but she now knew its purpose was anything but. Sienna's vision seemed to glaze over for a moment as she remembered what Bastian had said.

"There is a small hole at the back of your collar, so small that you can hardly see it. The same goes for Aela's bracelets. The only way to remove the steel is to coat the key in the blood of the Crown before placing it within the lock.

I would unlock it for you now, but given how long your beast has slumbered… to awaken it without preparation, well, you might not be able to contain it. You could lose all control and be even more savage than before. If that were to happen, there's a chance you would be caught before the castle was even out of view. When the time is right, ask Kieran to help you. Get him to set you free, Sienna."

Sienna's feelings toward Bastian were tangled. He had risked his life to free both her and Aela tonight, and so had Len. Yet despite this, anger still simmered beneath the surface of her thoughts. He had watched her slowly wither away for years, *decades*, shackled by her cursed collar, feeling each day like a slow death. He must have known that suppressing her other form—her true nature—was a form of murder, one that killed not just her body, but her soul. And still, he had done nothing, not until Aela had been taken as well; not until he heard his brother quote the prophecy.

It wasn't until the Night of Shadows that Sienna had also learned about the hidden passageways—how Len, and even Bastian, used them to move freely through the castle, unseen and unnoticed by the other guards.

Len had revealed to her a concealed door behind the armoire in her bedroom, cleverly hidden and perfectly placed. The door had always been there, as if silently mocking her ignorance. The door behind the armoire led to the very tunnels Bastian and Len had used to navigate the castle tonight. It was also how she had been sneaking down to the dungeons in secret to see Aela over the last few weeks. The very thought of it made her feel sick, the irony of her situation gnawing at her insides; she could have escaped *decades* ago if she had known; she could have slipped away in the dead of night like a ghost in the shadows.

Now, as the boat cut through the dark water, the castle shrinking in the distance, she couldn't help but feel the sting of missed opportunities. She thought Len had been her friend, so why hadn't he told her about them, helped her escape? How different her life would have been if he had.

But that was a question for another time. For now, she would focus on the journey ahead.

She turned toward Aela, who was staring vacantly into the dark sky at the front of the boat.

{Protect.}

The word echoed in her mind once more, as it always did when she thought of the girl. Lex sat beside her, subtly casting glances every few seconds in the direction of her friend. Sienna didn't know Lex, but it was clear that she cared for Aela, maybe not in an obvious way, but there was a protectiveness there that Sienna could relate to.

Sienna's heart twisted as she watched the young girl, barely even a woman, lost in her grief. Aela had collapsed after learning the truth about who she was—about who she loved. The revelation had shattered her.

Kieran had reluctantly gathered the fragile girl into his arms, scooping her from the ground and carrying her onto the boat as if she weighed no more than a child.

Sienna couldn't fathom what it must feel like—learning that your entire life had been a lie, that everything you'd trusted, everything you'd known, was false.

Her gaze lingered on Aela's frail form, but she pulled it away before tears could escape her eyes. No, she wouldn't cry, not now. She had to stay strong—strong for Aela, strong for herself, strong for her people. She could be weak later, when it didn't matter, but for now, she had to hold it together, just a little longer.

The sound of the waves gently lapping against the side of the small boat was the only thing that broke the silence. Sienna inhaled deeply, tasting the water's salt in the air on her tongue. Kieran was standing at the front of the boat, several feet from Aela and Lex. His shadows enveloped the group, hiding them from sight and pushing the boat forward through the water with ease. His power was so vast, so absolute, that it seemed to come without effort, a quiet strength that made her wonder what else he was capable of, what else he had hidden within him. Using his magic didn't seem to drain him, did not seem to cost him a thing. It was as though his shadows were a part of him, and he a part of them.

Sienna's lower lip quivered as the castle finally disappeared from view, the night's darkness finally swallowing the stone fortress. For the first time in decades, she felt something stirring within her—a sensation she had long since forgotten. For the first time in a long time, she felt a spark of joy.

She was going to Alethia.

She was going *home.*

·····)) ● (((·····

THE END

Printed in Great Britain
by Amazon